TRUTH POKER

TRUTH POKER

....

stories

Mark Brazaitis

Autumn House Press

PITTSBURGH

"Autumn House Press" and "Autumn House" are registered trademarks owned by
Autumn House Press, a nonprofit corporation whose mission is the publication and
promotion of poetry and other fine literature.

 Autumn House Press receives state arts funding support through a grant
from the Pennsylvania Council on the Arts, a state agency funded by the
Commonwealth of Pennsylvania and the National Endowment for the Arts,
a federal agency.

ISBN: 978-1-938769-03-0
Library of Congress: 2014955381

···

For Julie, Annabel, and Rebecca

and for Katy

and for the memory of my father

Acknowledgments

No work is entirely an author's own. I am grateful to the people in my life who have shaped and supported my writing: my mother, Sheila Loftus; my sister, Sarah Brazaitis; my brother-in-law George Gushue; my in-laws, John and Jean Penn; my colleagues Katy Ryan, Kevin Oderman, Ethel Morgan Smith, Dennis Allen, and James Harms; my fellow writers Valerie Sayers, William O'Rourke, Peter Anderson, Renée Nicholson, Janet Peery, Michael Blumenthal, Tony D'Souza, and Joan Connor; my favorite radio host, Diane Rehm, and her producer, Susan Nabors; my mentor, John Coyne; and—as always, and with the deepest love my heart knows—my wife, Julie, and my daughters, Annabel and Rebecca.

I am also grateful to the editors of the journals in which the following stories first appeared:

"The Blind Wrestler" in *West Branch*
"Cuts" in *Beloit Fiction Journal*
"Barbados" in the *H.O.W. Journal*
"The Ghosts of Girls" and "The Girl on the *Subte*" in the *Notre Dame Review*
"The Eye Man" and "The Bribe" in *The Sun*
"Blackheart" in *Witness*
"In the Village of Mourning" in *Bryant Literary Review*
"What to Expect When You Say You're Expecting" in *Lake Effect*
"The Meet" in *Mid-American Review*
"Pistachio" in *Talking River Review*
"Truth Poker" in *Carve*

Contents

∙∙∙

part one

....

BLINDNESS

The Blind Wrestler

∙∙∙

Katherine's son was about to wrestle a blind boy, a senior at St. Lucy's High School whom the local paper had written up the day before in a front-page story. The blind boy had been wrestling since he was in middle school, but, as the story tried to conceal, he wasn't very good. This season, he had lost all six of his matches. Her son, she feared, would destroy him.

Katherine sat four rows up in the collapsible stands of Sherman High's gym, which smelled like twenty-five years of sweat and the coffee parents had sneaked in this Saturday morning. St. Lucy's fans, on the other side of the gym, numbered two dozen, and they cheered the blind boy with half-hearted enthusiasm. Doubtless they'd seen him lose too often to think he stood a chance.

The blind boy's eyes were shielded by wraparound sunglasses, secured beneath his headgear and so dark and narrow they looked like a blindfold. His uniform was black, a contrast to his milk-pale skin. His 160 pounds were distributed over a sapling frame. He was taller than her son by a couple of inches but looked far less sturdy.

Her son pressed his palms against the blind boy's, and the whistle blew. For a moment, there was a standoff, the wrestlers like thin towers leaning against each other. But presently her son wrapped his arms around the blind boy's waist and drove his left shoulder into his chest. The blind boy gasped—from the blow or surprise at the blow, Katherine wasn't sure. An instant later, her son pinned him. Light applause filled the gym.

After standing, the blind boy extended his hand, and her son clasped it and said something and the wrestlers left the floor, the blind boy's coach helping him to the bench. Katherine's husband, sitting beside her, shouted congratulations, but their son was too cool to acknowledge his words. She could hear his teammates teasing him about beating a blind boy. What was next, one of them said, an opponent with one arm? Katherine realized she hadn't clapped at all.

For dinner, she served steak, as she always did after her son's matches. Her husband and son talked about her son's college options. He had been offered a partial wrestling scholarship to Ohio Eastern, the campus of which began eight blocks from where they lived, but his dream was to wrestle at Ohio State, whose coach had invited him to walk on.

She'd always hoped he would attend one of the excellent small schools in the state. Kenyon. Oberlin. Ohio Wesleyan. She'd pictured him inviting her to sit in on a lecture or attend a play. But she had overestimated his interest in books, studying, knowledge. He cared about what most boys his age cared about: video games, sports, girls. His girlfriend was another complaint of hers. She'd been the girlfriend of his two best friends. "So now it's his turn?" she asked her husband one night when their son wasn't home. "Is this a game of hot potato?" The blind wrestler, she remembered from the newspaper article, had been accepted early at Princeton. He intended to major in classics. He'd been studying ancient Greek since the ninth grade.

The phone rang. She left the table to answer it. It was her stepdaughter, who lived outside of Chicago with her husband and their three children, all under the age of five. "How are you, Katherine?" her stepdaughter asked in the inflated tone of someone who couldn't care less.

"I'm wonderful, as always. How are you? How's Brent? How are the kids?" Sometimes Katherine made a game of these phone calls, seeing how long she could keep them going, how uncomfortable she could make her stepdaughter, who was fourteen when Katherine married Simon and viewed her as an especially annoying secretary when all she wanted was to see the boss. But after her opening volley of questions, Katherine realized she lacked the stamina for the game tonight. Even before her stepdaughter had finished answering, she shouted, "Simon! Telephone!"

After her husband brought the phone to his ear, he exploded in a hearty, "Hey there! Long time, no hear!" It had been, Katherine calculated, no more than a week since they'd spoken. She looked around for her son, but he had retreated to his room. The sounds of her husband's enthusiastic conversation were inescapable so long as Katherine remained in the house, so she stepped outside. She wasn't wearing a coat. Her cotton sweater was thin, its buttons dainty. Examining it under a streetlight, she was appalled to think it made her look grandmotherly.

She headed north, weaving her way down side streets and across pot-hole-pocked intersections. Although she'd lived in Sherman since she was eight, these streets, lined with century-old houses, were unfamiliar. Several of the streets were made of brick, and their unevenness made them seem like an undulating sea. At the end of a cul-de-sac was a stone house, evidently abandoned. Behind its black metal gate and fence, its lawn was overgrown and gnarly. The glass in one of the second floor windows was missing, giving the house the appearance of a face with a gouged eye.

Off to her left, she heard whistling. She turned and saw a white dog, a square-headed Labrador. Behind the dog was the blind wrestler, bundled in a trench coat, his wool hat pulled down to the tops of his dark glasses. The wrestler and his dog strode toward her before, abruptly, stopping. Had they sensed her presence? Before she could retreat, the wrestler turned to the gate and pulled it open. He followed his dog up the front walk. A few steps shy of the front porch, they turned left, following a path she couldn't see because of the overgrown grass, and slipped around the house. To pursue him, she knew, was wrong. But curiosity overruled her conscience. She slipped past the gate, detoured down the path, and looped around the house. Here, she discovered woods, where the wrestler and his dog had no doubt gone. She sighed, disappointed.

There was a back door to the house, with a pair of concrete steps leading to it, the sides crumbling like a sand castle. She doubted the door was unlocked, but when she tried it, it flew toward her. She stepped into a mudroom at the same time she heard a dog's furious bark.

Beyond the mudroom, on the floor of the adjacent kitchen, sat the wrestler and his Lab. Pot smoke floated toward her, familiar from long ago. She wondered if this was a high-school hangout, a den of mild iniquity. The dog hadn't stopped barking, and the wrestler said, "Who are you?" several times.

"It's all right," Katherine said. "I'm not the police."

"What are you doing here?"

Good question, she thought. "I don't know." Although honest, her answer didn't sound reassuring. "I was hoping to get high." Her voice rose on the last word, a question more to herself than to him.

"How did you know I'd be coming here?" His voice had lost its nervous edge. His dog had quieted.

She thought about this. "I had a feeling," she said.

"I'm not a dealer," he said.

"I didn't say you were. And I didn't mean to scare you. Or your dog."

"It's okay," he said, although his tone indicated otherwise. She kneeled across from them on the linoleum floor. The light was murky; it was as if she was seeing him in a grainy photograph.

"You have a beautiful dog."

"That's what all the girls say."

Katherine was flattered to be included with the girls.

The wrestler dug in the inside pocket of his jacket. She could barely see what he removed. Presently, he held it out to her. She reached toward him, her hand accidentally wrapping around his wrist. "Hey, we're not signing a peace treaty," he said.

"I can't see," she said.

"Join the crowd."

Her hand moved up his and discovered the roach. "Got it!" she said, as if she'd caught a fish.

"Need a light?"

She slapped her pockets futilely. "Please," she said.

He reached into his coat pocket again, and soon a flame blazed in the space between them. She hadn't smoked pot since college. Roach in mouth, she dipped toward the flame. She nearly choked on her first puff.

"Get out much?" he asked her, chuckling. "Are you at Sherman High?"

She didn't know if he was serious. Couldn't he tell her age from her voice?

"Or do you go to Ohio Eastern?"

College? Could she pretend to be in college? "No," she said. "I don't go to school."

"You work then?"

"Yeah."

The wrestler didn't pursue the subject. "Cool" was all he said. He tilted his head and released smoke.

"How did you find this place?" she asked.

"Buster"—he indicated the dog—"specializes in sniffing out crack houses, gambling dens, houses of ill repute."

"Oh," she said.

"I'm joking."

"Right," she said. "I knew that."

"My girlfriend found it. Whenever we needed a little space, for whatever"—he paused and she nodded, although remembering he couldn't see, she said, "Got it"—"well, whenever we needed space, we'd come here. It wasn't long before Buster knew the route by heart, so when Emily, my girlfriend, went off to Brown in the fall, I kept the tradition alive.

"Emily came back for Christmas," he added. "It was freezing, remember? But we still managed a few trips over here. I'll be moving to the East Coast in the fall, so we'll see more of each other."

She asked him what he would be doing on the East Coast, although she knew, and he told her about Princeton and studying classics. "Homer is my hero. What can I say? It'll be the blind studying the blind." Although he'd doubtless used this line before, she laughed appreciatively. He told her about the other school subjects he liked, and why he enrolled at St. Lucy's rather than Sherman High—because St. Lucy's had a superior chess club as well as the only teachers within fifty square miles trained in instructing the blind. He didn't mention wrestling.

"What about you?" he asked. "You have a boyfriend?"

She thought about this. "Kind of," she said.

"Uh-huh," the wrestler said. "Not going where you want it to go?"

"Maybe," she said.

"What does that mean?"

She didn't know. She told him so.

"Up in the air," he concluded. They talked more before he said, "I better head home."

"Do you need help?" she asked. "I mean. I'm happy to—"

"I'm good," he said. "Buster could find his way home with his eyes closed." He laughed and laughed again. "I don't know what's funny," he said, laughing.

She laughed at the way he was laughing, like he was being tickled. "Hell, you'd think we'd smoked weed," she said.

As he stood, he said, "I'll be here Thursday, same time. If you want to come by." A pause. "No pressure or anything."

"If I can," she said, "I will."

"Cool," he said. "What's your name, anyway?"

"Katie," she said, which is how she'd been known in college.

"I'm Ben." In the darkness, he held out his hand, and they shook. Then he and Buster slipped out of the house.

A few minutes passed. She didn't feel like leaving. She liked imagining she was in college again. She didn't want to think about going home to Simon. She thought about him anyway, remembering the day they'd met, at the Book and Brew, where she worked during her sophomore year at Ohio Eastern. He was twenty-one years older than she was, and sometimes she noticed. But he was unfailingly sweet and attentive, and he was smarter than anyone she'd ever dated. (Admittedly, she hadn't factored in the advantage his age gave him; nor had she considered that his competition numbered exactly two). She had been studying English because she thought she would be a good English teacher. But she might have changed her mind. When she became pregnant, he was eager to marry her. For him, marriage was no big deal. He'd been married before. For her, it was like falling backwards and hoping someone would catch her. She quit college. She'd held a few part-time jobs, years apart and unmemorable. Occasionally, she thought of going back to school.

As she'd told her friend Elsa last month when they'd met for coffee at the Book and Brew, "I didn't know what I was doing."

"Who does?" Elsa said.

On Thursday night, Ben was where she'd found him the first time, Buster by his side. "Katie?" he asked.

"Hey," she said.

She slid across from him, sat Indian style. There was a silence, and Katherine heard Buster breathing, quick intakes of cold air. The darkness was like a photograph shot in evening without a flash, although Ben's pale face, moon-round, was distinct. Dark glasses covered his eyes. The house smelled of mold and talcum powder or aspirin or flour.

"You want to light up?" he asked.

"If you do," she said.

He sighed. "Do you mind if I skip it tonight? I have a match tomorrow."

"A match?" she said. She felt bad about playing the innocent. Deceiving a blind boy.

"I wrestle," he said.

"Neat."

"It would be if I was any good."

"I bet you're good."

"Why would you bet I'm good?" His curiosity seemed sincere. When she didn't respond, he said, "Because in wrestling, blindness isn't the kind of handicap it would be in football or hockey?"

"I don't know," she admitted.

"You were being polite. The truth is, I suck."

She wondered what she was supposed to say. "I'm sorry," she tried.

"It doesn't matter." He paused. "I didn't start wrestling because I loved wrestling. I started wrestling so I would get into Princeton. You know, blind boy refuses to allow handicap to stymie his Olympic dream." He laughed. "I started wrestling in the eighth grade, and I've won a grand total of two matches. One of them—I kid you not—was against a deaf boy."

"That's a good story," she said.

"Don't get me wrong: I don't like to lose. But I never aspired to be great. I have other interests." There was a pause. "Would you like to light up?" he asked, reaching into his pocket.

"No," she said. "It's okay."

He put his hand on Buster's head and massaged the dog. "I won't wrestle in college. I'm not good enough. Not by a long shot. But I'll miss it."

"You will? Why?"

"What do people do when they see a blind person? They clear out of the way. They're afraid they'll trip me or I'll run into them. If they do come close to me, they're usually crouching, saying hello to Buster."

"He's cute."

"And I'm not?" He laughed and ran his hand down Buster's back. "In wrestling," he said, "no one clears out of the way. They're required to do the opposite. Do you know what I mean?"

"I think so," she said.

"It's wanting to feel contact," he said, "to have a hold on someone."

She remembered how, until he was ten or so, her son saw her body as a chair, a pillow, a jungle gym. He hugged her without shame. He didn't turn from her kisses but puckered like a fish. He lounged on her lap as they watched movies. At night, she read to him in his single bed, both of them under the covers, their legs entwined. Gradually, he stopped wanting this closeness. It was like he was weaning himself a second time.

"It's about the weight of another person against you," Ben added. "Weird to think I'll miss that, right?"

"No," she said. "I understand."

Katherine had been standing in front of her bathroom mirror for fifteen minutes, brushing her hair, applying eyeliner and lipstick, and rouging her cheeks, before she realized her audience wouldn't—indeed, couldn't—notice.

"Have an affair," her friend Elsa had told her that afternoon at the Book and Brew. "You'd have zero problem finding a lover." But Katherine didn't think she could do this to her husband, who remained the kindest man she'd ever known.

"What are you going to do after college?" she asked Ben. "What does a person do with a degree in classics?"

They were sitting on the kitchen floor in the stone house. The night was especially dark. Only when he drew in on his roach could she see his expression. Buster's breathing was the most pronounced sound in the silences between their conversation.

"Become a Rhodes Scholar," he said. "Afterwards, go to grad school. Harvard or Yale."

"And afterwards?"

"Become a professor. Be the next great translator of *The Iliad* and *The Odyssey*. Narrate a PBS special on ancient Greece."

"You're not joking," she said. "What about your girlfriend? What about a family?"

"A wife before I'm thirty-five, a family before I'm forty," he said. "But I can't control so much what happens in my private life."

"But the rest of it is in your control?"

He thought about this. "My dad could lose his job and we could go broke and I could wind up at Ohio Eastern instead of Princeton. But I'd still be gunning for a Rhodes Scholarship."

"Sounds easy," she said.

"It's not easy," he protested. "But it's what I want to do, so I'll do it."

"You could be president if you wanted." She was only half teasing.

"Definitely," he said, "if I had a social bone in my body. But, no, when I want to smoke weed, I sneak off to an abandoned house. If I were social, I'd do it at parties like everyone else."

"Where do you get the pot?" she asked.

"My dad. He's a sixties radical who never became unradical. He just became rich." They drew in on their roaches. They blew smoke into the darkness. Buster shook his head, as if in disapproval.

"Why do you come here to smoke?" she asked him. "If it's okay with your dad, why not stay home?"

"It wouldn't be okay with my mom."

"Right," Katherine said. It wouldn't be okay with her either. As a mother. But as a—what was she when she was here?—it was fine.

"What about you?" he said. "How old are you, anyway?"

She didn't answer.

"I think I know."

"You do?" she asked, her heart trembling.

"I think you're twenty-one."

She wondered if he was flattering her. "Close."

"Twenty-two?"

"Close enough."

"Damn," he said. "Think about how cool I'd be if I could say I'd hooked up with a twenty-three-year old." Before Katherine could say anything, he added, "Too bad I'm happily married. Emily can probably hear me right now and I can expect a month in solitary confinement." He laughed, drew in smoke, exhaled it.

"What's Emily like?"

"Smart and sighted. But I thought we were talking about you."

"I'm only a Sherman girl who never left."

"Haven't left yet," he said. "Besides, what's wrong with that?"

"It isn't exactly a Rhodes Scholarship."

"A Rhodes Scholarship probably isn't even a Rhodes Scholarship. You think it's one thing and then it turns into something else. You study at the world's greatest university and ten years later all you remember of the two years is the crush you had on the girl at the newspaper stand around the corner."

"It sounds like you know her."

"Who?"

"The girl at the newspaper stand."

"I do! The Arctic Emporium, downtown Sherman, the summer I was fourteen. I was at an arts camp, and every afternoon we'd go for ice cream. She served me for five straight days. Her voice. Like marshmallow supreme with chocolate sauce. I can still hear it."

A few weeks before their wedding, Katherine and her husband-to-be went to the Hope Theater to see a revival of *Last Tango in Paris*. She had assumed the movie was about tango dancing, although she couldn't picture Marlon Brando as much of a dancer. She knew him as the enormous actor from *Superman*. "It's a different kind of tango," said her husband, who had picked the film.

She didn't think much of his comment until the movie started. Every so often, she glanced suspiciously at Simon, who always met her gaze with a small grin, which was probably intended to reassure her but struck her as sinister. *You don't know who the hell I am*, his grin said.

She remembered the movie today because the actress who had played the girl had died. The *Sherman Advocate and Post*, perhaps short on local stories, had printed a long obituary of her. The obituary quoted her saying she felt "a little bit raped" by the movie. Despite her roles in other films, she was forever the *Last Tango* actress, the girl Brando had had his way with in a desolate apartment. The designation haunted her; it may have contributed to her being, on several occasions, institutionalized.

"She was only nineteen when she acted in *Last Tango*," Katherine told Simon. Simon's hair, which had gone gray in his fifties, was now a Santa Claus white. It stood out against the black of his television chair. "Imagine making a decision at nineteen and having it determine the rest of your life. It ruined her."

"Ruined?" he said, puzzled. "No one would have heard of her if it hadn't been for that movie. I've never heard of an actress wanting anonymity."

There was a silence. She said, "Why did you take me see to that film, anyway?"

Another silence. "Honestly..."

When he didn't continue, she said, "Honestly what?"

"I think it was an obviously misguided attempt to encourage the sex back into our life."

"You took me to *Last*—." She stopped. "I was pregnant. And I was sick as hell during all but maybe three days of my pregnancy."

"Maybe I thought you were sick of me."

"Sick of you already? We'd known each other barely a year."

"The movie was supposed to be erotic." He sighed. "Those cravings seem a little juvenile now."

"What cravings?" she asked.

"For different kinds of sex. Anonymous sex. Anal sex. Sex in the lotus position." His smile was rueful. "What one craves now is closeness. Words in one's ear. A hand on one's heart." In a softer voice, he said, "Perhaps I'm speaking only about myself." His eyes flashed over her face. "Is everything all right, Katherine? You've been disappearing every few nights for these walks. I can't help wondering."

"What?" she asked. Did she think her husband hadn't noticed? Perhaps she'd thought he didn't care.

"Of course I'm thinking you've found some man, some younger man..."

He was right, in a fashion. "No," she said. "They're only walks." She tried to laugh so as to dismiss his worry. "I like the time to myself."

"She was only nineteen," she told Ben as they sat in the kitchen of the abandoned house. "She said yes to a movie and it made her life miserable."

"She might have been miserable anyway," he said.

"How can you say that?"

"Think about how an actress would handle it today," he said. "For a savvy one, it would be only a stage in her career. Afterward, she would do Shakespeare in the Park or Chekhov on Broadway. She'd adopt a kid from Bangladesh or the Sudan. She'd cut a CD of children's songs. She'd pose pregnant on the cover of *Vanity Fair*."

"But it wasn't only a stage in her career. It was *Last Tango in Paris*. It was stunning. It was controversial. Hell, it was pornographic—except she was the only person to expose herself. Even without the butter scene, which she said wasn't in the original script and was excruciating to film...well, the movie *was* her career—no, it was her *life*."

She should have stayed in school after she got pregnant, she thought. But at the time, it wasn't what young women in small-town Ohio who were knocked up and too terrified of hell or their parents to have an abortion did. They disappeared into marriage or worse. "I guess I feel..." She was surprised to find herself choked up. She drew in a breath. They hadn't been smoking. Ben would wrestle his last match the following afternoon. The following week, Emily was coming home for her spring break. "I guess I feel bad for her. She was only fifty-eight-years old."

In the darkness, she gazed at Ben, Buster at his feet. She wondered how the world would hurt him. Or how else it would hurt him. He'd been born blind, he'd told her, the result of Leber's congenital amaurosis. He'd had the defining moment of his life at its inception.

"When we think about forces we can't control," Ben said, his voice soft, conciliatory, "we usually think about hurricanes or floods or even drunk drivers who fly across the median and slam head-on into a family of five's station wagon. But I hear what you're saying. When you're cast as the female lead in *Last Tango in Paris*, the current is powerful. It's hard to swim back to shore."

"You hope you don't go over a falls," she said.

When Katherine walked into her son's bedroom, he was sitting at his desk in front of his computer. His face wore an absorbed, mesmerized look. Katherine was young enough to understand why her son's generation loved computers—loved them as much as her husband's generation loved cars—but old enough not to have fallen completely under their spell. "Do you have a minute?" she asked him.

He looked up, looked back at his screen. Reluctantly, he looked up at her again. He gave her a slight smile. "What's up?" he said.

Instinctively, she began to make his bed, a quick straightening and rearranging. She fluffed his pillow.

"Thanks," he said, his eyes back on the screen.

She sat on his bed. "You'll have to do this for yourself in college," she said.

"I know."

"I can't come with you."

He looked up at her. He was better looking than Simon. He was taller, and his eyes were larger and more welcoming. Of course she'd known only the forty-and-over Simon.

"Sure you can come with me, Mom," her son said. "You can have my bunk bed. I'll sleep on the floor." He gave her a teasing grin. Even as he did so, he managed to punch letters on his keyboard. Clack, click, clack.

"Actually, I was thinking you might be better off going to Ohio Eastern," she said. "The wrestling scholarship is a real honor. You could live here your freshman year. You could ease into college life."

His typing had ceased, but he wasn't looking at her. "At this point, I'm leaning toward Ohio State." His eyes danced around her face, settled south of her chin. "It isn't so far away."

"But the scholarship..."

"If I manage to walk on at Ohio State, the coach'll give me a scholarship." He narrowed his eyes. "We can afford the tuition, right? It's not like dad is...We're okay—financially, I mean—aren't we?"

"Of course, of course." She waved her hand.

"You always wanted me to go off to college somewhere else in the state, right?" Again, he wasn't looking at her. "Out of the house but not out of the state. Isn't that what you said? Besides," he said, "this way you and dad can get to know each other again. A second honeymoon. Whatever."

She was going to protest his implied assessment of her marriage, but his cell phone rang. He held up a finger as if she might dare speak over the cacophonous clash of the ringtone. "Brittney, what's up?" It was his girlfriend. Katherine felt the usual rush of mild disgust, although this time she recognized another emotion in the brew. Brittney wasn't the brightest girl, but she knew enough to protect herself, ensuring that her high-school lovers became nothing more.

She retreated from her son's room. Absorbed in his conversation, he didn't acknowledge her departure.

In the ten days she didn't see Ben because of Emily's visit, she thought often about what he might be doing. One evening, with her husband on the phone with his daughter, she walked over to the abandoned stone house. She was hoping to glimpse Emily, to see if she was as she'd imagined—a younger version of herself. But no one came to the house; no one emerged from it.

On Monday evening, with Emily back at Brown, Katherine left by the back door so as to preclude Simon, who was watching television, from asking her where she was going. When she reached the house, she saw a sign jammed into the front lawn: Remodeling by Frank & Frank. There was a stepladder on the porch. Otherwise, the house appeared untouched. She slipped around to the back door, which was locked. Was Ben inside? She tapped against the wood. She tapped louder. "Ben?" she whispered. "Ben?"

"Right here," he said, and she stifled a scream. He was behind her, Buster at his side.

"My God, you scared me." She told him about the sign on the lawn and the locked door.

"Well, crap," he said. "Do you know of any other abandoned houses in the neighborhood?"

Only my own, she thought to say.

"Let me try something," he said, and Buster led him up to the door. He removed a set of keys from his pocket and hunched over the lock. She heard the scrape of metal on metal.

"What are you doing?" she whispered. As she spoke, a wind kicked up, fierce and cool. The door whooshed open. "How'd you manage that?"

"Practice," he said as they stepped inside. When they'd found seats on the kitchen floor, he added, "When I was a kid, my parents gave me all sorts of stuff to take apart."

"You'd make a good thief."

He laughed at this. "I have higher criminal ambitions: International assassin."

"How was Emily's visit?" She'd wanted her voice to sound neutral, disinterested.

"Great," he said. "For the first forty-five seconds."

"What do you mean?"

"She broke up with me." His voice quivered. She couldn't see him; she wondered what his face showed.

"Why?"

"She said I have my life planned down to the minute. She said I lack spontaneity." He paused. "I told her every day of my life is full of spontaneity. I'm never 100 percent certain my next step won't be over an abyss." He sighed. "Of course then she admitted she was seeing someone else."

"Who?"

"Some sighted asshole, of course. If she had gone with a deaf dude, I would have said, 'Well, fair fight.'" His words were sarcastic, but his voice betrayed his pain.

"I'm sorry," she said, and she felt like comforting him, wrapping him in her arms.

He shrugged. "What can I do? I can't even stalk her." He tried to laugh.

They sat in silence before he said, "You still hanging around with that dude you mentioned?"

She hesitated. The age difference between her and Ben was the same as between her and Simon. If she had felt inclined, could she have pursued something with him without it seeming absurd and scandalous? "Yeah," she said.

"Too bad." There was more silence. "I didn't bring any weed tonight. My dad's having second thoughts about supplying me."

"Bastard," Katherine said.

Ben laughed. "You said it." He ran a hand down Buster's back. "But I shouldn't be too critical. He's taking me and my mom to Greece this summer. My graduation present and their twenty-fifth wedding anniversary gift. We'll be leaving the day after I graduate."

Their conversation was interrupted by sounds of voices outside. Ben stood up. "Are they coming in?" he asked. Presently, they heard the sound of a key in the back door lock. "Oh, shit," Ben said. "We need to hide."

"Where?" she asked.

"The basement." There was a snapping sound; whoever was outside had locked the unlocked door. Puzzled murmurs followed.

"This way," Katherine said. "Do you mind if I—" But he held up his arm, and she grabbed it. With her cell phone as a flashlight, she led him and Buster to the door at the front of the kitchen, then guided them down the wooden steps. "There's a wine cellar here," he whispered, and she found it in the corner, opened its door, and moved them all inside, shutting the door behind her. Profoundly dark, the cellar was only a little larger than a phone booth or a Port-O-Potty. They sat side by side, their hips and legs touching. Buster sat in Ben's lap. He made no sound. They could hear footsteps upstairs and muffled voices, a man's and a woman's, discussing stripping floors and removing wallpaper and installing insulation.

A minute passed in which she heard nothing. She was about to declare coast clear when the man's voice said, "I don't know what to suggest with regard to the basement. Do you want to have a look?"

Footsteps again, louder, approaching. "There's nothing special down here." It was the man speaking from immediately outside the door, his flashlight's beam slipping under it. "Except maybe the wine cellar." Katherine expected the door to open. She could use their surprise to her advantage, race past them up the stairs and out into the night. Ben would be able to identify her only as Katie. It could have been a scene in *Last Tango*.

"Would you like to look inside?"

Katherine heard the man grip the doorknob. From Buster came a soft growl.

"It isn't necessary," said the woman. "Besides, I think my stomach is telling me it's dinnertime."

There was more conversation, but it drifted from the wine cellar, then up the stairs. When they could no longer hear voices, Katherine and Ben broke into quiet, relieved laughter. Buster's tail thumped against Ben's chest.

"Close call," Ben whispered. "Thank God Buster growls like a stomach."

"I guess our safe house is no longer safe," Katherine said.

A long silence followed as their nerves calmed. Eventually, Ben said, "I have a request. Please feel free to say no."

"All right," Katherine said.

"May I touch your face?"

"Touch my—. Oh. To—"

"You know, for blind people, our hands are our eyes."

"Right. I think I knew that."

"Our elbows are our noses."

"They are?"

"Our little toes are our brains. But our mouths are in fact our mouths."

"You're funny."

"But I was serious."

"Oh. Well, sure." Katherine wondered if he would feel her years in her face. She wondered what he would say if he did.

Presently, she felt his fingers on both cheeks. They were surprisingly warm, and she told him so.

"I've had them on Buster's back. He's an electric blanket with paws." He moved his fingers to her chin, around her lips. He drew a long finger down her nose. His gestures felt careful, precise, and she couldn't remember ever being known like this. It felt like a languid, sweet prelude to deeper intimacies. She wondered if this is what he was hoping for. But his fingers remained on her face, tracing her eyebrows and her forehead (and perhaps its creases) and her temples and her hairline. Her body warmed and yearned, not for him but for the touches she'd never felt.

He removed his hands as water pooled in her eyes and slid down her cheeks. She wondered at her sentimentality or self-pity. "You're very beautiful," he said, his voice even-handed, almost detached. "I can tell."

"Thank you."

"I guess it must be late," he said, standing. She followed.

"I think so."

"There's no wine around here, is there?"

"I think we would have bumped into it by now."

"Well, we can drink a toast anyway." He reached for her hand, and when their hands were clasped and suspended at chest-level between them, he said, "Cheers." Their faces were so close they could have drunk from the same glass.

Was this it? she wondered. Was this their goodbye? "Let's wrestle for it," she said.

"For what?" he asked.

She didn't know. She knew she wanted to delay their parting. She wouldn't see him again, not in such an intimate place, not where she could be in her twenties again. She couldn't have said who made the first move, but a moment later, they were grappling, pulling, twisting, laughing. He was even thinner than he seemed but also stronger, and when she squeezed his shoulder, she did so roughly and felt his bone. He had his hands on her back and pulled her toward him, their chests colliding, their breath intersecting.

Buster broke into worried barking. Their closeness held, then Ben eased back. "It's okay, boy," he said, crouching to pet his dog. He looked up at her. "I guess the referee is saying the match is over."

They stepped out of the wine cellar and into the basement, her cell phone casting a weak yellow glow onto cobwebs in corners. Ben looked over at her. "If you want to learn to wrestle, I know someone." There was a personal trainer, Maggie Ray, who in addition to leading her clients in the usual weightlifting and treadmill exercises at Women's Work(out) in the Sky Lake Mall, he said, gave one-on-one lessons in Greco-Roman wrestling. She was a former state high-school champion—boys' division, no less—in the 101-pound weight class. She'd given a pre-match pep talk to St. Lucy's wrestlers last season. "I was so inspired I lost my match in thirty-two seconds," he said, smiling.

"I haven't done anything athletic in decades," she said.

He didn't comment on her word choice, though the smile he gave her in the yellow light suggested he knew how old she was. "It isn't too late," he said.

Her son decided to go to Ohio State. Although Columbus was only a two-hour drive from Sherman, she knew he wouldn't come home often. She knew she shouldn't want him to.

On the day he announced his decision, she thought about heading off to college herself. Starting over. It wasn't impossible. There were women in her position who had. She spent a couple of hours on her computer, calling up the web sites of universities across the country. Even some of the top schools had rolling admission. She could begin again somewhere—Amherst, Massachusetts; Ann Arbor, Michigan; Charlottesville, Virginia. When she thought of Simon, she felt miserable. *He did nothing wrong. But neither did I.*

Later the same day, she hopped in her car and drove mechanically out of town. Drives had lately replaced her walks to the abandoned house. Half an hour later, she found herself at the Sky Lake Mall. She stopped in at Banana Republic and bought clothes for her son that he wouldn't like or need. As she returned to her car, she saw a storefront she'd never noticed. It was Women's Work(out), and she remembered what Ben had said about it. She tossed her shopping bags into her trunk and headed to the door. A trial membership was free. She asked about Maggie Ray, the wrestler. The front-desk clerk, a blond man with the tattoo of an upside down anchor on his right forearm, said Maggie had an opening in her schedule at six-thirty the next morning.

She finds her way back to who she was—or she thinks she does—not by running off to another city, to another life, but by working her body into the form it was when she was half her age. She spends fifty minutes three days a week on a wrestling mat, straining to bring someone fifteen pounds lighter, but five times as strong, down. ("You're getting better," her opponent, who is also her teacher, tells her one morning. "I'm actually having to try a little bit.") She spends two hours two days a week lifting weights and peddling a stationary bike and even throwing punches at the neglected heavy bag suspended from the ceiling at the back of the gym. On weekends, she sometimes wakes up before the newspaper has been delivered, dresses in the dark, and runs past familiar landmarks, one of which is an old stone house, its lawn mowed, its broken window replaced. "Resurrected," she says about the house, and it's also what she thinks about herself—except when the euphoria born from her exercise wears down at the end of the day to aches in every part of her body and she glances in the mirror and there she is, gray sprouting from her crown in defiance of the dye job that was supposed to last longer. Her muscles are tauter, but her eyes are the same, greeting her with sadness, confusion, and accusation, as if over a betrayal.

On the day her son was to leave home, his room seemed like a tree whose leaves had fallen. He had removed posters from his wall. He had swept shelves clean of baseballs and CDs. Instead of a broken alarm clock and programs to Ohio Eastern sporting events on the table next to his bed, there was only a layer of dust. It was as if he didn't plan to come back.

She found her son and husband standing by the front door. The car was loaded. Katherine wore the black, body-hugging outfit she used for her wrestling lessons. Her son was wearing shorts and a gray T-shirt, her husband a nondescript polo shirt and jeans. The laces on his left shoe were untied. His white hair was half-combed. For him, it seemed, it could have been any Saturday morning. "Ready?" he asked her.

She looked at her son. "I have one request before we go," she said.

"What, Mom?"

"A wrestling match. The two of us."

Her son looked around as if she might be speaking to someone else. "Are you serious?"

"No going off to college until we've wrestled."

He turned to his father. "Is she serious?"

"I'm serious," she said. "In the living room." She motioned.

"I don't know, Mom."

"Come on."

"This shouldn't take long." This was her husband. "I mean, Katherine, he's hoping to walk on at Ohio State and you—."

"I'm what?"

"Never mind."

They knew she worked out at six-thirty every weekday morning. She hadn't told them what she did in the workouts.

In the living room, she pushed aside a couple of chairs. There was a red rug over their hardwood floor. It wasn't the size of a wrestling mat, but it would do.

"Are we betting on this?" her son asked.

"Nope," she said. "We're only wrestling."

"Dad, I guess you'll be the ref," he said, and both men laughed.

"All right," Simon said. "When I say, 'Bell,' the match starts." He paused. "Bell."

She attacked his midriff, wrapping her arms around him. He stumbled backwards. She wondered if he was going to fall, but he righted himself. "Mom, come—." He grunted as she pulled him down to the carpet. "Jesus, Mom. All r—." He struggled, and even in his squirming, she felt how warm he was, how soft in places, as she remembered. He didn't seem to know where to grab her, where to put his force. Even as he tried to escape, he exhibited a familiar passivity, a customary surrender. *Baby*, she wanted to say. *Sweet baby*. He twisted from her.

"Come on, you two," her husband said. "We need to hit the road."

She had her son locked in her arms, his back to her, the left side of his body against the floor. He had been her joy, her burden. He had been her excuse. When he was gone, she could no longer claim he was in the way of what she could be.

"Okay, Mom, you won."

"No, I haven't," she insisted, feeling his heart beat against her hand, smelling his hair. She thought, *Let go. You need to let go.* But she didn't—she couldn't—even when her husband grabbed her wrists and strained to pull her free.

The Juror

··

How could you condemn a boy to death if you couldn't imagine his life?

Or, in this case, two boys. Brothers. Moon and D'Shawn, known sometimes by their nicknames, Half and Black Shawn. They were nineteen-year-old fraternal twins and were accused of killing a junior at Ohio Eastern University named Brad Marshall, a white boy whose father owned five car dealerships in Columbus. Brad had been their rival in Sherman's illegal drug world.

The charge was first-degree murder. William Haywood was certain his fellow jurors would find the boys guilty.

William, who was named after W.E.B. Dubois, had never had a nickname, not even Bill or Will. Although he'd grown up in Washington, D.C., where even the mayor had a drug problem, he'd never indulged in drugs, much less sold them. He'd attended Woodrow Wilson Senior High, which was ninety percent black, but he'd taken all AP classes, which were ninety percent white. His parents could have sent him to Sidwell Friends or Georgetown Day School. As a black student with near-perfect PSATs, he would have received a full ride. But his parents, sixties semi-radicals (they marched but never went to jail), believed in public education. Besides, they knew Wilson had a school within a school. Those AP classes. The chess club. The golf team.

From Wilson, he'd gone on to Harvard, then to the Fletcher School of Law and Diplomacy at Tufts. Afterwards, he'd joined the foreign service. Before moving to Sherman twenty months ago to become the Robert Alphonso Taft Distinguished Visiting Professor of Global Studies, he'd spent most of the past twenty-five years abroad. Guatemala. Ghana. Nicaragua. Niger. His last post was as deputy chief of mission in South Africa. At forty-nine-years old, he'd been in line to become an ambassador. But his mother had become ill—she'd smoked all her life, and lung cancer had caught her—and he received an unpaid leave from the State Department so he could be with her. His mother had died a month ago. When the semester ended in two weeks, he would return to the foreign service. He was scheduled to become deputy ambassador to Benin in mid-June.

William's father, who had died of a heart attack two years into William's first overseas post, was black, his mother white. Until he was fifteen, he had blamed the strangeness he felt in the presence of both whites and blacks on his mixed race. When he turned fifteen, he blamed it on his homosexuality. But eventually he decided that neither his mixed race nor his sexual orientation, either alone or in combination, explained entirely why the only people he felt at ease with were from countries besides his own.

Save Spanishville, a few square blocks inhabited by immigrants (documented and otherwise) from Central America, Sherman was white. Ohio Eastern University, although it claimed a black population of seven percent, was the same. When he'd accepted the visiting professorship, William decided to treat it like another foreign posting. He taught one class a semester, served on two university-wide committees, and gave two public lectures each year on U.S. foreign policy. Otherwise, he spent time in Cleveland, which was an hour-and-a-half drive from Sherman, and with his mother, who'd lived in the carriage house behind his rented four-bedroom before, in the last six weeks of her life, he moved her to a hospital bed in his living room.

The only time his routine had been disturbed was in his first February in town, when he'd been bombarded with requests to speak—in classes, in community centers, at a diversity training session sponsored by the university's provost. When he'd expressed his surprise to a black colleague, she'd said, "Don't you remember? February is Black History Month. It's the shortest month of the year, so we have to cram all our blackness into 28 days—29 if we're leaping."

Even during his brief time in town, he'd been called to jury duty three times. On the first two occasions, he'd avoided it, his mother his reason. But the third time, the judge refused to excuse him. His mother was, after all, dead. "Three strikes and you're in," the judge said.

Tim Kovitch, a tall, thin man with broad shoulders who owned the Book and Brew, had been elected jury foreman. After the jurors settled in seats around a rectangular wooden table, he said, "I think we should... maybe...have a nonbinding poll. You know, guilty or not guilty. To see where we stand." He looked around at his fellow jurors.

Betty, a white-haired former fifth-grade teacher, turned to the man sitting next to her, a forty-year-old Roto-Rooter plumber named Rick, and explained what "non-binding" meant. Rick told her he'd figured it out, having become an aficionado (his word) of binding foods thanks to his unfortunate recent propensity (his word again) for loose stools.

"So why don't we go around the table," Tim said, "and give a thumbs up or a thumbs down...I mean, say, 'Guilty' or 'Not guilty' or...I guess... 'Undecided.'"

Ten jurors said "Guilty." William said he was undecided. So did a twenty-one-year-old senior at Ohio Eastern named CeeCee.

"Okay," Tim said to William and CeeCee. "Should we talk about it? Where are your doubts?"

"Where is your certainty?" CeeCee said. She looked like the sorority president she was: She had blonde hair and an artificial tan, which made her glow like a tropical sunset. She was double-majoring in government and wildlife biology. Mike, a financial planner, had brought in Trivial Pursuit so the jurors could play during breaks in the five-day trial. CeeCee hadn't missed a question.

"For starters, Moon and D'Shawn are the biggest drug dealers on campus," Tim said. "Or they were, before Brad Marshall decided to enter the market."

"All they were selling was a little weed," CeeCee said.

Tim tapped his fingers against the table. "Second, you heard three—no, four—witnesses testify that they'd heard Moon or D'Shawn or both say they wanted to kill Brad." He tapped again, like a drum roll. "Third, both brothers were at the crime scene during the murder."

"So were a hundred other people," CeeCee said. "It was a party. But no one saw the actual murder."

"Both brothers were upstairs when the murder was committed. Witnesses saw both brothers run after the shots were fired."

"Of course they ran," CeeCee said. "Who sticks around after shots are fired?"

"So why didn't they testify?" asked Betty. "Why didn't they tell us why they ran?"

"They aren't required to testify," CeeCee said.

Betty frowned. "Instead they sat at the defense table, looking guilty."

"How did they look guilty?" CeeCee said.

"I'm sure they don't own those suits," Betty said. "I'm sure taxpayer money bought them. My money, your money."

"What do their suits— " CeeCee began.

"The suits looked cheap," Mike said. "They kind of shined, like maybe they'd been dry-cleaned too much."

"I'm not sure what guilty looks like," CeeCee said. "I thought both of them looked tired."

William knew he should say something, if only to support CeeCee. He could at least point out that if Moon and D'Shawn had been at all successful as drug dealers, they would have bought their own suits. But he wasn't as credible an advocate as CeeCee was. She wasn't the same color as the defendants.

"Three witnesses," Tim said, holding up three fingers for emphasis, "said they saw Moon with the gun earlier in the evening"

"Not *the* gun," CeeCee said, "*a* gun."

"How many college kids are carrying guns to a party?" Betty said.

"You'd be surprised," Rick muttered.

"One witness said Brad had a gun too," CeeCee said.

"A witness who was talking to one of the killers half the night," Mike said.

"She seems like an articulate and clean and nice-looking young African-American woman," Betty said. "I'm disappointed she would lie in order to protect someone who isn't any of the above."

"I agree that D'Shawn isn't a woman," CeeCee said, her sarcasm delivered with a smile. "But he seems clean and nice-looking enough to me. Why do you think she was lying about the gun?"

"Because no one found a weapon on Brad," Mike said. "He was defenseless."

"Someone could have taken it," CeeCee said.

"The defendants had a motive," Tim said. "No, a double motive. They were competitors. And the victim was sleeping with Moon's girlfriend."

"Ex-girlfriend," CeeCee said. "You heard what, what—what's his name said. Their friend. Chris Little. Little Chris."

"The midget." This was Raylene, an administrative assistant in the biology department at Ohio Eastern.

"He isn't a midget," CeeCee said, sighing. "God, do I have to defend the witnesses too?"

"He *is* on the short side," Tim said.

"He said Moon broke up with *her*," CeeCee said.

"Moon was jealous," Mike said. "He didn't want anyone dating his ex-girlfriend. Pure O.J."

"No one testified to Moon being jealous," CeeCee said. There was exasperation in her voice.

"Three witnesses saw Moon with the gun," Tim said.

"*A* gun," CeeCee repeated. "And the police didn't find the gun on either Moon or D'Shawn. It was in the toilet tank on the second floor." She looked at William, as if to ask, Are you going to say anything? William offered her a smile and a nod but remained silent.

"They weren't invited to the party," Betty said. "They just showed up."

"Everyone just showed up," CeeCee said. "It wasn't a wedding."

"They'd been talking about killing him ever since he moved in on their territory." This was Glenn, who fixed GE refrigerators. His specialty was lucrative, he'd told them, because there were thousands of GE refrigerators in town and they broke down all the time. He didn't understand why people continued to buy them. "This isn't a hard call. They wanted to kill him. They told people they wanted to kill him. And guess what? They killed him."

"Thank you," Betty said.

"I've said I've wanted to kill my sister," CeeCee said. "It doesn't mean I will."

"I think we know what kind those two are," Glenn said. "I think we're being polite because the professor's in the room." He nodded toward William. "Without the professor in the room, I think we'd have wrapped this up already."

"What about *me*?" CeeCee said.

"Brad Marshall was a student," Betty said. "Those two are full-time drug dealers."

"D'Shawn is taking 18 hours—that's more than a full load," CeeCee said. "He's a finance major."

"So he can learn what to do with all his drug money," Betty said.

"Personally, I think he put his brother up to it," Glenn said. "Moon doesn't look like...well...the brightest star in the universe."

"How can you know?" CeeCee said. "You haven't heard either of them speak a word."

William could see the frustration in CeeCee's face decline toward resignation. "They're maybe looking at the death penalty," she said softly.

"Our decision," Tim said.

When William received his class schedule on his first day of high school, he noticed he'd been assigned to non-accelerated classes—all except for math, his best subject. For math, he'd been placed in the remedial group. He told his homeroom teacher what the problem was. His teacher, a black man from South Carolina whose glasses were as round and conspicuous as an owl's eyes, said, "Give it a week or two. See if they might not be the best classes after all."

After homeroom, he'd gone to the main office in order to speak to the principal, but he'd been intercepted by the guidance counselor, a gray-haired white woman (she looked, in fact, like Betty), who pulled his file. Inside the file was a junior-high-school photograph of William. He'd forgotten about Picture Day, and in the photo he looked uncharacteristically un-groomed. The guidance counselor's eyes returned to the photo frequently, and it was to the photo she spoke when she said, "I don't see what the problem is."

His mother had to come to the school before he was allowed to take the classes he was qualified to take.

Guatemalans in the rural areas he visited thought he was from Livingston, a town on the country's Caribbean Coast settled, or so local myth said, by Africans who escaped a sinking slave ship. In Ghana, he was sometimes thought to be Nigerian. When he was in South Africa, he was asked on occasion if he was from Botswana. He liked being from somewhere he wasn't. It excused whatever preconceptions people had about him.

"Three witnesses," Tim said. "I keep coming back to three witnesses who saw Moon with the gun."

"*A* gun," CeeCee said, irritated.

"A gun very similar in description to the murder weapon."

Since his return to the States, William did most of his shopping online. But when he'd wanted a new suit for his mother's funeral, he'd gone to Marvel's, a men's store in Sherman. Marvel's was an anachronism, a first-rate store in an otherwise moribund downtown, its walls and shelves full of suits, shirts, and ties imported from England, France, and Italy. He'd been greeted by the store's owner with standard courtesy, and the owner had been nothing but professional toward him. But as he tried on suits and gauged the attractiveness of various ties, William noticed a young man, a Marvel's employee, against the far wall. He appeared to be of Eastern European descent, and his eyes, deep-set and suspicious, followed William wherever he moved. At one point, the owner left to retrieve a suit, and William stared at the employee, hoping he might embarrass or shame him into looking elsewhere. If anything, however, the man's gaze became even more resolute.

Guilty before the crime. Guilty a priori.

In high school, William was one of two black students (the other was a congressman's daughter, her presence in public schools a political calculation) who didn't ride the charter busses from downtown. He'd never made friends with a single boy or girl who poured off the busses every morning, although he became familiar with their faces in the hallways. Every few days one of them would be called into the principal's office, guilty of infractions William sometimes knew about (a classmate named Mookie had punched an assistant football coach) and sometimes didn't. Since elementary school, he'd been afraid of being called into the principal's office, worried it would mean a permanent mark on his record and therefore confirmation of what he knew wasn't true about himself.

Instead of friends, he acquired lovers, first an older boy in his neighborhood, later men in bookstores and bars in Dupont Circle. His longest relationship, in his senior year, was with José Ferreras, who worked as an administrative assistant in the Portuguese embassy and had a wife and daughter back in Lisbon. José's tour ended around the same time William graduated. From José, William learned he wanted to escape. And he learned how he could.

"It would be nice to finish this up before the weekend," Betty said. "Do we really want this hanging over ours heads?"

"We all heard the judge," Tim said, turning to CeeCee. "There's reasonable doubt. And then there's fanciful doubt. Few cases will be airtight. But there's significant evidence here. The history between the accused and the victim. The threats to kill. The gun three people saw. The suspects fleeing after shots were fired."

CeeCee looked worn down. She stole a glance at William. Soon every eye in the room focused on him.

"What troubles you here, professor?" Tim asked.

This was the moment, he knew, when he should be Henry Fonda in *Twelve Angry Men* and slap a pistol identical to the murder weapon down on the table. But he'd never owned a gun, not even in South Africa, where half of his colleagues carried handguns. (He'd never heard of any of his colleagues fending off armed criminals, although one, drunk and fuming one night, had shot his wife to death.)

He looked at his watch. It was inching toward four o'clock. Moon and D'Shawn were probably guilty, he thought. They were boys off the charter busses, Mookies who instead of employing fists to right whatever injustices they saw in their world or assert the power they believed was rightfully theirs had used a gun. He had declared himself "undecided" on principle. It would be unseemly, he thought, to sit through a five-day trial, then reach a verdict in five minutes. And the evidence, as D'Shawn's and Moon's public defenders had stressed, was all circumstantial. Even so, he wanted the trial to be over as much as Betty did. He'd begun packing. No later than the afternoon of his last class, he planned to be on the road to D.C., where he would stay until his assignment in Benin began.

Nevertheless, something restrained him, and it wasn't only the depleted and depressed look on CeeCee's face.

He said, "I think we should use the weekend to think it over."

He could tell his fellow jurors, minus CeeCee, hated him. He hadn't felt such animosity in a long time.

If William had despised his square, two-story house with gray vinyl siding before his mother died, he doubly despised it now. There was only one room in the house he liked, his first-floor office, where he sat now.

He had enough to do to last him the weekend—student papers to grade, an article he was writing in which he compared Egypt's current unrest with the civil discord Cleopatra faced—but he was restless. He answered emails (one from the ambassador to Benin). He looked up an old boyfriend on Facebook. He clicked on the television and watched news of a country he'd never visited but which nevertheless seemed familiar.

He was usually in bed before ten, but he didn't think he would fall asleep easily tonight. He decided on a walk, although he braced himself for what he might face: The suspicious looks of neighbors who should have known him by now. A slur from the college-student occupants of a passing car. (Two months before, he'd been called a faggot from such a vehicle, although he believed the insult was random. He dressed, he believed, like the most un-ostentatious heterosexual, and he'd never had an affair in Sherman. When he wanted company, he drove to Cleveland, where he'd become reacquainted with a lover he'd known in Niger.) Presently, he stepped outside and into a night infused with a soft, enticing mist.

The judge had warned jurors to stay away from the crime scene, and William had no intention of disobeying her. Nevertheless he found himself, as if carried by a dream or drawn by an overpowering desire, standing outside 418 Elm Street, a three-story redbrick house with one of its attic windows boarded up in cardboard. The house was not in mourning—unless it was the kind of mourning he'd seen in Guatemala, where wakes had the revved-up energy of a new year's party. The wraparound porch hosted a dozen college students, the orange ends of their cigarettes illuminated in the April night like fireflies.

If someone here identified William, the judge would call a mistrial. He knew he should turn around, but he heard a voice from the end of the porch: "Moon, what the fuck, man?" He saw two young black men, illuminated— barely—under the only working light bulb on the porch. They wore black leather jackets over red turtleneck sweaters and khakis. William wondered if "Moon" was now a common name.

William veered right, stepping across the grass and into a garden of azaleas. From where he stood, he could hear, but not see, the men on the porch.

"We need to turn the fuck around if you plan to wave your gun at him," the same young man said in a hard whisper. "I don't trust your hothead self."

"Fuck no," the other said. "He needs to know fear."

"We'll let him know some other time."

"People need to see him wilt."

"Another fucking time, Moon. Another fucking place. Too many goddamn people here, all right?"

"The world needs to see who's boss."

"I'm telling you—."

"Go the fuck home, man."

"You know I won't leave you."

"I got Little Chris."

"Little Chris hooked up with that cheerleader. He's gone, all right?"

"It don't matter."

"He'll kill you, Moon. He'll claim self-defense and kill you."

"Fuck him." There was a pause, and Moon spoke under his breath. "I want him terrified."

"Let me have the gun, Moon."

"Fuck no."

"You're fire, I'm ice. Remember?" The voice was soft, conciliatory. "We need ice in charge of your gun tonight."

"Gun control, Black Shawn style. Here, motherfucker. Enjoy."

When William backed up, he saw the boys—or young men: they seemed baby-faced-new-to-the-world to him—striding toward the front door. They were the same boys—both of average height, Moon with a face as round as his name, D'Shawn's narrower, darker—he'd seen hours earlier, in court. This was impossible because both Moon and D'Shawn, having failed to post bail, were in the Sherman County jail.

William was tired—too tired to see or hear right. It was late, and nothing good could happen to him. But as if the front door were a magnet and he metal, he drew toward it. Inside, music beat against the walls as hard as hammers. He'd never understood the appeal of music as a string of expletives. But here it was: every synonym for fornication, every derogatory name for a woman. Smoke hung in the air as over a metropolis. He smelled marijuana, acrid but sweet. He wondered where the two brothers had gone. To the attic, he decided, where the murder might be about to happen.

No, he reminded himself, it *had* happened.

But in the far right corner, behind a brown couch and a trio of barstools, he saw Brad Marshall holding onto a blonde woman's elbow as he gestured at her with the drink in his hand. A young black woman in a white sweater and a sky-blue skirt held the blonde woman's other elbow, apparently hoping to lead her from the scene. William recognized Brad from photographs the jury had been shown. He recognized the young black woman from the witness stand.

It wasn't easy to negotiate his way toward them. People appeared periodically to block him. One was a young man who couldn't have been taller than five feet. "Little Chris," William said.

Little Chris looked up at him. As he had on the witness stand, he wore nerdy glasses fashionable with African-American athletes. "What's up, my man?" Little Chris said, and offered his hand not in a handshake but in another hand-powered ritual of greeting, one that William failed to enact properly, leaving Little Chris with a puzzled and disappointed frown.

"What happened to your cheerleader?" William said.

"Fucking boyfriend was waiting for her in her bedroom. Shit, he wanted me to do her while he was watching. But I ain't no exhibitionist."

"Quite so," William said, speaking, he thought, like one of the Nigerian elite for whom he was sometimes mistaken in Ghana. "I've got to speak to him," William said, gesturing toward the corner.

"With Brad motherfucking Marshall?" Little Chris shook his head and said either "racist pig" or "rapist pig." William couldn't hear well above the music's pounding beat.

William left Little Chris and reached the far corner. At William's arrival, Brad released the blonde woman—William wondered if she was Moon's ex—and she and her friend immediately disappeared into the thick of the party. Brad was wan, with black hair and a collection of pimples on his forehead. He wore a two-sizes-too-large sweatshirt and loose jeans. He was a few inches shorter than William, although he tried to rectify their difference in height by standing erect. "You need something?" Brad asked him.

William was so astonished to be talking to him, he said, "You're supposed to be dead."

Brad flushed. "What?" he said loudly, and several faces turned toward them. When they'd turned back, he said in a soft hiss, "Who said? Moon?"

"You need to leave," William said. "Fast."

Brad looked William over. He drew in a breath and seemed to relax. "Are you their father?" Slowly, he pulled a silver pistol from behind his back and wiggled it at him. "Tell Half and Black Shawn I'll be waiting for them upstairs." Grinning, Brad slipped past him.

Get the hell out of here, William told himself. But after glancing at the front door, he headed toward the staircase in the other corner. Brad must have ascended quickly because when William stood at the bottom of the stairs, he saw no one above. Little Chris moved past him. "He's up here, isn't he?" he muttered. "He'll kill him. He'll fucking kill them both." Little Chris raced up the stairs. William turned to see who might be following, but no one was.

Halfway up the stairs, William stopped to catch his breath. Presently, he resumed his climb, his feet clapping against the hardwood staircase, and reached the hallway. In front of him was a bathroom, its door open. Three young women stood before the mirror, applying something to their eye-lashes and lips. Upon seeing him, one winked and motioned him in with her index finger.

William turned left and stepped into a bedroom. Four white college students, wearing Ohio Eastern sweatshirts, sat cross-legged on the hardwood floor beneath a bunk bed, a Ouija board between them. Bottles—beer, vodka, whiskey—surrounded them. They passed a joint around. At the back of the room, next to a window, D'Shawn was speaking with the same young black woman he'd seen downstairs. William couldn't hear their conversation clearly but occasionally caught words: "summer," "internship," "Cleveland or Capitol Hill."

He found the other three rooms on the second floor crowded with weed smokers but absent Brad and Moon. Little Chris was in the third room, speaking with a red-haired woman in a corner. William remembered the attic, the murder site, but none of the four rooms offered an entrance to it. Perhaps it was accessible only via pull-down stairs from the ceiling of one of the rooms. He was about to search all four rooms again when he remembered how, on first arriving in Sherman, he had toured several rental houses, one more dilapidated than the next. Access to the attic in two of the houses was via a staircase in the second-floor bathroom.

The young women who had occupied the bathroom were gone. William entered and stepped toward the door at the back. A voice behind him said, "You planning to piss or is it my turn?"

William turned to find D'Shawn filling the doorframe, the faint bulge in his jacket doubtless his brother's gun. Moments after D'Shawn closed the door, William heard two quick shots, followed by a silence, followed by the sound of feet pounding wood. The back door opened, and Moon, his eyes filled with fright, his lips quivering, appeared, a pistol in his palm. It was Brad's pistol, silver and small. William guessed what had happened: Brad had pulled it on Moon and Moon, in the ensuing struggle, had wrested it from him and shot him.

To his brother, D'Shawn said, "Where the fuck did you...Are you fuck-ing...?" But maybe he, too, had divined the truth. "Wipe your prints, damn it."

Moon pulled the bottom of his turtleneck from his khakis, wrapped the gun in it, and rubbed furiously.

A siren sounded.

"Give it to me," D'Shawn said. Moon dropped his gun into the bath-room towel D'Shawn held in front of him. D'Shawn rubbed the towel over the weapon before allowing the gun to slide into the open toilet tank.

"What the fuck were you doing?" D'Shawn barked. "What the fuck did I tell you?"

"He wanted me scared. Said he was going to— ."

"Come on, man. Let's go!" They slapped the door open, and their feet smashed against the steps on their way down.

The three young women who earlier had occupied the bathroom peered in from the hallway. The one who had beckoned William with her finger now pointed at him and said, "He's a killer!" The other two young women shrieked, and all three turned and descended the stairs.

Glancing out the window and down at the yard, William saw D'Shawn and Moon dart off into darkness, Little Chris trailing them. Brad, he remembered from the coroner's report at the trial, had died instantly.

William thought of his classmates on the charter busses, how he'd never tried to befriend any of them. They would have scorned him anyway, he thought. He'd heard them in gym class, how they said faggot as they might say child molester. But he couldn't say he didn't know them or they him. They never talked, but they shared a world within the world.

He's a killer. And other things he wasn't, truly wasn't, but to some minds was and always would be.

The siren grew louder. He raced down the stairs, rushed out the open front door, and ran until he reached his house.

When, presently, silence was restored and his breathing fell into its regular rhythm, he wondered if he'd gone anywhere at all.

Diplomatic immunity. William had heard the phrase long before he knew what a diplomat was. (His father was complaining about a car with a diplomatic license plate double-parked in downtown D.C.) Even later, when he understood, he conceived of diplomatic immunity as an all-powerful force, a prophylaxis against persecution of any sort. To have diplomatic immunity was to have protection against everything shy of death.

He'd seen diplomatic immunity at work. He'd been with two colleagues when they'd been busted with marijuana outside the Managua International Airport. But after they flashed their credentials, the pair of policemen who had been about to arrest them, looking disappointed and confused, turned from the scene.

Diplomatic immunity didn't apply to William or any of his colleagues when they were in the States, of course. If they were caught with marijuana, they faced the same consequences as anyone else. No, according to the statistics—how many of his charter-bus-riding classmates had ended up in prison after drug busts?—William would face worse consequences.

Although he was freer in any foreign country than he was in the land of the free, he'd long understood that his career choice might be seen as a kind of exile—or an abdication. He sometimes asked, as if he were speaking to an imaginary inquisitor, a woman who looked like Rosa Parks and could quote everything Martin Luther King had ever said, "Do you blame me?"

But it was CeeCee to whom, a year-and-a-half later, he might have explained, if only to elucidate his behavior as a juror. She'd come to Benin as a Peace Corps Volunteer. All 127 Volunteers had been invited to a Thanksgiving dinner at the ambassador's residence in Cotonou. CeeCee looked every bit the sorority sister she'd appeared during the trial. If William had to bet which Volunteer was having the most success, he would put all his money on her. She recognized him immediately as he stood in front of a cheese spread beneath photographs of President Obama and Vice President Biden. "Professor," CeeCee said, extending her hand and reintroducing herself unnecessarily. They talked about their respective work in Benin before she mentioned the trial.

"I was hoping we'd win the day," she said. "I had a new strategy. I'd been thinking about it over the weekend, which you'd been smart to suggest we use to consider everything. Both brothers were being accused of first-degree murder, but no one saw D'Shawn with a gun. And it wasn't D'Shawn whose girlfriend or ex-girlfriend was part of the mix. I don't even understand why he was being charged."

"The law of brother as keeper," William said, thinking he was making a joke.

But CeeCee didn't smile. "It was probably hopeless," she said. "The ten other jurors had probably made up their minds as soon as they saw who was being accused."

William wondered if she was being unfair but doubted it.

"Anyway, I guess we'll never know. A mistrial." She shook her head. "And the judge wouldn't tell us why."

"One of the jurors visited the crime scene."

She looked at him. "Is that what happened?"

He nodded, although he'd never understood how to classify what he'd experienced. Hallucination? Nocturnal daydream? Or simply an overpowering conviction about what had happened?

In front of his fellow jurors, he would have found it impossible to explain, however obliquely, his insight. They would have ascribed his assurance, and the sympathy he would have shown the accused, to his being black. He understood this as the burden of any black man or woman in America, of any person of whatever dark shade: to know the truth, *to know it without a doubt,* but to have one's knowledge ascribed to racial solidarity or to a calculated effort to balance scales weighted down on one side by centuries of wrongful convictions, lynchings, and slavery or simply to anger and a desire for revenge.

But the judge, he'd thought, might be convinced. She was educated, she must understand the law's racial biases, she looked—and perhaps this is what had ultimately convinced him to speak with her—like CeeCee plus thirty years. When he'd spoken to her, it hadn't been with the intention of excusing himself from the jury or having a mistrial declared. It had been with the hope—foolish and fantastic, he realized now—of having the case thrown out. He'd stood in her chambers (not the book-lined, wood-paneled room of movies but an office as efficient and neat as an insurance company executive's) and spoken of what he knew—or at least knew was possible. His conviction must have seemed like lunacy.

Clarity, he thought, can be a kind of madness.

"I wonder which juror…" CeeCee began. But she found the answer in his face.

"It probably wouldn't have mattered," she said. "I bet we would have been a hung jury. But, well, who knows. If you and I had come in Monday and done our best…I guess you'd have to believe in miracles." She put cheese on a cracker and ate it.

He thought to ask her what had become of Moon and D'Shawn, but he decided he didn't want to know. He asked her again about her life, and this is what they talked about until she excused herself and drifted off into the crowd. He glanced at the portraits above him before, hearing a trumpet—the first note from the Gangbé Brass Band—he turned and rejoined the party.

Cuts

∙∙

Sitting in his car outside his son's middle school, the radio broadcasting a story about prison or war, the father can't concentrate. He is thinking about his son, who is inside the school gym. It is the last day of basketball tryouts. Cuts will be made today. Since the tryouts began at the beginning of the week, the father has been rehearsing how he will comfort his son when he fails to make the team. He has been recalling his own stories of failure, although of course he will not use the word failure when he speaks with his son. He will call it a setback, a roadblock, an opportunity to do something else. He will say, "You're only in the sixth grade. You'll make the team next year. Guaranteed." His son's game, although by no means weak, is far from complete. He can't dribble well with his left hand, and on defense he tends to lean back on his heels rather than lean forward on his toes, which makes him slow to react to his opponents' moves. The truth is, his son could use more practice. He spends far more time on his computer than on the basketball court.

When his son isn't appeased by his reassurances, the father will say, "Let me tell you a story." He could begin with the famous story of how the world's best basketball player, as a sophomore, was cut from his high-school team. But the world's best basketball player, retired a decade now, is only a name to his son. He never saw him play. The father doesn't know if the players his son likes have equivalent stories of failure. The father will, therefore, speak about his own failures, and his son will be comforted because his son admires him, wants to be like him. He said as much a month or two ago. Or perhaps it has been a couple of years now. He will share his own basketball story, from junior high, about how, to fill a twelve-boy team, only thirteen boys showed up for tryouts, which were conducted over a single afternoon. When the tryouts ended, at dusk, with darkness visible in the windows above the bleachers, the coach stood at center court and called the names of the twelve boys who had made the cut. It reminded the father of a beauty contest, except instead of giggling and blushing, the chosen boys slapped hands and thumped their chests.

After the twelfth name, there was silence. He expected the coach to come over to him and say something, offer encouragement, condolences. But the coach retreated to his office beyond the far basket. The other boys raced into the locker room, and he thought he could hear them singing. He slipped into the cold October night, his hair damp with sweat, his cheeks wet from the tears he couldn't stop. He walked the mile-and-a-half home and found his father in his easy chair in the living room, his reading glasses propped on his nose, the afternoon paper spread between his hands.

He broke down again, although he knew his father hated tears.

"I guess I don't have to ask whether you made the team," his father said, his smile suggesting satisfaction at his observation.

"I'm sorry," he told his father, although whether because he was crying or because he had failed to make the team, he didn't know.

Perhaps his father offered mild words of comfort. Perhaps he immediately returned to his newspaper. What he remembers is racing to his room, closing the door, and shoving his face deep in a pillow.

He didn't remain a failure, although he never again played an organized sport. He could have tried out for the team the following year, but when he saw the notice about tryouts posted on the school's bulletin board, he remembered the coach calling out the names of the boys who had made the team and the subsequent silence. How often in daydreams had he imagined his name being the last called? How often had the fantasy dissolved, leaving the genuine, awful memory?

But if he had failed as an athlete, he had succeeded elsewhere. He had gone to an excellent college, the only person in his high-school class to gain admission to the prestigious school. In college, he knew boys—they were inevitably boys—who'd had life handed to them like keys to a new car. They strutted around the place like roosters who knew they would never meet the ax. If there was a chance they would fail, their fathers bought off the committees, the judges, whoever might say no. They had a monopoly, it seemed, on all the pretty girls, even the pretty girls who were, or should have been, smart enough to see them as illegitimate owners of success.

You don't want to be one of them, he would tell his son. You don't want your victories handed to you. You don't want your victories to be unearned.

The father, whom everyone called Johnny in college, although he always introduced himself as John, roomed with one of these boys. Kenneth—never Ken or Kenny—was in the same eating club his father and his grandfather (and generations of Kenneths before them) had been in. If Kenneth had ever had an original thought, John concluded, it must have occurred in a different life. In their sophomore years, both John and Kenneth fell in love with Elizabeth Wright, who lived down the hall from the two of them. She had hair like a movie star from the thirties, thick and red-brown, and she liked chess, which she played with John a few times a week in the atrium in the student center. With a smile he often conjured to help himself fall asleep at night, she sometimes referred to him as "my check mate." But of course it was Kenneth she dated. Of course it was Kenneth she agreed to marry.

Soon after their engagement, when all three of them had graduated and were living in the same city, John tried, in intentionally dramatic fashion, to make Elizabeth change her mind. He met her at a coffee shop where they occasionally met to play chess (its name was the Lost World, which would come to seem appropriate) with a bouquet of roses. When he told her he loved her, had always loved her, and would love her forever, the embarrassment on her face was so pronounced he turned toward the window. Outside, a bearded homeless man, perhaps drawn to the scene by the flowers on the table, shook his head in sympathy. It was as if following the roll call of names at his junior high basketball tryouts, John had grabbed a ball and shouted, "You'll change your mind, Coach, when you see what I can do!" and, in attempting to dribble like a Globetrotter, had bounced the ball off his foot.

"Okay," he told Elizabeth, his voice a mix of humiliation and self-loathing, "that didn't work. Will you still play chess?" But she said she had to go. He never saw Elizabeth again, although he did see Kenneth, who always greeted him warmly but with a smile that suggested he knew everything and thought it was hilarious. John tracks their lives now via the alumni magazine. They have four children and live in a suburb of Atlanta.

He wonders if he should tell his son this story. But what is its lesson? If at first you don't succeed in romance, try again? He has tried. He's been married—and divorced—twice.

He checks his watch. It's six o'clock, which is when the tryouts are supposed to end. He steps out of his car. The air is noticeably chillier than when he arrived half an hour ago. It's darker, too, autumn's colors dissolved in gray-black. Across the street, on the front lawn of the middle school, an oak tree's leaves flutter and fall in the wind. He walks across the street and across the lawn to stand outside the wide double doors to the gym. Two dozen other parents have gathered here, and he sees the anxiety in their faces. He nods to the several he knows. To stem his nerves, he hums a song. Almost immediately, he stops, the song bitter with recent memories.

He had seen the audition notice in the *Sherman Advocate and Post*. Three weeks later he was standing on the stage in the Metropolitan Theater, singing in front of a director, an assistant director, and eight hundred empty seats. *Carousel* was to be a collaboration between the drama department at Ohio Eastern University and the amateur singers and actors of Sherman. In his wildest fantasy, he would be given the part of Billy, the angry, depressed lead. But he would have settled—gladly—for a role in the ensemble. In prep-aration, he had sung along to the 1956 movie soundtrack in his car, in his house. Once he woke up at five-thirty and sang it in its entirely before he drove to work. To be sure he wasn't using the professional singers' voices to hide the insufficiency of his own, he downloaded the karaoke version of "You'll Never Walk Alone" from iTunes and sang it a dozen times a night. He had the liberty to do so because he and his girlfriend of a year-and-a-half had broken up the previous month. When he wasn't singing, his house felt too quiet.

His audition time was from ten to ten-ten in the morning. He'd taken the entire day off from work at the law firm where he'd made partner five years before. It was a small firm. He sometimes wondered how he would have fared at a large firm in a big city. In the alumni magazine, his classmates boasted of their successes in Boston, New York, Philadelphia, L.A. He arrived fifteen minutes early to the audition. His throat felt raw from all his practic-ing. He wished he had swallowed a spoonful of honey, as he had on other days.

When he was called onto the stage, he could hear his heartbeat in his ears, like explosions. He hadn't sung in front of an audience since his junior-high-school graduation, when he and his classmates had entertained their parents, grandparents, and bored siblings with an off-key rendition of "Inch Worm." But he sang well—he knew this about himself, even if he hadn't allowed anyone to verify it. He regretted not pursuing musical theater in high school and college, if only to gain experience singing in front of people. Instead, he'd captained the debate club in high school and had appeared in two Shakespeare comedies in college, stepping in to minor roles when a student-director friend of his had failed to find enough actors.

At the audition, he sang the full sixteen bars he'd prepared. He believed this was a propitious sign. (He'd been warned he might be cut off.) Later, he learned the director, in an effort to foster good relations with the good citizens of Sherman, had permitted every amateur to sing all sixteen bars of whatever they'd prepared, no matter what they sounded like. Meanwhile, he stopped the drama students at Ohio Eastern after a single note if they didn't hit it correctly. After he finished singing, the director thanked him. John bubbled like a teenager. "I hope to see you again!" he exclaimed, as if at the end of a first date.

The director gave John a smile, familiar from somewhere, a smile both self-satisfied and amused, as if at a joke only its teller understood. Only when John received no call back—only when he read the full cast list in the *Sher-man Advocate and Post*—did he understand the smile's message.

He could share this story with his son. As before, however, he wonders what moral he might impart. If you don't audition, you'll never know how lousy a singer you are? Wouldn't the illusion have been preferable to the truth?

But his stories aren't required to have morals, are they? They are simply ways to comfort his son, to ease his son's disappointment. Your father tried and failed, and he isn't...what? Unhappy? Would this be the truth?

Years are supposed to enhance the good memories, soften the bad. But whatever mechanism in the brain is in charge of this distillation is, in John, broken. Good memories fade easily; bad memories burn. A day doesn't go by that he doesn't think about the last time he saw Elizabeth.

The doors to the gym burst open, and he recognizes the rejected immediately. Their heads are bowed, their eyes are red-rimmed and averted. They walk into the dark evening as if into a headwind. And there is his son, off to the side, wandering like a blind man whose seeing eye dog has abandoned him. He steps toward the boy, a lightness in his heart. His stories are ready. Like water to the thirsty, they will revive him. You'll never walk alone.

The next moment, he realizes the boy, despite his too-long hair, his too-long nose, isn't his son but his son's one-time friend, Daniel. He hears: "Over here, Dad!" His son approaches, bookended by a pair of boys, their faces beaming. He feels the lightness in his heart burn to black, leaving a familiar residue. What long ago had expressed itself as tears now resides within him as something seared. "I made it!" says his son, but John turns from the boy's smile as if from a judge's damning sentence.

Barbados

When Eddie saw the job candidate's name, he smelled the Chesapeake Bay, its saltwater and jellyfish, its speedboat oil. He saw the moon roll a thin silver carpet across the water. He felt his blood fill him everywhere, deliciously, and he felt hands on his chest and in his hair and on his cheeks. He felt lips on his lips as cool and inviting as the night.

But the Alvaro López Eddie knew had returned to Guatemala after the summer they were counselors at Camp Go in Edgewater, Maryland. He had plans to go to college in Guatemala City, buy a coffee finca, live with his future wife and children on the shore of Lake Atitlán. The Alvaro López Eddie knew was history.

Eddie was supposed to meet with this other Alvaro López at two-thirty on Friday. Alvaro was the last of three finalists for the position, a late replacement for a candidate who had withdrawn. Eddie had met already with the two other finalists, whom he had found adequate if uninspiring. He wasn't on the four-person search committee and had no vote on who was hired. The committee simply wanted his input.

A note at the bottom of Alvaro's schedule said a copy of his dossier was available from the unit's administrative assistant. But when Eddie asked to see it, the assistant said one of the committee members had taken it home.

Who needs a candidate's file, Eddie thought, when there was the Internet. But when, sitting at his desk in his third-floor office with its view of downtown Sherman, Ohio, he Googled Alvaro López, he was greeted with hundreds of Web links to three musicians, one a drummer, another a guitar player, the third a saxophonist. He tried to narrow the search by putting "Alvaro López Guatemala" into the search field. This yielded stories about a drug lord and links to YouTube videos of the guitar player strumming in a dust storm.

Late to pick up his son from preschool, Eddie raced down the stairs to the parking lot and his Nissan. During their summer by the Chesapeake, he had driven an ancient Volkswagen Beetle, which smelled of dirt and Alvaro's nectarine-scented cologne. On their nights off, he and Alvaro sometimes drove into Washington, D.C., to watch movies and drink beer in Georgetown. One time at the Alligator, a club on K Street, Alvaro, who was five-feet, seven-inches tall only by the most generous measurement but had brilliant black hair, skin a color somewhere between copper and gold, and dark eyes with lush eyelashes, spent an entire night dancing with the young women in the club as Eddie watched from a table. Alvaro spun them, twirled them, drew them into his chest. He was masterful, and Eddie found himself becoming jealous, which was, he suspected, Alvaro's intention. Later in the Volkswagen, before they reached the camp parking lot, Eddie pulled to the side of the dark road, lined with maple and oak trees, and after clicking off his headlights, grabbed at Alvaro's slacks in a gesture as much angry as lustful. "Gently," Alvaro said twice before it was over.

Having propelled himself into the past, Eddie didn't remember the turns he'd made to reach the Discovery Center, where his son, Adam, was in his second year of preschool. Eight minutes late, he sprinted the ten yards from his car to the front door, his breath filling the February air. "Are you feeling all right?" asked Sabrina, the Discovery Center's director, after she opened the door for him. She was tall and thin, with straight, gray-black hair and a repertoire of sneers. He had never liked her, but she was a high-school classmate of his wife's, and he did his best to be friendly.

"I'm fine, thanks," he panted. He peeked into the playroom, glad to see he wasn't the only late parent. A blonde-haired girl—Lila or Layla, he couldn't remember—was flicking paint from a brush in the general direction of a piece of paper tacked to an easel. He remembered Ona, the art teacher at Camp Go, who was only two years older than he but was rumored to have been divorced. She had brownish-blonde hair and enormous breasts the likes of which he'd encountered only in dirty magazines. He wanted to sleep with her, but his desire made him awkward, and he mostly found himself answering her questions about Alvaro. "Do you want me to arrange a threesome?" Alvaro asked him one night as they dried themselves after a swim in the bay. He said, "No," with a kind of panic, unwilling for Ona—or anyone—to know the extent of his relationship with Alvaro.

"Where's Adam?" Eddie asked. The answer came from Adam himself. He burst from the bathroom at the far end of the room, his pants down by his knees. "I'm here!" He had a piece of toilet paper in his right hand and a Matchbox car in his left. The blonde-haired girl made a squeaking noise before resuming her painting. Eddie ushered Adam back into the bathroom, where he tidied him up.

On their way out of the Discovery Center, Sabrina, who stood beside the door like a witch awaiting trick-or-treaters, said, "Please say hello to Jenny for me."

Sabrina was the only person Eddie knew who called his wife Jenny. It spoke to an intimacy they had once shared, and from time to time, on little evidence, he speculated about how intimate their relationship had been. "I will," he said, and passing by her, he drew in a breath of her perfume, as strong as a reproach.

In his car, he thought about the candidate. What if he was the Alvaro López he knew? What if he was hired? How long would their history stay secret?

"Go, Daddy!" Adam shouted from the back seat of the car. "Go, go, go!"

Eddie dug in his pocket for his car key, but he realized he had already put it in the ignition. He started the car, then turned around to look out his rear window. His eyes fell on his son in his car seat. With his reddish-blonde hair and pinpoint orange freckles, he looked like Jennifer. He wondered how he would feel if his son grew up to be gay. Of course what he and Alvaro had done at Camp Go had nothing to do with being gay; they were simply young and curious and full of displaced lust. He wondered if what they'd done had been a never-to-be-repeated experiment for Alvaro as well. He wondered what Alvaro would think of Sherman, whose voters had recently declined to reelect the two openly homosexual city council members because they had proposed a gay-pride parade.

He turned on a CD—*Free to Be You and Me*, his wife's nostalgia purchase—and listened to two babies speculate about whether they were boys or girls as he and Adam drove home. They lived in a two-story redbrick house in The Summit, a gated community in the hills on the west side of town. The realtor had spoken of the spectacular views, and while it was true one could see the Sky River from the guest bedroom, the most prominent landmark within eyesight was the coal-fired power plant north of town. Eddie had once compared it to a serial masturbator, its long, thin smokestack shooting carbon dioxide into the sky in a never-ending orgasm of pollution.

His wife wasn't home, but the house was Jennifer personified. There were photos of her, and her and Adam, and her and the three of them, on the piano, on the mantel, on top of the television. The rooms were painted, by Jennifer herself, in her favorite colors. The place smelled like she did, of a perfume Eddie remembered from their first date; of coffee, which she drank by the pot; and of horses, which she rode twice a week at a stable half an hour outside of town.

"Well, what do we want to do, A-man?" he asked his son. Adam wanted to watch TV, which Eddie wasn't supposed to encourage; Jennifer thought TV stifled originality and creativity. She was right, of course, but Eddie was tired, so he grabbed a beer out of the fridge. He walked back into the living room and plopped down on the couch. Adam had already commandeered the channel changer.

An hour and twenty minutes later, when he heard Jennifer's car pull into the drive, he turned off the television to a cascade of disapproval from Adam and rushed out to the back porch to bury his four Sam Adams bottles in the recycling bin. Jennifer had been horseback riding, and she smelled of horses and hay. Adam raced up to her, wrapped his arms around her legs, then darted off toward his toys at the back of the house.

"Welcome," Eddie said, suppressing a burp.

"What've you been doing?" Jennifer asked, glancing around, suspicion in her eyes.

"Relaxing," he said.

"TV?"

"Father-son time. All good."

"I'm starving," she said. "I don't suppose you made dinner."

Eddie snapped his fingers. "Forgot."

She shook her head, but she was smiling as she slipped past him and into the kitchen. He might have joined her to peel carrots or cut apples, but the beers had made him languid, and he plopped back onto the couch. The sounds from the kitchen were a soporific; anything shy of a thunderclap would have been. Before he closed his eyes, he tried to remember the last time he and Jennifer had made love.

He awoke to his son's loud voice: "No more dreams, Daddy! No more dreams!"

At several points during dinner, Eddie thought he might bring up Alvaro's name, if only because Alvaro wouldn't leave his thoughts. He was relieved when Jennifer finished dinner and asked Adam if he wanted to take a walk. Eddie had declined these outings so often Jennifer had stopped inviting him. He heard them leave with a soft shutting of the front door.

What would Jennifer say if she learned he'd had sex with a man? Would she be horrified? Probably. But he would explain that his relationship with Alvaro had occurred half a lifetime ago, when he didn't know himself, when he was experimenting with everything. She might ask him if he had been afraid of AIDS. He probably should have been, but he and Alvaro were so young, it didn't occur to him to worry. If Jennifer blanched at his disclosure, however, he could point to her own experiments in same-sex sex. During college, she'd become involved with a fellow horseback rider, also named Jennifer. Eddie had found something comic about a Jennifer bedding a Jennifer or vice versa, and his reaction had been to laugh and tease her. He doubted she would find his revelation funny. Besides, the time to confess had been early in their relationship.

Presently, he found himself in his and Jennifer's bedroom, standing in front of the full-length mirror nailed to the closet door. He removed his sweater and T-shirt and stared at his chest. Hair swirled around his nipples, met in the middle of his breastbone, and cascaded toward his bellybutton. He'd borne this hirsute letter T since he was sixteen. What was new, or new within the last half decade, was the relative flabbiness of his chest, his budding man-breasts, his rub-a-dub-dub-three-men-in-a-tub paunch. He used to run and lift weights, but since Adam's birth, he'd given up regular exercise.

He remembered how he and Alvaro, at midnight, used to leave their campers dreaming and slip down to the shore. They would walk to the end of the pier and strip in the moonlight, piling their clothes into two tiny volcanoes. Alvaro's chest was hairless and flat, like gold slate. His other features—his feet, his thighs, his ass—were as small, as dainty even, as a girl's, and sometimes Eddie would have him before they dove into the water. After swimming and floating on their backs and talking in the radiant moonlight, he would have him again on the dry dock.

Eddie had pushed his trousers and underwear to his feet, and he was gazing at his naked body, at his tangled brown pubic hair and his circumcised penis, swelling in his hand.

"What're you doing, Daddy?" Adam stood in the doorframe, gazing at him with a half smile. He marched next to Eddie. "Can I show the mirror my penis too?"

Before Eddie could answer, Adam pulled down his pants. He mimicked the solemn look on Eddie's face. A moment passed. "What are we doing, Daddy?"

Eddie thought to say something about a testicular exam. But Adam would follow up with questions, and his lies would find their way to Jennifer. He sighed, gazing at himself. Somewhere beneath the body he owned now was the body he'd owned when he was eighteen, like a beautiful, hard Russian nesting doll. He said, "We're seeing who we are."

Adam puffed up his chest in imitation of his father. "Yes, we are," he said.

But when Eddie heard Jennifer coming up the steps, he quickly pulled up his underwear and pants and whispered, "The show's over."

As Jennifer read a goodnight story to Adam, Eddie grabbed his running shoes from the closet. They were at least five years old, but they looked new, the silver outlines on the black swoops shining. They even had a new-shoe smell. He changed his clothes and put on sweatpants and a T-shirt. He popped into Adam's room to tell Jennifer where he was going. "Running?" she asked, as if she hadn't heard him. But she gave him an encouraging smile.

Outside in the crisp air, he felt exhilarated. This lasted all of ten seconds before his body recognized what it was being asked to do. He felt a dull ache from feet to ears. His breathing became the breathing of someone on Mount Everest whose supplemental oxygen had run out. But even as his body said stop, his brain, fearing a capitulation to soft and flabby, urged it on. He ran a mile to Sherman High School and ran two miles around the school's track. The route on his return was uphill and he found himself slowing to a near walk. But he never gave in entirely, and when his house was in sight, he sprinted like a man in pursuit of a medal.

In the kitchen, Eddie dropped to the floor. He was on pushup twenty-two when he heard Jennifer's steps. He continued, finishing thirty (he'd wanted to do fifty). He collapsed and looked up at her standing in the door-frame. It was only nine o'clock, but she had on pajamas. They were baby blue and baggy and hid all of her curves, which were subtle to begin with. "You're very cute, in a mid-life crisis kind of way," she said. "Keep panting, I'm going to change."

She returned in black underwear and a black bra, and after a brief attempt at sex on the kitchen floor, which proved cold, hard, and the bearer of two smashed grapes, they walked upstairs to their bedroom. She threw a towel over the lamp and turned on the CD player on their bedside table. It was Tori Amos's latest, her voice high and elongating syllables beyond recognition.

Eddie remembered one night when lightning and rain had spoiled their midnight swim, he and Alvaro sneaked into the boathouse, whose second floor hosted the camp's drama classes. Alvaro discovered a long, red wig and a toy pistol, and after he slid the pistol over to Eddie, he put on the wig and pretended to be Tori Amos singing "Me and a Gun." Eddie had heard the song a few times, and he found its lyrics chilling and disturbingly stirring, but Alvaro changed the words, and Barbados became not a place to dream of while being sexually assaulted but an oasis they were creating, a paradise of heat, lust, and soon-to-be fulfilled desire.

In their queen-sized bed with rose-colored sheets, Eddie and Jennifer climaxed simultaneously, something they hadn't achieved since before Adam was born. "My God, that was good," Jennifer said, collapsing next to him. "I don't know why we don't do that more often."

Although Eddie had reviewed Alvaro López's dossier that morning and realized exactly who the candidate was, it was hard to accept him as real, so profound a part of his fantasy life had he become. But after Seymour Stolzenberg, the unit head, with his crooked glasses and gray beard stubble, said, "Fifteen minutes and I'll be back," Alvaro—*his* Alvaro—was alone in his presence. Eddie's first impulse was to rush up to him, embrace him, say, "How the hell have you been?" This, he remembered, was how the two cowboys in *Brokeback Mountain* had reunited. No, they'd done an embrace one more by kissing like they hoped to pull the breath from each other's lungs. But he hadn't loved Alvaro. They'd been two boys full of life and lust, and he, anyway, had outgrown this manifestation of his curiosity and desire. At the same time, he remembered lying on the dock with Alvaro after their swim, after sex, and staring at the stars, talking about whatever they wanted. He seemed to remember holding Alvaro's hand.

Alvaro hadn't changed aside from his face, which seemed heavier around the mouth and chin. His hair was the same vivid black, and he was as slim as an exclamation point. "Come on in, Alvaro," Eddie said, and he offered him his hand to shake. Alvaro's hand was cool, small, smooth. "Here, have a seat."

As Alvaro sat in the hardback chair in front of Eddie's desk, Eddie found it difficult to read his expression. Was he nervous? Pleased? He couldn't have been surprised: Eddie's name had been on Alvaro's interview itinerary. He'd had time to wonder if Eddie was *the* Eddie. Their eyes connected, moved off each other, connected again. "Well," Eddie said, and he was about to launch into his usual speech about what he did at the company when Alvaro said, "It was because of you."

Eddie's heart rumbled. He'd wondered if his employment with the company was the reason Alvaro wanted the job. To have his suspicion confirmed scared him. But beneath his fear, there was something less frightening or, rather, frightening in a thrilling way.

"My career," Alvaro said. "You helped start my career."

Eddie released a breath, relieved but also disappointed.

"Do you remember how, during the inventions contest at camp, you built the solar shower?" Alvaro asked.

It was a twenty-gallon tank lined with tinfoil and surrounded by magnifying glasses to intensify the sun's rays. For three straight days before the judging, the skies were overcast. The water in the shower was as chilly as if it had been pulled from a mountain creek. "It was a colossal failure," Eddie said, smiling.

"For the contest it was, yes. But do you remember a few days afterwards, during the evening of a very hot day?"

They'd tested the shower together, first in their bathing suits, then, assured no one was around, without them, and the water had been perfect, a few degrees shy of hot. He nodded, smiling more cautiously this time. He didn't want to engage Alvaro in a reminiscence of their relationship. He was worried it would give him permission to mention their connection casually to whomever he met today. "It was long ago," he offered.

"Yes, but it was the spark I needed. I went back to Guatemala and I founded my company, and soon we were selling low-cost solar ovens in poor villages in the oriente. And before long, we were even selling—yes," and he smiled warmly, and Eddie, recognizing his smile from a lifetime ago, smiled back, "solar showers."

There was a long pause. The smile left Alvaro's face. "But then I had to leave the country."

"Why?"

"The war. We had begun selling in the Petén, and when you sell cheap to campesinos in a war zone, no matter the profit you make, the army thinks you are a communist. So I began to receive death threats. And, one day, as I was driving in Chiquimula, far from the war zone, an army jeep pulled next to me and—." Alvaro made a pistol of his right hand.

For Eddie, there had always been something at once terrifying and titillating about the casual violence in Alvaro's country. He justified his occasional roughness with Alvaro by thinking of what he might be facing at home. "They shot at you?"

"They shot at my engine. Destroyed my car." He paused. "It was a warning."

"So you came to the States," Eddie said. "And you've been working here ever since."

Alvaro nodded.

"You're a U.S. citizen now."

Alvaro gazed at him. Was his look conspiratorial? "I was married. It lasted two-and-a-half years. No children."

"I have a son," Eddie said. He didn't mention Jennifer. There was more Eddie wanted to know about Alvaro, more he wanted to tell about himself. But the situation precluded this. "Why would you like to work here?"

Eddie half expected him, perhaps even wanted him, to say, "Because you're here."

"Your great spirit of invention," he said. "There is cautious invention, and there is your fearlessness. You risk ridicule. You continue anyway."

Eddie wondered if "you" was intended to refer to him or the company. They'd been so reckless; it was amazing the entire camp didn't know about them. He was terrified they would be discovered. But night would fall, the camp would settle down into cricket chirps and sleep, and he and Alvaro would escape to the lake. *Yes, I haven't seen Barbados—but I'm going to tonight.*

"I'll mention this to you only," Alvaro said, his voice lowered. "I have another offer, from a company in Spain. It's attractive, but I love what you do here. This is where I'd like to be."

Eddie felt his heart race again. What if Alvaro moved to Sherman? He'd ask him to keep their past a secret, and they could be friends. He would introduce him to Jennifer. It might all work out.

There was a brief silence before Eddie said, "I'll tell you a little about what I do here."

"I know what you do," Alvaro said.

Eddie must have looked surprised because Alvaro held up his hand and, smiling gently, said, "But of course I would like to hear this from you."

"All right," he said, and he began his usual spiel. It was as if he had memorized lines to play a part, and because he knew them perfectly, he could think about anything as he spoke. He wondered again what would happen if Alvaro was offered the job. He felt terror, and beneath it something like the opposite. He reached the end of his talk at the same time Seymour Stolzenberg opened his door and said, "All done?"

The answer, Eddie thought, depended on what his colleagues decided about Alvaro.

Alvaro stood and so did Eddie. "Nice to meet you, Alvaro." Eddie couldn't keep the grin off his face as he shook Alvaro's hand.

"Very nice to meet you, Eddie. Very nice." A smile—and a wink? Eddie might have imagined it—and Alvaro was gone.

Distracted, his mind wandering, Eddie didn't finish what he'd hoped to at work until late. It didn't matter. It was Jennifer's turn to pick up Adam, and he'd called and told her he wouldn't make it home in time for dinner. It was eight-thirty by the time he left the office.

His route home took him downtown past the Hotel Sherman, where Alvaro was staying. He slowed and pulled into a parking space across from it. A doorman in a ridiculous red top hat stood outside. Eddie was happy to see he was sneaking a cigarette. Eddie considered what would happen if he walked into the hotel and asked whoever was at the front desk to let Alvaro López know he had arrived. Alvaro would invite him up to his room. He would open the mini bar. They would have a drink.

But he didn't allow himself to imagine what would happen next. He wasn't like some reckless politician who would risk everything to consort with pages and prostitutes, videographers and interns. Such men—and they were inevitably men—had no foresight. They couldn't see past the pleasures of their blowjobs and sock-wearing tumbles in hotel beds with Russian émigrés who haven't outgrown their acne but charge a thousand an hour. They couldn't see how stupid it is to treat a good, steady life—a life anyone would envy—like a chip on a roulette table.

Alvaro had only a one in three chance of being hired. If he didn't get the job, Eddie might never see him again. He could at least say hello, catch up a little more on his life. He stepped out of the car, but only, he decided, to breathe the air. The doorman tossed his cigarette stub into the street. It rolled, its orange light sparking. He and Alvaro could have a drink, couldn't they? Two old friends? This wasn't reckless or stupid. This was civil and polite.

From somewhere nearby, Eddie heard a baby crying. He remembered the night he and Jennifer had brought Adam home from the hospital. At three in the morning, Adam, sleeping in a Moses basket in the middle of the bed, had released such a terrible howl that Eddie sprung immediately for the phone, prepared to dial 911. But Jennifer wasn't concerned, and she quieted their son soon enough with her breast. Eddie had been unable to fall back to sleep. He had realized his life would now be dedicated to staving off whatever would cause Adam to feel such anguish.

He returned to his car and drove home. The house was dark. Jennifer had forgotten to leave the porch light on. She'd locked the front door, and in the darkness, he put the wrong key in the lock. For a moment, he thought it might be stuck. But he was able to extricate it with force. He stepped under a streetlight in order to find the right key, then returned to his front door and let himself in.

Jennifer had gone to bed but had left his dinner on the kitchen table. The salmon and asparagus were cold but he didn't put the meal in the microwave. He drank a beer with dinner and drank another in the living room, the lights off. He thought about Alvaro. He thought about Adam's cry. There was something—no, everything—primal about its anguish and plea. But if a baby's or a child's cries had simple remedies, an adult's—a man's—well… *But I should be happy. I* am *happy. I am.*

The weekend came, and if Eddie hadn't forgotten Alvaro, even for an hour, he had saved serious thought of him for private moments, when Jennifer and Adam were asleep, when he had the night to himself. On Monday, he picked up Adam at preschool, and it was Adam's teacher, Veronica, instead of Sabrina who remained after school. Veronica was his age, slim and dark-haired and unmarried. If he'd wanted to have an affair, here was his chance. But there were good reasons he'd chosen a life straight and narrow. He was a good father, a good husband, and this mattered to him. It would be easy to make his life implode, but he wasn't this dumb.

The next day, there was a knock on his office door. He opened it to find Seymour Stolzenberg and the three other members of the search committee standing outside. After Eddie invited them in and they'd sat down, Seymour said, "Well, as might have been expected when we decided on a four-person committee, we're deadlocked. Instead of flipping a coin, we thought we'd employ you as the tiebreaker."

"Alvaro," Eddie said, as if he'd been prepared for the question. At the same time, he was stunned by his impulsiveness, his reckless desire to have his cry answered the only way it could be. He saw the future light up in fire, but his heart dashed like a boy racing toward the bay. "Alvaro López," he said, as if they might misunderstand.

Seymour looked at his colleagues before turning back to Eddie. "He wasn't one of the two we had in mind."

Already Eddie had bolted ahead to Alvaro's welcome, to the help he would give him in finding a place to live. He imagined the realtor waiting on the front porch as they revisited the second floor, the master bedroom.

Eddie recovered, offered the name of another candidate. But after the committee members left, he heard the echo of his voice enunciating Alvaro's name—like a lover would in bed—and he felt transparent, exposed. It was as if they'd known about him and Alvaro and had only been seeking his confirmation. They'd wanted to embarrass him. They'd wanted him to speak his humiliating desire.

But of course they didn't know anything.

The Ghosts of Girls

....

1

Phantom white, the girl raced from the trees, her hair blown back in the wind, and stopped in front of Joan Worthington's Saturn, waving. Joan swerved left but felt a thud, like someone waking her from a dream. She knew she had killed the girl. Joan understood what to do next—stop, verify the awful fact, call 911—but her foot remained on the gas pedal and she drove another hundred yards before she pressed on the brake. Her Saturn came to a stop on the dark road. She slipped the car into park and stepped outside.

There were no streetlights. If there were houses tucked behind the trees lining the road, their lights were off. She looked down the road. There was only darkness. She marched into it unsteadily. As she did, she heard a whip-crack of thunder. Presently, it began to rain. She had left her car door open; she had left the headlights on and the engine running. She was drunk and high, although she couldn't say to what degree.

When she was half a minute down the road, the rain picked up, and now it was impossible to see. "Hello?" she called into the night. "Hello? Can you hear me?" But the only reply was the smack-smack-smack of rain on asphalt. She thought about the party she'd come from, hosted by Allison Hall, her childhood friend who had returned to town this summer to become an associate dean of Ohio Eastern University's business school. After the other guests left, she and Allison smoked weed, left over from Allison's husband's losing fight against brain cancer, and finished what remained in at least three wine bottles.

She and Allison had been best friends from kindergarten until their graduation from high school. Although they had lived on opposite sides of the country, they hadn't lost touch. They sent each other Christmas cards, and they spoke on the phone every so often, especially in the wake of loss (Joan's husband, of a heart attack, followed by her son, killed in Iraq, followed, less than a year ago, by Allison's husband). On Allison's back porch tonight, as the wind whirled around the pair of weeping willows in her half-acre yard, Joan and Allison had touched on the sorrows in their lives but had quickly moved on to happier subjects from their past: their matching pink bicycles, their third-grade teacher and his lisp, their Girl Scout troop's rain-soaked weekend camping trip to Murderers' Cove.

"Hello? Hello?" The night replied with only the steady beat of rain. She took two more steps forward but decided she would be better off in her car. She ran, then walked, then staggered the final few steps to her Saturn. She fell into the driver's seat, closed the door, and wheeled the car around. She lowered her window and drove slowly, but the girl, or her body, wasn't on the road. Had the impact sent her flying into the weeds beside the road? Or, injured, had she staggered into the trees? Joan turned her car around again and drove back the way she'd come, this time peering intently into the darkness on her right and left. But with the rain, she could see nothing. Again she stopped and turned around.

She saw only the dark and rain until a car appeared behind her. It was a police car, she was sure. She slowed, prepared to pull over. But now she saw it was a pickup truck, with bright lights. The truck tailed her, pulling close to her bumper. She couldn't see into its cab. She flipped her rearview mirror to the right so as to banish the reflection of its bright lights. Moments later, the truck pulled beside her. In the passenger seat was a girl of high-school age, blonde and pale, a bandana around her neck. Her window was open. She was facing Joan, and her mouth was moving in an exaggerated imitation of speech. Or perhaps she was saying something to Joan, an insult, a curse, an accusation. The girl's mouth closed, and she gazed at Joan as if expecting a reply. "What?" Joan mouthed to the girl, but the truck raced ahead and Joan watched with relief as its taillights grew faint and disappeared.

She considered whether to continue her search, but she worried about another vehicle coming. She drove until she was at an intersection familiar only from tonight. She turned right and, half a mile later, pulled into the long driveway. Allison's $566,000 house came with indulgences her friend didn't need such as a tennis court (Allison had never picked up a racquet in her life) and a four-car garage. Widowhood allowed Allison the freedom to be lavish. "I loved Ray, of course," she'd told Joan as they sipped their wine tonight, "but he was as frugal as Scrooge with everything but his bad jokes."

Joan stepped out of her car and moved toward the front door, her legs wooden. She rang the doorbell and heard six chimes in succession, each in a lower register than the previous. When no one answered, she rang again. Before the last chime sounded, Allison opened the door. She was dressed as she had been at the party, in blue jeans and a red blouse. Her hair, which she'd dyed copper, was skewed to one side, as if a stiff wind was blowing it. Her eyes were red.

"I'm lost," Joan said. This wasn't what she had meant to say. She had intended to speak about the girl.

Allison's expression collapsed into tenderness and concern. "It's all right," she said. "Why don't you stay here tonight and we'll send you home tomorrow morning. I can't believe I allowed you to leave in the first place."

Allison stepped aside, waving Joan into her house. The place smelled of marijuana. Joan noticed a roach burning in the ashtray on the coffee table. After they were seated side by side on Allison's blue couch, Joan said, "When I was driving home, I think I hit a girl."

There was a pause. "You did? Or you only think you did?"

Joan told her what she'd seen, what she'd heard. She told her about her fruitless search.

"You couldn't find her?" Allison asked.

Joan shook her head. "But it was dark, and then the rain came, and who knows where she might have gone. Into the trees. To die."

"What the hell would a little girl be doing on a lonely country road at two-thirty in the morning?"

"Should I call the police?" Joan asked. "I could meet them at the spot where I hit the girl."

"Did anyone see what happened? Was there maybe a man or a woman— parents—somewhere nearby?"

"I don't think so. I think there was only the two of us."

Allison released a breath and removed her arm from the armrest. "I think I know what happened." She paused. "I think you hit an animal, maybe a stray cat or a possum or a baby deer."

"Are you serious? I don't know. I don't think—."

"It's late. We've been drinking and…We're in altered states."

"But I saw the girl. She looked up at me. Like a girl on the cover of a children's book, the perfect rosebud lips, the blonde curls."

"Your description is telling, Joannie. 'The cover of a children's book.' You're probably confusing what you hit with what you saw at your store before you came here tonight."

Joan owned Wonderland, a children's toy-and-book store in downtown Sherman. She had spent half an hour the day before in the book section, giving recommendations to a succession of pre-teen girls. More and more, customers solicited advice from Joan about books and games, then walked out of her store and bought them online or at Wal-Mart.

Joan sighed. "I guess I'm hoping you'll say, 'Call the police. It isn't too late. There won't be any bad consequences.'"

"Too risky," Allison said.

"What do you mean?"

"You'll end up arrested no matter what you hit—and I'm sure it wasn't a girl. They'll have you up on a DUI. And whatever the equivalent is for smoking pot. Think of the ramifications. And the police will come here, I bet. Can you imagine the fallout? Less than a month into my new job, I'm caught with enough pot to make a Mexican drug lord turn dollar-bill green with envy."

In high school, Allison was two people, the serious student during the week, the serious party girl on weekends. But even when she was drunk or stoned, Allison was never anything but calculating and rational. It was Joan who confessed to her friend all kinds of embarrassments. Their dynamic tonight was familiar.

"So what do we do?" Joan asked.

"We sleep it off. If in the light of day and sobriety, you still believe you struck a girl and not a doe or a large rodent, we'll go to the spot of the alleged incident and have a look."

"And if we find a body?"

Allison sighed. "If we find a body, there's nothing we can do, is there?" Allison put her arm around Joan. "This will all look better after a little sleep."

Later, between the cool sheets of the guest bed, Joan thought of the young woman in the pickup truck. She imagined the woman on the witness stand in a courtroom. She imagined her pointing a long finger at her. "She's the killer!"

Joan didn't think she would sleep, but she must have because when she opened her eyes, sunlight had penetrated the pinholes in the white Venetian blinds and Allison was kneeling at the side of her bed. "I forgot I have a breakfast to go to." She wore a smart yellow suit. Her makeup covered whatever fatigue had accumulated on her face. "Listen to me, Joannie: It's a bad idea to call the police at this point. Legally, I mean. And I maintain that it's impossible that you hit a girl. In the middle of nowhere. In the middle of the night. All right?"

Joan knew it wasn't impossible, but she nodded.

"You're welcome to stay here all morning—all day if you like," Allison said. "I won't be back until sometime after two. But I'll call you." She paused. "In the meantime, please don't...don't..."

"Don't?" Joan repeated.

"Don't panic."

"All right," Joan said, and Allison was gone.

Joan closed her eyes, but she knew she wouldn't be able to sleep again.

She recalled the moment before her car struck the girl. She recalled the girl's face, her eyes wide with surprise and fear. She heard the soft, terrible thud.

I should have stopped the car immediately. I would have been able to help her.

She rose, dressed, ran a brush over her tired brown hair, gazed too long into a mirror at her exhausted brown eyes. After leaving Allison's house, she examined her front bumper and saw a dent, perhaps a foot in length and as thin as a crescent moon. She slumped into her car, turned the ignition, and drove. Approaching what she thought was the fatal spot, she slowed down, gazing out the driver-side window, expecting to see a body curled in the weeds. Presently, she pulled to the side of the road, cut her engine, and clicked on her emergency lights. She stepped out of her car. Although it was only nine o'clock, the day was already hot and humid.

About twenty feet separated the side of the road from the beginning of the forest, all filled with Queen Anne's Lace and weeds, some as tall as her chest. She didn't want to walk into the weeds. She feared staining her clothes; she feared thorns slicing into her skin; she feared snakes. But from the road she was having no luck spotting the girl.

She was sweating and her hands were trembling. She felt light-headed and knew she should have had something to drink before leaving Allison's house. She turned back to her car. Maybe Allison was right. She had been tired and her senses had been compromised by the wine and pot. Maybe she had only imagined a girl.

There was a buzzing sound in her ear, and she flicked her hand to strike the mosquito or bee. But there was no insect. A hundred yards down the road, she saw a motorcycle, ridden by a young blonde woman without a helmet, her hair blown back. Joan walked quickly toward her car, but she didn't make it before the motorcycle pulled up beside her. The rider was the girl from the night before. A single gold earring pierced the left side of her nose. Her cheeks were red from sunburn or the wind.

"Did you lose something?" the girl asked, cutting the engine.

"No, no, I didn't," Joan said.

"I saw you looking on the side of the road."

"You did?"

She pointed behind her. "I saw you from the hill."

In the distance, the road rose, more a bump than a hill.

"I saw you last night," the girl said. Although her eyes were as dull as an overcast sky, there was something intense and menacing about how unblinking they were. "Did you hit something?"

For a moment, Joan didn't speak.

The girl craned her head to look at Joan's front bumper. "Or someone?" the girl added.

Did she know? Joan wondered. Impossible. "Last night, I thought I hit a baby deer. I was…well, I was curious about whether I did, in fact…I thought I'd take a look this morning." She added, "No big deal."

"I know you, don't I?" the young woman said. Her nostrils expanded, receded, expanded, receded. The gold earring glinted. "You're the lady who owns Wonderland."

Joan wanted to say, You're mistaken. But she nodded.

"Let me help you." Before Joan could protest, the young woman hopped off her motorcycle and began scanning the weeds. She moved down the road's shoulder with the swift curiosity of a bloodhound. No more than a minute later, her voice, filled with fascination and horror, pierced the morning: "Holy fucking shit!"

With terrible resignation, her heart thudding, Joan walked to where the young woman was standing. Five feet from the road, down a small slope and surrounded by weeds three feet tall, was a blonde-haired girl, her legs tucked in the fetal position. She looked like she was sleeping, but Joan knew otherwise. She thought she should say something, but she could think of nothing to lessen the awfulness of the scene. She felt like falling down, head in her hands, and screaming. A pair of flies buzzed around the girl's eyes.

"This fucking sucks," said the young woman. Turning to Joan, she asked, "Were you drunk when you hit her?"

Joan looked at the young woman's face. Her blue-gray eyes, she thought, were set too far apart from each other, giving her the faint appearance of an alien. Her blonde hair hadn't been washed recently and limp strands clung to her shoulders like tentacles. She was thin, and her breasts were insubstantial. Or perhaps they were only hiding beneath her pale blue T-shirt, two sizes too large.

"Were you drunk last night?" the young woman repeated. "You looked out of it when I saw you."

Joan thought of how, after she had left Allison's house the previous night, she had stood in the driveway, staring at the moon until it had been swallowed by clouds. If she had only gone immediately to her car and driven off, she never would have hit the girl.

The girl. Who was the girl?

To the young woman, Joan said, "What's your name?"

"Grace."

"And you live around here?"

There was a pause. "I'm in transition."

"What do you mean?"

Grace stared at the girl's body before turning her gaze back to Joan. "If you don't want to report this, it's fine with me. I won't tell anyone. The girl's dead, right? It won't be long before someone finds her."

Joan felt something unpleasant fill her nostrils. Was the girl's body already decaying? The smell disappeared, replaced by the smell of the day's growing heat.

"But if you do call the cops, don't tell them about me, all right? I don't need them in my life, you know what I mean? Are we cool?"

Mutely, and without even understanding what Grace was asking her, Joan nodded.

"Cool," Grace said. She stepped over to her motorcycle, hopped on, and turned the ignition. It sounded like a lawnmower. It looked like a glorified bicycle. "Don't worry," Grace said. "You didn't mean to hit her." She frowned and shook her head. "But the cops wouldn't understand. They'd say you left the scene. Well, fuck them."

"Where are you going?" Joan asked because she didn't know what else to say.

"To buy cigarettes."

Joan thought to inquire if she was old enough, but she only nodded.

"It's okay," Grace said. "There's nothing anyone can do. Better leave it like it is. You don't want the cops in your life."

"Thank you for the advice," Joan said, "but I think I'd better do what's right."

Grace shrugged and drove off. Joan watched her until, several hundred yards distant, she made a right turn. No other vehicle had come by in the time Joan had been here, but now she grew nervous about the possibility. She returned to her car, slipped into the driver's seat, and drove back to Allison's house. In Allison's driveway, she removed her cell phone from her purse. She phantom-pressed 911 half a dozen times. She could tell the police she thought she had hit an animal, but this morning she discovered she had actually hit...She knew she wasn't thinking clearly. She was exhausted, hungover.

Her phone rang. The sound so surprised and scared her, she dropped the phone under the pedals. She scrambled to pick it up and answered, breathless, "Hello?"

"Hi, Joannie, I'm just checking in to see—."

"She's dead, Al. I found her on the side of the road." She drew in a breath. "I'm sitting here in your driveway, about to call the cops."

"Absolutely not."

The quickness of Allison's response shocked Joan into silence.

"Did you hear me, Joannie?"

"Why?" Joan managed. "Isn't it better to call, to end this nightmare the right way?"

"They'll ask you why the hell you waited a day to contact them. You would be admitting to fleeing the scene of an accident. They'll ask you what you'd been doing driving on a backwoods road at two-thirty in the morning, and—I know you, Joannie—you'll give them all the incriminating details. Tomorrow it will be in the paper and all over radio and TV. Imagine what people in town will say. What do you think becomes of a toy-store owner who admits to a hit-and-run accident involving a little girl? Do you think your business would survive?"

Joan's business was in peril as it was. Even so, she wondered how much of Allison's concern was selfish. Was she worried about her role in the accident's prelude and aftermath? Was she worried about being an accessory?

"Did anyone see you today?" Allison asked. "Did any cars pass by?"

Joan thought of telling her about Grace, but she anticipated Allison's reaction—exasperated, critical ("Why didn't you just tell her you were having car trouble? Oh, Jesus, Joannie"). So she said, "No."

Allison's sigh was full of relief. "All right. We're in the clear."

"What do you mean? Leave the girl where she is?"

"The girl's body, you mean? Yes, Joannie. Go home. Forget this ever happened."

"I'm not sure I can."

"I'll come by tonight, all right? We'll talk, and I'll show you how it's going to work out fine. All right?" A pause. "All right?"

Their interaction was familiar from a lifetime ago, and Joan answered the way she had when she was eight and twelve and sixteen. "Yeah," Joan said. "All right."

2

The story appeared two days later, on the front page of the *Sherman Advocate and Post*.

Girl's Body Found on Side of Wildflower Road
Hit-and-run accident suspected; police seek witnesses

By Marilyn Baker
The body of a young girl was discovered yesterday afternoon on the side of Wildflower Road between Route 44 and Baker's Ridge Parkway. A local resident, T. J. Holmes, discovered the body after chasing down his two beagles, who had escaped from their backyard enclosure.

"I thought they'd found roadkill," Holmes said.

Holmes immediately called 911.

"Her condition is compatible with a high-speed car accident, although we are looking at other possibilities," said Sherman County Sheriff Edwin Wall.

Neither Wall nor Sheriff's Department spokesperson Melissa Zeiger would speculate on why the young girl might have been walking on Wildflower Road or why her absence wasn't reported.

Holmes said, "It's something I never expected to see. It's so sad. Someone's lost their little girl."

Hit-and-Run Victim Identified,
Was abducted by "violent" dad

By Marilyn Baker

The eight-year-old girl whose body was discovered two days ago on the side of Wildflower Road has been identified as April Morningstar of Tallahassee, Fla. Her mother, Patricia King, had been looking for her since June, when the girl's father, Joseph Morningstar Jr., abducted her from a picnic hosted by King's company. At the time of the abduction, King had full custody of her daughter and had secured a restraining order against Morningstar.

Reached in Tallahasee, King said, "This is a nightmare on top of a nightmare." She said she planned to fly to Sherman today to claim her daughter's body.

Law enforcement officials in Tallahassee had put out an Amber Alert the day April was abducted.

Sherman County Sheriff Edwin Wall said he has organized a countywide search for Joseph Morningstar. "Evidently he's worse than a deadbeat dad," Wall said. "He's a violent, disturbed man."

Dead Girl's Father Found;
'I did not kill my baby'

By Marilyn Baker

Joseph Morningstar Jr., the father of the girl whose body was discovered Monday on Wildflower Road, says his daughter ran away from their campsite on Saturday night and, despite his all-night search, he failed to find her. Morningstar turned himself in to Sherman County Sheriff's deputies yesterday.

Morningstar said he and his daughter had been camping in the woods beside Wildflower Road after his car broke down, according to Sherman County Sheriff Edwin Wall. Morningstar hoped to find an auto parts store so he could fix his vehicle.

Wall said Morningstar, who is in custody in the Sherman County Jail, insisted that he had nothing to do with his daughter's death. "He must have said fifty times, 'I didn't kill my baby,'" Wall said. "It's never smart to trust these types, but he was shook up good."

Ohio AG Vows Max Penalty
for Hit-and-Run Driver

By Marilyn Baker

Killing someone in a hit-and-run accident in Ohio is a third degree felony, punishable by up to five years in prison, and a five-year sentence is what Ohio Attorney General Mark Spangler will seek in the death of April Morningstar. An autopsy has confirmed that the girl's death was the result of a collision.

Every morning after reading the newspaper, Joan cried, shouted, pounded walls, tables, furniture, the sides of her head. She didn't deserve this. She especially didn't deserve this so soon after her son's death. It had been five years, but it felt like five days, five minutes sometimes. And April Morningstar didn't deserve to die—she didn't deserve her entire, sad life. She and April were collateral damage to some terrible joke, some cosmic mistiming.

Yes, she had been drunk and high—she never should have left Allison's house in such a compromised state, but lately she had been opening Wonderland on Sunday mornings because the first-communion and baptism crowds sometimes bought gifts and she needed every penny—but she hadn't been speeding. Or if she had—so what? The road was straight and empty. Or it should have been empty. No matter how impaired she was or how fast she was driving, she couldn't be blamed for hitting the girl on such a road at such an hour. (It horrified Joan to think that April had been signaling to her for help. If she hadn't been high and drunk, or if she'd had better reflexes, she could have avoided her, saved her, driven her triumphantly home to Tallahassee and her mother's grateful arms.)

There had been no way to anticipate this, no way to prepare. No matter what condition you're in, you don't slip behind the wheel of your car bracing for the possibility of killing someone—a child, for God's sake. It wasn't like being a soldier in a war, when you accept the possibility of killing innocent people, even children, because neither weapons nor the men and women who use them are perfect. This is what Carl, her son, had said to her in response to a report on TV about an Afghan school bombed by mistake. He said it coolly, clinically. He hadn't yet been to war, but already he was hardened.

They had never spoken about the possibility of him being killed, although of course it was all she thought about. Was he expected to contemplate his own death with similar indifference? She wondered if detachment was as valuable a weapon in war as guns and bullets and unmanned drones.

He wasn't innocent—he'd signed up to kill—but she couldn't help but think of him as innocent. His death was no accident—the roadside bomb outside of Baghdad intended murder—but it was an accident of chance that he'd been assigned to this particular job on this particular day in this particular part of the country. It was an accident of chance that he'd been sent to Iraq at all. He could have been sent to Afghanistan and lived to be a hundred.

She found herself screaming her son's name as if it was he she had struck on Wildflower Road instead of April Morningstar.

Inevitably, Joan's crying and racing thoughts were interrupted by the phone's ring—Allison—who told her everything was going to be better soon.

"I don't deserve this," Joan said on the seventh morning after the accident.

"In no way, shape, or form," Allison assured her.

"I should turn myself in."

"You would deserve the consequences of turning yourself in even less."

"So what do I do, Al? What do I do?"

"You know how to deal with adversity. You've done it before. You know the terrible drill."

Joan had been certain she wouldn't survive Carl's death. After a month or two, her friends stopped calling and coming by with food. When, after a year, they saw she remained distraught and depressed, they became even scarcer. But she had showed up at Wonderland every day, and if her interactions with customers lacked mirth, she was at least able to keep her business solvent.

"It's going to be fine, Joannie. All right?…All right?"

"How in the world is it going to be fine?"

"It will, Joannie. Trust me. It will."

3

The bells on the door of Wonderland jingled. It was 1:45 on a Tuesday afternoon, a dead time, and Joan looked over at the door, curious about who might be coming in. Five seconds passed before Joan recognized Grace. She had cut her hair short, like Twiggy, although Grace couldn't possibly know who Twiggy was. And the mod effect was muted because a couple of stray hairs stuck straight up, like alien antennae. Standing beside Grace was a young man, maybe twenty years old, who sported a faint black mustache. His hair, black and unwashed, was longer than Grace's. His tongue pressed against the right side of his mouth. Joan felt sick with dread. She put her hands on the sales counter to steady herself.

"I haven't been here in years," Grace said. "What a funhouse."

Joan followed Grace's gaze. There were Beanie Babies, WebKinz, life-sized and life-like koala bears. There were board games, from the traditional (Monopoly, Clue, Life) to the sure-to-be ephemeral (High School Musical, Hannah Montana, Wall-E). Deeper in the store were train sets and Harry Potter novels and an assortment of girls' dresses, skirts, and pajamas and boys' T-shirts, cowboy vests, and superhero socks. There were witches' hats and magicians' wands. The aisles were narrow, and toys poked from the shelves like hands from a crowd.

The man stepped in front of Grace, and Joan read his expression and knew all she needed to know about him. He grinned or smirked and, turning to Grace, said, "Whose birthday is it today?"

Joan looked at Grace, who was blushing, giggling. Joan placed her hand on the telephone in front of her. But who could she call? She wished someone would walk into the store. At the same time, she wished no one would. She doubted another presence would alter what was about to transpire.

"Whose birthday is it today?" the man repeated.

Grace wouldn't look at Joan. "I don't know, Kyle. Whose birthday is it?"

"It's my birthday," Kyle said, and he began pulling games from the shelves—Stratego, Risk, Sorry!—and piling them in his arms. "Come on, help me, sweetheart," he said, and Grace walked past the sales counter, again without looking at Joan, and pulled down a pair of spider monkeys.

"Don't be cheap," Kyle said, and Grace took one swift glance back at Joan before grabbing a Barbie Horse and Carriage.

"More!" Kyle insisted, but Grace shook her head and said, "Let's go, baby."

"Go?" he said. With a child's whine, he added, "But there's so much I want!"

Grace giggled nervously. "Later," she whispered.

"It's a shame you're not in the mood to celebrate." Kyle turned and looked directly at Joan. "But we'll be back." His voice was a slow hiss. "We'll be back to celebrate an early Christmas."

"Don't come back," Joan said softly but firmly as they headed toward the door, their arms full of loot.

Kyle turned around, grinning. Although weighted down by his plunder, he managed to hold up his right hand and spread his fingers. "If you don't want us back," he said, "say hello to five years in a cage."

Grace tugged his shoulder, but Kyle's gaze held Joan's until she turned away. She didn't turn back until she heard the jangle of the bells. Her only consolation: Grace had left the Barbie Horse and Carriage on a shelf by the door.

"It will be fine, Joannie. Nothing has happened so far. So it's a safe bet nothing will happen."

Allison leaned over the table. They were having drinks at Wild River, which was two miles out of town in the opposite direction from where Allison lived. Photographs of fishermen and their catches shared wall space with canoe paddles and fishing rods. Joan hadn't been here in three years, when she'd come on a blind date. She'd liked the guy; he'd never called.

Their waiter came, and Joan ordered another beer. Allison hadn't touched her gin and tonic.

"There's something I didn't tell you," Joan said. Now she did.

"Oh, for fuck's sake," Allison said. "How many times have they come to your store?"

"They came in together the first time. Then he came back yesterday, asking for what he called a loan. He wanted five hundred dollars. I gave him two hundred. He said he'd be back for the rest."

There was a long silence. "Why don't you shut down your store for a month?" Allison said. "Go on vacation. Everything will blow over."

"I can't afford to shut down the store."

"It doesn't look like you can afford to keep it open either." Allison slapped her hand against the table and leaned back in her chair. "Christ." She sighed before leaning forward. "Maybe you should think about selling it."

"To whom? And for how much? The price of a bus ticket out of here?"

Allison picked up her gin and tonic and had a long sip. "I should never have had that fucking party."

"I should have called the police as soon as I hit the girl."

"Shhh," Allison said, looking around. "God, Joannie, let's be discreet, please."

"I've been discreet—at your insistence. Now I'm being blackmailed by a punk."

Allison lifted her glass, stared at it, put it down. "All right," she said. "I'll give you the $300 to pay him off. But when you hand over the money, look him in the eye and say, 'This is it. We're done.' All right?"

"And if he says we aren't done?" Joan recognized the hopelessness in her voice.

Allison leaned forward, leaned back. She put a hand on her glass, removed it.

"Don't you think I better cut my losses by calling the police?" Joan asked. "I don't have to tell them I was at your party. I could say…well…"

"It isn't the party I'm worried about," Allison said. "What I'm concerned about at this point, Joannie, is the fucking attorney general and his promise to give maximum jail time to the driver." In a softer voice: "I'll give you the money. Maybe that will do it. Maybe the teenage prick will tire of the game."

It was a Wednesday, and so far, she'd had a good day. She'd sold $138.42 worth of WebKinz to a white-haired woman visiting her grandchildren from Nebraska. It had been four days since she'd seen Kyle. Perhaps he'd moved on to other distractions. But every time the bells on the door jingled, she looked up in fear. At 4:22, Kyle stepped into the store with the air of an absentee landowner. He was smoking a cigarette. Remembering what Allison had told her about acting tough, Joan said, "Do you mind, Kyle. Children come in here."

He looked at her as if he didn't know what she was talking about; perhaps he didn't.

"The cigarette," she said.

"Oh," he said, nodding in exaggerated fashion. "Right." He turned to his right and the display of Webkinz. He pulled a turtle from the stack and snuffed out his cigarette on its shell. If she'd had a gun behind the counter, she wouldn't have hesitated to blow out his brains.

He strolled to the counter and, without saying a word, held out his open palm. She thought about refusing. But she saw his next step: an anonymous call to the Sherman County Sheriff, with details. She had the $300 in an envelope in the register. She might as well have had his name on it. She popped open the register, retrieved the envelope, and filled his pale hand.

"Do I need to count it?" he said.

"Cut the tough boy act, Kyle," she said, although her voice betrayed her; it quivered. Nevertheless, she continued, "This is it, understood? This is the end of our arrangement."

"So I should go ahead and turn you in?"

He stared at her. She turned from his idiotic mustache, his skinny body. How had her life reached the point of becoming in thrall to an upstart blackmailer? She knew she was doomed.

The door's bells jingled like hell's Christmas, but at least he was gone.

The next morning, Grace stepped into her store ten minutes after it opened. She was red-eyed and looked sleepless, and she glanced quickly at Joan before looking away. Joan sat behind the counter, behind glass boxes of earrings and key chains and refrigerator magnets. She had change for a fifty-dollar bill in her register. She suspected Grace was going to ask for more.

For a long time, Grace stood in the store entrance. She rubbed her temples. She touched the earring on her nose. If Joan's initial reaction was to tell Grace to go to hell, she softened. The girl seemed distraught, lost. "Are you all right?" Joan asked.

Grace nodded quickly, stopped, nodded a few more times. She stepped forward, stopped, stepped forward. Stopped. "I'm sorry," she said. "I shouldn't have brought him here. I shouldn't have told him."

To have said, "It's all right" would have been a lie. So Joan said, "Why did you?"

"He was my boyfriend."

"Was?"

"I don't want to be with him after what he did." Grace stepped up to the counter. She reached into the pocket of her jeans and pulled out a crumpled wad of bills, which she placed on the counter in front of Joan.

"What's this?" Joan said, collecting the bills in her palm. She counted $143.

"I stole it from his wallet this morning, while he was sleeping. He told me what happened here yesterday."

"So you stole what he stole from me."

"It isn't everything, I know."

"No, it isn't everything." Joan looked at Grace, whose eyes were an overcast sky. "But I'm grateful." Grace's eyes lightened, becoming almost pretty.

"He'll be back, though, won't he?"

There was a pause before Grace nodded.

"It'll never end," Joan said. "It'll never end until I go to the police and tell them what happened. And when I do, I'll have to tell them about you and Kyle."

"I wish you wouldn't."

"You're a minor. Nothing much will happen to you."

"They'll send me back."

"Back where?" Joan asked.

"Back to my dad."

"Is that so bad?" By Grace's look, Joan could tell that it was.

"I've been living with Kyle and his older brother, who's never around. But after this morning…"

Joan registered the concern and fear in her eyes. "What do you plan to do now?"

"I can't let him find me. Kyle can be very sweet but he has a temper I'm scared to death of. And sometimes this look comes over him. It's the look I saw on this boy in my neighborhood when I was growing up—this look he had when he tortured field mice and barn cats."

The image made Joan recoil. "Can you stay somewhere else?" she asked.

"I was hoping..." The door jingled and whooshed open. It was Helen Davidson, who had ordered three sets of the *Little House* series. She taught homeless women at the Day Center how to read, and she always rewarded their efforts with books the women could read to their children.

As Helen waved hello, Grace leaned over the counter and whispered, "I was hoping I could stay with you."

Carl, her son, had been loyal and devoted, and he was always concerned about her wellbeing. He couldn't have been older than five when one morning he found her gazing out of the kitchen window and asked, "Are we all right, Mommy?" He was the boy everyone in the neighborhood entrusted to look after their dogs and cats when they were out of town. When Martha Cavander, who had been delivering the *Sherman Advocate and Post* since she was in junior high, had chemotherapy, Carl filled in for six months. He was ten years old and had to wake up at five o'clock every morning. He never failed to climb out of bed with anything less than determination.

Perhaps he'd been so responsible because he'd had to become the man of the house at such a young age, stepping in for his father, who wasn't much of a presence even when he was alive. She knew she couldn't ask for a better son, and yet sometimes she'd secretly blamed him for the long hours she had to work, for the dearth of men interested in her. After Carl's death, these complaints struck her as the epitome of selfishness and self-pity. She had been lucky, lucky, lucky to have such a son.

She knew what Carl would have done if he had struck a girl late one night on a country road. He would have looked for her until he found her; if he'd had to, he would have stayed in the rain all night. Even if he was drunk and high, he...But he never would have been drunk or high.

Sometimes she balked at what she used to think of as his rigidity. She felt his disapproval when she drank too much or dressed provocatively for one of her rare dates. One of these dates resulted in a boyfriend, Hugh, who owned a used car lot on Two-Mile Road. Although Hugh was separated from his wife, Carl objected to her dating a married man. He had smaller objections to Hugh's weight (he was close to 300 pounds) and his overuse of cologne. His contempt became, subtly, hers. In Hugh's presence, she grew cool and unenthusiastic. Even so, she felt angry, bereft, and humiliated when, eight months into their relationship, Hugh returned to his wife.

Carl saw everything in stark contrasts. Good and bad. Right and wrong. For Carl, there was rarely a middle. After graduating from the ROTC program at Ohio Eastern, he was eager to fight in Iraq. He believed the United States was right to turn the country, "a backwater of terror and tyranny led by a nuke-obsessed madman," as he defined it, into a peaceful, democratic place. "It needs us," he said.

On one occasion, when she'd had too much to drink (which didn't influence what she said but gave her the courage to say it), she suggested there might be better solutions to what was wrong in Iraq than war.

Carl smiled at her with what, in her husband, she used to think of as smugness. "We are the world's only superpower," he said. "Might doesn't make right, but when you're right—and you have might..." He trailed off, before concluding, "When you have the advantage, take advantage."

She wondered if this was a maxim he'd memorized in Military Science 101.

Joan lived at the end of a cul-de-sac on the east side of town, flanked by two rentals, one of which was unoccupied. A graduate student in physics rented the other house but he had a girlfriend in Akron and was never home. Sometimes she felt like Laura Ingalls Wilder, isolated on the prairie. On Grace's first night in her house, the girl asked about the photograph on the mantel. It was an eight-by-eleven, in black-and-white, of Carl in high school, posing, arms crossed, against the trunk of a buckeye tree.

"He was a beautiful boy," Grace said.

"Yes, he was."

Grace glanced at her, glanced back at the photograph. "Why did you let him go?"

"Go where? To Iraq?" The question irritated her despite the softness of the girl's tone.

"It's easy to understand why my mom let me go," Grace said. "She didn't care what happened to me. But I'm sure you were the kind of mom who kept your kid beside you all the time."

It was true, Joan thought. "In the summer, I used to take him to my store, to Wonderland, every day. All he wanted to do was sit in the corner and play with Revolutionary War soldiers." Joan smiled at the memory.

"Thank you for letting me stay here," Grace said, turning from the photograph. "It's weird how this all happened." She shuffled her feet on the wood floor, a kind of nervous dance. "Maybe it isn't right to say this, but I'm glad it did."

"You don't plan to go back to him, do you?" Joan asked.

"No," Grace said softly. She followed this with a more emphatic "No," as if to assure Joan. It did the opposite. Grace was sixteen. If she was anything like the sixteen-year-olds Joan knew, and had been, she could be gone tonight. But she wanted to believe Grace. Maybe Grace had a little of Carl in her, Joan thought. Maybe the Carl in her would help her see Kyle as the budding psychopath he was. Maybe, with Joan's help, she would find her way to a better life.

Maybe—probably—I'm a fool.

When Kyle failed to appear in Wonderland for seven days, Joan allowed herself to hope he had moved on to other amusements. But Friday morning, he reappeared, the same terrible grin on his face. He had the gaunt, hollowed-eyed look of a heroin user. He appeared in dire need of a shower and a haircut.

"Did you miss me?" he asked her as he fingered the rack of Webkinz.

"I thought we had settled everything, Kyle." She spoke as evenly as she could, but her voice vibrated with the uncertainty of someone attempting to reason with a snake.

"I took a little holiday in the big city," Kyle said. "Cleveland. Spent all I had, which wasn't as much as I thought I had. In the meantime, it seems my girlfriend disappeared on a little holiday of her own." He turned to her with his hollow eyes and his sinister ghost of a mustache. "You didn't have anything to do with her disappearance, did you?"

"What do you mean?"

"You didn't, for example, kill her?"

"What do you want?" She couldn't keep the anger out of her voice.

"I want an Xbox, an iPod, a Wii, and a few DVDs. You'll order them for me, I bet." After he strolled over to her, he produced a list from the back pocket of his jeans and dropped it onto the counter.

For a long time, she didn't look at it. Finally, she drew it across the counter and glanced down to read it. "And that'll be it?" she asked. "Once I order everything you've written here, we'll be done. All right?" She tried again: "Understood?" Each time she spoke, her voice lost a degree of authority and assurance.

Kyle laughed and said, "I'm a high-school dropout. I don't have a job. What do you think?"

She drew in a breath. "Okay. So when will we be done? When you find a job?"

"When I'm president of the United States."

His laughter was punctuated by the jangling of bells. He kept laughing as he passed Rachel Sampson on his way out the door. After Rachel, a seventy-year-old she had known all of her life, bought a pair of chocolate-smelling erasers for ninety-five cents and said, "Keep the change," she cried for everything that had disappeared from her life.

"Do you know what I would do if I had any guts?" Allison asked the next day. Joan had closed Wonderland early so she could visit her friend.

"What's that?" Joan replied. She and Allison were sitting on her back porch, sharing a joint. It was approaching six in the evening, and they had already downed a bottle of pinot noir. Toward the end of the bottle, the wine tasted like sweet grape juice. Allison was both drunk and high, but Joan felt nothing. She was too tense, too upset.

"I would kill him," Allison said. She laughed, but Joan didn't. The thought was too omnipresent in her mind, too desirable, to speak of lightly.

"How would you do it?" Joan asked.

"The next time he comes into your store, you could shoot him. When he's dead, put a gun in his hand and tell the police he was coming to rob you. You shot him in self-defense."

"Wouldn't they trace the gun I tried to frame him with?"

Allison sighed. "I didn't say I'd thought out all the details." She drew in a deep drag and released the smoke. It smelled, Joan thought, like burning leaves, like fall. At the end of Allison's backyard, beyond the weeping willows, was a forest, the leaves of its trees turning red and orange.

"You could stake out his house," Allison said. "When he steps outside, blow his fucking head off."

"And what about his neighbors?"

"Maybe no one will be around."

"And maybe I'll like the electric chair."

Allison drew in another deep drag, released the silver-gray smoke. "This plan depends, of course, on Grace either not suspecting or not caring who killed her boyfriend—or ex-boyfriend, if we can trust this designation. Maybe you'd have to kill her, too, although this is complicated by the fact— and it amazes me to say this—that she is living with you."

"If I did anything to Kyle, I don't know what she would do. As it is, I keep waiting to come home and find she's cleaned me out."

"Maybe she's just waiting to line up the moving vans. How long has she been living with you, anyway?"

"Eight days. I was sure Kyle would come by to claim her—or kill her. But he either doesn't know where she's living or he doesn't care."

"He has daily access to Wonderland. What more does he need?"

"He's asking me to order stuff I don't have. An iPod, DVDs...I don't even know what."

"Of course he is." Allison stubbed the roach onto a plate with a Garden of Eden motif, a snake wrapped around Eve's leg. "I guess it's the end game. I've been asking—discreetly—about lawyers. You should be doing the same."

"I'll end up in jail."

"And I may end up unemployed."

"I won't mention your party," Joan said.

"This may come to trial, Joannie. You'll be under oath. I wouldn't ask you to lie." Allison reached across the table and held Joan's hand. "Maybe things will fall our way. But find the best lawyer you can. Look in Cleveland or Columbus if you have to."

"I don't have the money for a lawyer."

"I'll help as much as I can."

They sat a long time in silence. Joan said, "When should I go to the police?"

"Now? Never? I don't know."

"I'll do it on Monday. Is Monday all right?"

Allison nodded. She squeezed Joan's hand before withdrawing it.

"Since the accident," Joan said, "everything I've done, every decision I've made, has been wrong."

"Maybe any decision would have been wrong," Allison said

4

As Joan drove from Allison's house, she thought about her friend's last words. Any decision would have been wrong. Wasn't this the definition of a dilemma? Any decision would be wrong now. She could either go to jail or go broke.

But there was a day-and-a-half before the deadline she and Allison had set, so maybe there was hope. Grace was on her side now. Perhaps Grace could somehow reason with Kyle. Perhaps she knew something damning about him and could threaten to reveal it unless he stopped blackmailing her.

Or perhaps she could sell Wonderland—perhaps someone from the church crowd would step in out of the blue to buy it tomorrow—and she— and Grace?— could move elsewhere, across the country even, and begin again. She knew she was being sentimental and unrealistic, but filled with fantasy, her mind had a chance to relax, even to feel pleasure. Everything outside the fantasy had become too complex, difficult, and ugly.

She was on the fatal road again, but unlike when she drove to Allison's house today, she didn't backtrack in her mind to the night she struck April Morningstar. For the first time, she thought, *Maybe something good will happen now.* The thought gave her a brief, hopeful rush, a feeling akin to what she experienced when a toy or game that had sat on her shelves for so long the manufacturer had gone out of business unexpectedly found an eager home.

A moment later, as her mild euphoria was subsiding, she saw a motorcycle in her rearview mirror. She thought of how Carl's friend Steven had received a motorcycle for his eighteenth birthday, and how she worried Carl would press her for one of his own. But Carl said, "You'll never see me on a motorcycle. You're safer on a hang glider." There were risks worth taking, Carl said.

Like going to a fucking war?

She felt herself tear up. Stupid, she thought, to think about Carl, to blame him for his death.

There were two people on the motorcycle, neither wearing a helmet, and she thought of Grace and Kyle. But because they came so quickly to mind, and because she had left Grace in her house only an hour—no, a few hours—ago, she didn't think they could be the motorcycle driver and passenger. But when the motorcycle pulled into the left lane to pass her, she recognized Kyle, his hands loose on the grips. Although his sunglasses obscured his eyes, his mustache was enough to identify him. The motorcycle gained speed and pulled next to her. She wondered what new girl he had on the back.

But of course it wasn't a new girl. Grace's short blonde hair danced in the wind like a mirage. She turned her head, and when she recognized Joan, a brief and unfamiliar expression came over her face. It wasn't embarrassment or shame; it was disgust. At herself for being caught? Or at Joan for having caught her? Now Grace was smiling at her conspiratorially, mouthing something to her. But the way Grace's arms were wrapped around Kyle's waist—affectionately, trustingly—told Joan it was she who was being deceived. Joan's expression hardened. In response, Grace laughed, and as the motorcycle picked up speed, she gave Joan a dismissive flick of her wrist.

Joan felt hurt burrow into the same place where her sadness over Carl's death resided. It was trailed swiftly by rage. To think Carl was dead and April Morningstar was dead and these two criminals were alive and laughing. She punched the gas petal, pulling even with the motorcycle. As Grace turned to her in surprise, she jerked her Saturn to the left and into Kyle's leg. It was a touch, a tap, the equivalent in words of a murmur, a whisper, nothing like Kyle's vicious extortion. Nevertheless, the motorcycle toppled over as if struck by a wave. Kyle and Grace flew off, their heads and bodies smashing against the asphalt.

As if she had only been daydreaming and had allowed her car to drift across the median, Joan veered back into her lane, her eyes on the road. Seconds passed. Although her heart was racing, she could imagine nothing had happened. She even reached to click on the radio, but when she glanced up at her rearview mirror, she saw a police car behind her, its blue and red lights whipping the air. Terror competed with relief within her as she pulled her car to the side of the road. *It's over. All of this is over.* But when she glanced again at the rearview mirror, she saw only the long, empty road. What justice the world didn't supply, her conscience imagined. She knew, however, that from this moment forward it would be self-defeating to think of what she did as anything but right. Internal debate would paralyze her, break her faster than Kyle had. She pressed the gas pedal and left the scene.

The *Advocate and Post* quoted the sheriff calling the incident a "single-vehicle accident." He said, "It could have been carelessness. It could have been a murder-suicide. It could have been a double suicide. These were two troubled young people." He had spoken to the motorcycle driver's brother, who described the teenage couple as "lost." The two deaths having occurred on the same road where April Morningstar died was, the sheriff said, "a mean coincidence."

Joan took no chances. She left her Saturn, scuffed on the left side, dented on the right, in her garage. She walked to work, and she bought all her groceries at the Carrot Club, a co-op located two blocks from Wonderland. When her sister, who lived in upstate New York, told her she was looking for a used car to buy her son, who'd just received his driver's license, she offered her Saturn. She drove it to Syracuse over Thanksgiving. Upon her return, via Greyhound, she bought a used Ford Focus.

Target joined Wal-Mart in the Sherman Mall, and now her customers had more cheap places to buy toys and children's books. In response, she inaugurated ten-percent-off Wednesdays. She sponsored local dance recitals, horseback riding shows, and mother-daughter fun runs. For a small fee, she opened Wonderland to sleepovers, telling ghost stories before bedtime and waking her guests in the morning with sugar cereal and strawberry tea. She managed to stay a few months ahead of bankruptcy.

Three days after the accident, Allison came into her store. She had called Joan twice since they'd seen each other last, but Joan hadn't returned her calls. When she'd rehearsed what she would tell Allison, it had sounded boastful and cold, even accompanied by the tremor she would doubtless fail to repress.

It was two in the afternoon, and there were no customers. Outside it was ninety degrees; inside, it wasn't much cooler, despite the central air, which pumped continuously. Allison remarked on the weather, and they discussed this topic for a few minutes, both of them knowing the oppressive September heat wasn't what was on their minds. It was Joan who said, "Are you all right?"

"I should be asking you," Allison said. She sighed, and there was a long pause. "I don't understand how or why any of this happened. I return in triumph to my hometown and reacquaint myself with my best friend, and now...Now..."

"Now what?" Joan said, surprised at how cool her voice was, how little patience it showed for Allison's hesitancy. She took strength by summoning Carl's clarity. She'd done what was necessary. *When you have the advantage, take advantage.*

"You think you know someone," Allison said. "You grow up with someone, and you think you know her. And—this is what's most surprising—you think you know yourself." Allison picked up a blue stuffed animal from the rack to her right. If it was supposed to represent a real animal, the designer had failed. "But you know what I thought when I saw the article about those...those two? I thought, 'This is either the best thing that could have happened or the worst.' So far, it's coast clear. But why am I not sleeping easy?"

"I don't know," Joan said.

"Are you?"

Joan thought about this. "I've never needed much sleep."

Circumstances being what they were, Joan thought she and Allison would drift apart, perhaps chatting amiably but superficially when they saw each other downtown or in the Sky Lake Mall. But two days after their conversation in Wonderland, Allison called to invite her to dinner on Saturday. Because Joan wasn't using her car, Allison picked her up.

On the drive, Allison talked about her job, making light fun of the people working under her. Before long, they reached the fateful road where their lives might have been ruined. It was empty; not even a squirrel or rabbit or deer—not even a fly—crossed their path. Joan thought to say something, but silence seemed the more appropriate, and more respectful, response. Perhaps Allison was thinking the same. Or perhaps they were only establishing how they would treat this time in their lives.

Although they saw each other several times a month over the next seven years, before Allison left Sherman to take a dean's position at a small college in California, where her daughter lived, the only girls they spoke about were themselves, as they had once been. Their ghosts, as it were, offered enough material to keep conversations alive, sometimes until the brink of morning.

part two

....

EYES, HEARTS, SUBWAY, SKY

The Eye Man

∙∙

The eye man came to town with doctors and nurses who carried suitcases full of medicine and Bibles. They were accompanied by boys and girls who dressed up like daisies and frogs and sang religious songs in English in the park. The eye man wasn't a doctor or nurse. And neither the doctors nor the nurses nor the boys and girls who dressed up like daisies and frogs knew, or would tell me, what he was. He was simply "the eye man." He made eyes.

I translated for the group of doctors and nurses during their two-day clinic in the Church of God, one of several Evangelical churches in Santa Cruz Verapaz, Guatemala, where I was a Peace Corps Volunteer. I didn't much care for these clinics. A few months earlier, I had translated for a Catholic medical group from the United States; during the half day they were in town, the three doctors and five nurses saw perhaps three hundred patients, and their diagnoses were, because of the limited time, based only on what the patients told them. There were, of course, no follow-ups.

I'd agreed to translate for the Evangelical group because Rosemary, the secretary in El Instituto Básico, where I taught English, had asked me to, and I liked her. Also, I enjoyed the challenge, the quick reconfiguring of words from one language into words from another.

The Evangelical group was more overtly religious than the Catholic. Patients were asked their religion, and if they responded anything but Evangelical, the nurses drew a frowning face on their prescriptions. Evangelical patients received a smiling face. Whatever their religion, they had to pray before receiving their medicine. A trio of Guatemalan ministers led the prayers in front of the "pharmacy" the group had set up on the right side of the church.

I worked with a nurse named Dolly, a blonde who wore bright pink lipstick. Dolly decided that all the stomach problems the patients had were due either to ulcers—she'd read that Guatemalans drank too much coffee, and thus were susceptible—or worms. For the latter, she prescribed the appropriate medicine along with a thirty-day supply of vitamins. Other problems—bad skin, headaches, dizziness—Dolly chalked up to poor nutrition, and people with these ailments received a double supply of vitamins. Dolly was pretty and affable, cooing effusively when women brought their children in with ripped pants and bare, dirty feet. "How adorable!" she'd say and then ask me to translate this to the mother. After three hours of prescribing vitamins and drawing faces on prescription slips, Dolly burst into tears. "I can't take this anymore," she said. "They're all so sad!" She joined the worshippers waiting at the "pharmacy," her prayers broken on occasion by a rush of tears.

The other doctors and nurses either had translators—two Evangelical missionaries doing time in Guatemala had come to assist—or spoke Spanish. One of the doctors was a Guatemalan from the capital, and he no doubt had a better understanding of the people's problems than Dolly, but he did as much cheerleading as work. Every few minutes, he would pause during his examination of a patient and ask in a loud, earnest voice: "Who loves me?" And the others in the group would respond: "Jesus loves you!"

The eye man worked at a desk on a stage at the back of the church. He had long, shaggy black hair, and he sat hunched over his work like a monk over the Bible. When Dolly abandoned her post, I went to observe him. The eye man didn't speak Spanish, but he evidently didn't need a translator. He'd already seen a dozen patients, and he wasn't expecting more; everyone needing an artificial eye had been told to come before noon.

Spread in front of him on the desk were several sheets with small, black dots at their centers. As I spoke with him, he painted one of the dots with a small brush. Beside him on the table was a palette, sprinkled with various shades of brown. His other equipment included a three-burner electric stovetop, three pots, and what looked like two halves of a gold jewelry box filled with a sort of putty. When I asked him to explain how he made the eyes, he winked and said, "Secrets of the trade." The process, he said, took a long time, so people had to return the next day to pick up their new eyes.

That evening, the Evangelical group held a service in the Church of God, which I watched while standing in the church entrance, unwilling to submit to an hour or more in a hard pew. The Guatemalan doctor, whose own dark brown eyes seemed to wander randomly in their sockets, began the service by speaking about his love of Jesus. Then he smiled, big and handsome, and asked the audience, in Spanish, "Who loves me?"

Not having been trained to answer correctly, everyone sat silently until Doña Alejandra, a widow who sold boh, the local moonshine, out of her two-room wood house, pointed to herself and shouted, "I do!" The doctor blushed, and everyone laughed.

The doctor was followed on stage by twenty-seven boys and girls dressed as daisies and frogs. They sang a song called "Jesus in the Garden" while dancing and hopping around.

To thank me for my translating work, the group invited me to dinner at their hotel, located on the far side of town. Built within the last five years, the Hotel Mundo wouldn't have been out of place in the United States. The dining room's varnished wood interior reminded me of a Swiss chalet. I sat beside the eye man. We ate broiled chicken and mashed potatoes—good American fare—and he said nothing until dessert arrived. He stuck a spoon in his jello and said, "I wonder what's living in there."

"Nothing," I said. "This is a good hotel. They use only agua pura."

"What?" he asked.

"Agua pura. Pure water. No bacteria, no amoebas. Nothing. Safe as can be."

"Oh," he said, turning to look at me. "I didn't mean that. As a kid, I always imagined men were trapped inside the blocks of jello. Kind of like padded cells for the insane."

"I see," I said, smiling.

"I thought the same of ice cubes, only they were for girls who'd gone to the beach and had brought back too nice a tan."

I laughed charitably, but he didn't join me or even smile. Not a hint that he was joking.

He looked around the dining room at the people finishing up their meals. "Has someone introduced you to Jesus?" he asked.

I thought for a second he might be referring to someone from the group, some doctor whose hand I hadn't shaken. "Jesus Christ?" I asked.

"Yes."

"Well, no. I'm not really...Well, I'm not a religious person. Spiritual, yes, but not religious."

"Jesus loves you."

"I'm glad."

"He really does. He loves me, too, although sometimes I forget." He leaned over and whispered, "Sometimes I do things only the devil would admire."

"Like what?"

He pulled away, looked around, then dipped his head again to my ear. "Sometimes when I'm riding my motorcycle, I imagine a girl sitting behind me and stroking my...you know."

"Oh."

"You see, one time it happened. Her name was Sally. We were riding down a back road. Countryside. She reached around and started rubbing my...you know. I got so excited I crashed. Broke one of my legs and both of Sally's." He looked at me as if trying to read my reaction. "I was very sad for a long time. But the next time I got on my motorcycle, I didn't think about the crash. I thought about her hand. It had felt so good."

"I bet." I'd heard about Jesus lovers with suspect pasts. Evangelism, it seemed, could be a sort of AA for the perverse.

"Jesus doesn't like it when I think like that."

"Hmm."

"But I love Jesus as much as anyone in this room does. And Jesus loves me. But he loves me the same as he loves everyone else. Jesus is like that. Fair."

"That's good," I said. "Otherwise people would get jealous."

He ran a hand through his hair. "You're right. You're absolutely right."

The next morning, Dolly was still in a state and wanted to worship all day with the preachers, so the Guatemalan doctor asked me if I would work with the eye man; the people he had seen the day before were scheduled to come pick up their artificial eyes and they might have questions. After our conversation of the night before, I was reluctant, but I consented and found him in the back of the church. On the desk in front of him was an old Monopoly box.

"Do you want to see?" he asked.

I was about to tell him I knew what Monopoly looked like, but before I could speak he opened the box. Inside, surrounded by azure silk, were a dozen eyes.

"Wow," I said.

The eyes, shell-shaped and with brown pupils, stared as if out of a celestial closet.

Don Hector, a wrinkled man of about sixty who sold tomatoes and onions in the market, was the first to come into the church for his eye. It was a surprisingly simple matter to place the eye in the empty socket; the eye man attached a small suction cup to the artificial eye, inserted it in the socket, secured it by placing the upper and lower flaps of skin from the socket over it, then removed the suction cup. With his new eye, Don Hector looked young enough to chase señoritas in the park.

When Don Hector gazed at himself in the eye man's mirror, he smiled broadly, revealing a mouth significantly short of teeth. "Next time," the eye man said, "I'll make you some dentures."

I translated and Don Hector smiled again. He thanked "el doctor" and walked out of the church. Perhaps I imagined it, but he seemed to be skipping.

Next came Doña Blanca, and she and the eye man had a conversation, with me as translator, about the Second Coming. The eye man said Jesus had already come but would reveal himself only when we recognized him.

"Where is he?" Doña Blanca wanted to know. "In the United States?"

"He's here," the eye man said, patting his chest. He pointed to Doña Blanca's heart. "And there."

It was five o'clock when the last of the eye man's patients, the bus driver Don Victor Hernandez, arrived, panting and covered with grease. He said his bus had broken down during its last run of the day, and he'd had to repair it, then run to keep his appointment.

"I used to own a school bus," said the eye man. "I lived in it for three years."

When he'd fitted Don Victor with the new eye, the eye man said, "Just remember: keep at least one eye on the road."

I translated, and Don Victor laughed.

"Well," said the eye man as the last of the patients was ushered from the church and the doors were closed, "it's over." The Guatemalan doctor was slumped in a pew. After a few moments, he began to snore.

"Where are you going next?" I asked.

"Honduras, I think," the eye man said. "Or maybe El Salvador. Mexico? I don't know."

There was a loud bang on the church door. It woke the Guatemalan doctor, who leapt to his feet as if he'd heard shots. "Qué pasó?" he shouted. Then, apparently remembering where he was, he sighed. "I'll get it."

He opened the door. I heard a woman's voice babbling in Pokomchí, the local Maya language. Then a boy's voice said, in Spanish, "My mother wants me to have eyes."

"I'm sorry," said the Guatemalan doctor, shaking his head. "I'm very sorry, but the clinic is closed."

The boy translated this for his mother, who spoke more urgently.

"My mother says I need eyes," the boy said. "Look, I have no eyes."

The Guatemalan doctor said nothing.

"What do they want?" the eye man asked.

"The boy's blind," I said. "He wants eyes."

The mother talked rapidly, then began to cry.

The doctor turned around and threw up his hands. "No, no, no, I'm very sorry," he said, although softly, and began walking toward the back of the church. The mother followed, pulling her son behind her.

"Bring them up here," said the eye man.

"But you're leaving early tomorrow morning," I said. "You won't have time to make eyes."

The Guatemalan doctor said, "You'll do it?"

The eye man smiled and waved for them to come up on stage.

As they approached, I realized I knew the boy. He lived in the village of Najquitob and was probably eight years old. He didn't attend the village's elementary school, but at lunchtime when the schoolboys played soccer, he was always standing under the pine trees beside the field, as if watching. Where he should have had eyes, there was nothing but dark slits.

I worked with farmers in Najquitob every Wednesday, and when there wasn't much to do in the fields, I'd play soccer with the boys. I'd once asked them what had happened to the blind boy. One boy said he'd been born like that. Another said that guerrillas had poked his eyes out when his father refused to give them money. A third said soldiers had poked his eyes out when they came looking for his father.

I gave up my seat to the señora. The boy stood next to her. The señora said something and the boy translated into Spanish. I then translated for the eye man: "She says she wants her son to see again, and she heard you make eyes."

The eye man whistled. "No, ma'am. No, ma'am. I'm not a miracle worker, just a sinner trying to please Jesus. Tell her I'll give her son eyes but they won't help him see."

I translated, and the boy translated, and his mother began to cry, then shouted something fierce.

I told the eye man that the mother didn't believe him.

She cried, her body heaving. Then she calmed somewhat and wiped her nose with her corte. Then she cried all over again.

"Darn," said the eye man. "Darn." He ran a hand through his long, black hair. He shook his head. "Okay," he said. "Okay, okay, okay. Here it is, right? Here it is: I can't make eyes that will help her son see. No, I can't do that. But I will make him eyes that will help everyone else see." He smiled. "Right."

"What do you mean?" I asked.

"You'll see," said the eye man, biting his lip, then grinning. "You'll see. Just tell her what I told you."

"It doesn't make sense."

"Just tell her."

"You want me to tell them that you'll make eyes that will help everyone else see?"

"Exactly. Tell them."

I turned to the boy and conveyed the eye man's message as best I could.

"Cómo?" the boy asked.

I explained again, and the boy told his mother what I'd said. She responded in Pokomchí, and the boy said to me, "She doesn't understand."

"I don't either," I said. I told all this to the eye man.

"Tell them I'll have them done in seven hours," the eye man said. "They can come back."

I explained this to the boy and he to his mother. The boy said they didn't want to walk back to their village—it would take them two hours—so they would wait. I decided I would come back to see the result. And I did. At midnight the eye man was still huddled over his desk, working in the dim church light.

"Almost done?" I asked him, stepping onto the stage.

He covered up his work with his chest. "Almost," he said. "Don't look until they're finished."

The señora was sitting in the first pew. Her son was asleep with his head on her lap.

"You've waited here a long time," I said to her. Then, remembering she didn't speak Spanish, I said, "C'alen," hello, one of the few words in Pokomchí I knew.

"C'alen," she responded.

I sat in the pew behind hers. I flipped through one of the hymnals. I put it back. I stood up and walked to the window. The street was empty. I looked at the eye man. He was working with some sort of fork or knife. I sat down again.

"It's very late," I mumbled to no one. I closed my eyes. I opened them a few seconds later. "It's very late," I repeated.

I lay down on the pew and stared at the ceiling. Paint was flaking from it. A rare, blue cushion was in arm's reach, and I pulled it to me. I rolled onto my side, brought the cushion under my head, and closed my eyes.

I woke to the sound of a bus roaring past. I sat up. The church was empty, the light gray. I looked at my watch; it was almost seven in the morning. The eye man was gone. I wondered what he'd made for the blind boy. I figured that, whatever it was, his mother was probably disappointed. In general, I found, Guatemalans had unreasonable ideas about the United States. And here was a mother who'd expected her son to be given new eyes. Real eyes.

The next week, I was in the village of Najquitob, working with a group of farmers in their communal cornfield. When I finished around noon, a chipi-chipi was falling. I walked to the soccer field and found it covered in a thick mist. At first, I could see only a lone boy standing in front of the near goal. Then I heard a shout, and a soccer ball emerged from the mist, followed by a boy chasing it, then a pack of boys charging like young bulls, laughing.

The lead boy kicked the ball hard, but the goalie moved left and trapped it between his feet, then kicked it up the right sideline.

"Play with us!" one of the boys shouted before disappearing up the field.

Glad for the invitation, I took off my work boots and socks. It was nice to feel the cool, damp grass on my feet after I'd worked all morning in the heat. I jogged into the mist, where it was hard to see. Then I heard a rumbling sound and saw a pack of boys coming toward me. The ball was well ahead of them, and when it reached me, I kicked it to the right and raced after it. I heard the boys reverse direction.

Seconds later, I was close enough to the goal to shoot. But as I drew back my leg to kick, I noticed the goalie. He was the blind boy. He crouched, as if ready to make a play.

As I stood there, a boy with curly hair came from behind me and kicked the ball out of bounds.

"Qué pasó?" the curly haired boy asked me.

"The boy," I whispered, pointing to the goalie.

"Sí," the boy said. He took my arm and led me over to the blind boy.

"Hombre," I said, "you have eyes."

The blind boy smiled. "Sí, pues," he said.

I was close enough now to see his new eyes clearly, but I couldn't believe what I saw: for irises, the eye man had drawn twin portraits of Jesus, each with long brown hair, golden skin, and a contented half smile, as if he had just told a joke or performed a miracle.

"Increíble," I said.

"Sí, increíble," said the boys, who had by now gathered around me.

"Increíble," I said again.

"Sí, increíble," the boys said.

There was a pause while all of us gazed at the blind boy's eyes.

"Juguemos," said the curly-haired boy. "Let's play."

"Juguemos," the other boys echoed.

"Juguemos," said the blind boy.

As I jogged with the curly-haired boy toward the ball, I inquired if his eyes were the reason the blind boy had been allowed to play soccer. No, the curly-haired boy said. The blind boy had been allowed to play because he'd asked.

The Bribe

Grace and I had agreed to pick up Paul at the airport in Guatemala City. Eva, Paul's girlfriend and our fellow Peace Corps Volunteer, had to build chicken coops in a village near Santiago and couldn't leave in time to meet him, so she'd asked us to go in her place. Paul didn't speak Spanish and needed someone to look out for him. Besides, he was bringing a bagful of novels, and Eva told us we could have first pick.

Grace and I caught the last public bus and arrived at the airport almost two hours early. We milled around the shops, where güipiles, T-shirts, and copies of Rigoberta Menchu's autobiography were sold for twice what they cost elsewhere. From the balcony above the baggage claim, we watched people trickle in from Los Angeles and Miami and Costa Rica. They lifted their bags off the conveyor belt, stood in line to have them searched, then exited through the large glass doors. Outside, beggars and cab drivers awaited them.

With an hour to go before Paul was due to arrive, we walked outside into the cool evening and sat on the grass in the park across from the airport. The taxis came and went, gunning toward the big hotels. The sky turned orange, then gray. Grace sat on my lap, and we kissed.

We talked about how we pitied Paul, coming to a country where he didn't speak the language. Without us, he wouldn't know how much a cab ride to the hotel cost and would end up paying three times the going rate. We'd have to teach him how to bargain in the market—just stand there and look indignant until they lower the price—and not to accept any food or drink from strangers, because it might be drugged. Anyone who didn't know Guatemala was ripe to get ripped off.

Grace and I were at ease in Guatemala, to the point where we considered ourselves locals. We laughed and kissed, and I ran my hand through her long brown hair. I put my other hand up her skirt and felt her smooth thigh.

"Uh-oh," Grace said.

"What?"

She was off my lap in an instant.

"Get up," a voice said in Spanish.

I turned around and saw three policemen, one of them shaking a billy club at me. Grace was on her feet and patting down her skirt.

"Yes, señores?" I said, standing.

The one who had the billy club smiled. He was the tallest and broadest of the three, and the only one with a mustache. "I think you have been doing something very bad in public," he said. The other policemen nodded.

"Excuse me?" Grace said.

"Oh, yes," said the leader. "Very bad." He grinned and turned to his companions.

"What do you mean?" I asked, preparing to play the dumb American.

"You and the girl have been having relations in a public place. This is against the law."

"We weren't doing anything," Grace said.

"We will have to arrest you."

I wondered if he was joking. I tried to smile, but it felt halfhearted. Grace narrowed her eyes.

"We weren't doing anything," she repeated.

The policeman looked at his two companions, and they grinned on cue. "We saw you," he said. "There's no question. You are North Americans?"

We nodded. The policeman nodded with us.

"In your country, perhaps, such sexual acts are permitted in public places. But in our country, things are different."

"Right," Grace said, seizing on an excuse. "We're used to a different standard in our country. We're sorry. De verdad. We're meeting a friend here, and his plane is due to arrive soon. If you'll let us go, we promise never to do anything like this again." Grace took me by the elbow, and we began to walk away, but the policeman put out his hand to stop us.

"This is not a satisfactory solution," he said. "What if the murderer said he would never kill again? Should he be let free?"

"But we didn't murder anyone," I said.

"The principle is the same, no?"

"We weren't doing anything," Grace said for the third time.

"But you just admitted you were."

"No, I didn't."

"Now you are lying. On top of what you have done, you are lying."

Even in the dim evening light, I could see Grace's face turn red. She shook her head.

"Come," the policeman said, "we must take you to jail."

I spoke up: "Isn't there some other way of handling this?" I suspected a bribe was what he wanted, but I wasn't positive. If I wasn't careful, he might use the suggestion against us. I pictured Paul stepping out of the airport into the gauntlet of cabdrivers and beggars, looking around for us. How long would he wait? He didn't even know at which hotel he was supposed to meet Eva.

"What other way could we handle this?" the policeman asked.

"I don't know," I said, not wanting to be the first to mention money.

"Well," he said, "why don't you suggest some possibilities?"

"No," I said, shaking my head. "Why don't *you* suggest some possibilities."

He gave his companions a sly look. "You are gringos, no? So you must know the great actor Sylvester Stallone. I would like very much to appear in one of his movies—even as a villain, if I must."

Was he joking? Grace and I had met more than a few Guatemalans who assumed that everyone from the United States knew Madonna and Michael Jordan.

Grace said, "I have a cousin who works for a film company in New York. He worked on Woody Allen's last film."

"Woody Allen?" the policeman said. He whistled softly and shook his head. "What you were doing in a public place warrants more than an appearance in a Woody Allen movie. I would consider Harrison Ford. But Sylvester Stallone is my first choice."

He turned to his companions, who laughed loudly.

"I know I cannot be in any of your movies," the policeman said, suddenly serious. "What else?"

"I live near a DIGEBOS office," Grace said. "They're doing a major reforestation project, and they've got a lot of nice pine saplings. I could get you some to plant in your yard."

The policeman looked hard at Grace. "So you think I have land? I'm a policeman. I make less than fifty dollars a month. How can I afford to own land? I live in an apartment with my family and my two brothers and their wives. Perhaps I could plant a tree in my bedroom."

Again, the two other policemen laughed.

"No," the policeman said, "you will have to think of something else."

I sighed. I figured it was time to bring up money. "Well," I said, "we're not tourists, so we don't have any dollars. But if money is an issue, I think we can take care of it."

"Ah," the policeman said, nodding. "You are offering me a bribe?"

I shook my head furiously. If I'd miscalculated, I didn't want to double our offense: sex in a public place and attempting to bribe a policeman. How many days, weeks, months might we spend in jail? I imagined a stinking cell in some obscure part of the capital. Would we be allowed a phone call? Would the phones even work?

"So you're not offering me a bribe?" he said.

"We're meeting a friend," Grace said, "and he'll be here very soon." Her teeth were clenched, and her blue eyes had begun to water. In desperation, she mentioned the names of two army captains she knew. She claimed to have their telephone numbers in her pocket. "I'll call them," she said. "I'll tell them what's going on here."

The policeman shook his head and curled his finger at me, motioning for me to come with him. He walked to a pine tree about twenty yards away. I followed. We faced each other. He was tall for a Guatemalan, but still two or three inches shorter than I.

"Your woman," he said in an even tone, "is threatening me."

"I'm sorry."

I know she is saying all this because she is nervous," he said, "but it is unpleasant." His shoulders slumped a little, and his dark eyes were round and large, like a curious child's. "As you know," he said, "it is illegal to offer a policeman a bribe."

"And illegal to accept one," I said.

"Yes, this is a problem, isn't it? But for most people, it isn't a problem. The bribe is offered and accepted, and the law doesn't matter." He sighed. "Some of our laws, I admit, are loco. But you and your girlfriend have broken our law, and if I were to enforce it, I would have to take the two of you to jail. And it would be very unpleasant there. You would be separated, and who knows what would happen to you. Someone from your embassy would come tonight or tomorrow or next week, and there would be publicity. There is always a reporter from *La Extra* at the jail, and this would be news. The story would help to sell newspapers. But who would profit? Not me, not you." He shook his head. "It's unfair. The government does not pay us enough to live on and then expects us to refuse bribes. This is like asking a starving man to refuse a piece of bread."

I glanced over at Grace. She was talking with the other two policemen, speaking loudly and quickly, mentioning someone else she knew, the owner of a plantation on the south coast who was a retired colonel and had many friends in the army.

"I do not like to think of my country as corrupt," the policeman said to me. "And this is what you will think if I accept your bribe. You will tell all your friends, 'Yes, Guatemala is very corrupt.' I shouldn't care. I am only one man, with two young daughters and a wife who cleans our neighbors' houses for money. And we are still hungry. Perhaps I should accept your bribe. Sometimes, in order to survive, people must become corrupt."

"It's hard," I said, trying to sound sympathetic. I didn't care about his dilemma. I was ready to pay the bribe.

"Before I was a policeman, I was a student," he said. "An art student. Painting." He made a drawing motion with his right hand. "But I could go for only one year because my uncle died. He was the one paying for my school."

"Sad," I said with as much feeling as I could fake. Where was this leading? Was he softening me up so I would pay a larger bribe?

"I paint very little now," he said. "Only playing cards."

"Playing cards?"

"Yes, I paint playing cards. I have a deck in my pocket, cards I have painted by hand." He smiled. "I think this is how we will solve our little problem today: you will buy a deck of my playing cards, and I will let you go meet your friend."

I wondered how much he was going to charge. I had a hundred quetzales in my pocket—around twenty dollars. If he asked more for his hand-painted cards, we would be right back where we started.

"How much?" I asked.

"The price is usually one hundred quetzales. But because this is an unusual situation, I will sell them to you for seventy."

"Okay," I said, relieved to be resolving matters. I pulled out my wallet and turned around so he wouldn't see how much money I had. Then I drew out three blue twenties and a pink ten and handed them to him.

"Thank you," he said.

When I began to walk away, he said, "Wait."

"What now?"

"Your cards."

"Right," I said. "The cards."

From his pocket, he removed a deck of cards wrapped in tissue paper. "Here," he said.

They weighed hardly anything; I doubted it was even a full set. I shoved the cards in my pocket.

"You aren't going to look at them?" he asked.

"Later," I said, and I walked over to Grace, threw my arm around her shoulder, and practically carried her toward the terminal.

"What's going on?" she asked me.

"I'll tell you in a minute," I said, stealing a quick look back. The policeman was standing with his head bowed, as if he'd lost something in the grass.

In the safety of the airport, I told Grace what had happened. I didn't mention the cards, just how much I'd had to bribe him.

She whistled. "Ouch. That's fifteen dollars—half a month's rent."

"Yeah, a goddamn rip-off."

We met Paul outside the baggage claim and hailed a cab to the Hotel Suizo. On the way, we told him about our adventure.

"Be forewarned," Grace said. "No sex in public places."

Eva met us at the hotel, and after dinner, the four of us went back to Eva and Paul's room and talked until late. Around midnight, the conversation began to fade, and Paul and Eva looked as if they wanted to be alone. But Paul still hadn't offered Grace and me any of the novels he'd brought, and we weren't about to leave without our bounty.

"Well," Eva said, "what should we do?"

"Anybody up for cards?" I asked, and I pulled out the policeman's deck, opened the tissue, and placed it on the center of the bed. They were smaller than regular cards, maybe three-quarter sized, and their backs were all painted dark blue. I flipped the deck over. The top card, the king of hearts, had a drawing of the Mayan god Quetzalcoatl in the center.

"Cool," Paul said, picking it up.

"Where'd you buy these?" Eva asked.

"Why haven't I seen them?" Grace said.

We flipped through the deck. The queen of hearts was La Llorona, the weeping woman. The jack was the Mayan corn god. There was even a pair of jokers: El Sombrerón, the guitar-playing midget. The colors were bright, the images simple and powerful. I could see why the policeman had been so eager for me to look at them.

"They're beautiful. Where'd you get them?" Eva asked again.

"From a local artist," I said.

"I'd like a set," she said.

"I'll buy one for you," Paul said gallantly.

The next morning, Paul took me aside and asked where he could buy a deck of cards like mine. Eva had talked about it half the night, he said. I told him I didn't think he'd be able to find an identical deck, but that I would sell him mine.

"How much?" he asked.

"Thirty dollars," I said, calculating my profit.

He didn't hesitate: "It's a deal."

But I regretted it later, after Grace had left me and I wished for some memento of our illegal embrace.

Blackheart

The moon is full, the sky cloudless. It is summer in Argentina—"All your friends in Ohio are shivering in the snow," her mother told her the other day—but the nights are cool. She walks across the garden's lawn toward the door on the other end. It is the door to the vineyard. Black Heart is behind it.

Her mother and Ed are eating dinner in Mendoza. It is late, but dinner always starts late in Argentina. The restaurants open at eight at night. Emily has eaten dinner at a restaurant in Argentina only once, and she fell asleep before dessert. Waking her, her mother said, "You'll never be mistaken for an Argentine." Ed had said the same in relation to her red hair and blue-green eyes, inherited from her father. Emily wanted to stay with her father in Sherman instead of coming here, but he has a new girlfriend and Emily's presence, he said, would be inconvenient now. There was a time between her parents' separation and divorce when her father wanted her to spend all her time with him. Her mother said this was only because he wanted to look good in the eyes of the divorce judge. After the divorce, he became busy.

So did her mother, who met Ed in an adventure writing class he'd taught in Cleveland. Older than her mother by sixteen years, he has a balloon belly and waddles rather than walks. He is a travel writer, a food writer, a wine writer. He has rented this house outside of Mendoza so he can write about Mendoza's foods and wines. Her mother is supposed to be home-schooling her—Emily's fifth-grade teacher gave her mother a packet to cover January and February, the months they would be gone—but most days, her mother and Ed drive off into the Uco valley, and Emily leaves her schoolwork and wanders around the vineyard singing songs she knows and songs she makes up. Beyond the last row of grapevines, there is an elevated spot, a grass altar where she likes to lie on her back and stare at the Andes Mountains, off to the west, snow-capped and shimmering like a picture in a storybook. Sometimes Maria, the wife of the man who looks after the property, finds her and asks if she's all right. Maria's Spanish is only a little better than Emily's. Maria and her husband, Daniel, who live in the two-room cottage next to the house where she is staying, are from Bolivia. Her mother says their first language is…Emily can't remember. It starts with a q, like question.

Daniel is in charge of keeping the robbers and the killers and the rapists out of the vineyard and out of the garden and out of the house. One night, she overheard her mother and Ed discussing what happened to a Canadian woman who owns a hotel in Mendoza. When her mother discovered her hiding behind the kitchen door, she said, "You don't have to worry, sweetheart. We have Daniel and the dogs."

Their house sits in the north end of the garden, and the garden is surrounded by a black iron fence topped with barbed wire. On three sides of the black fence, separated from it by a ten-foot-wide corridor, is a chain-link fence, also topped with barbed wire. On the fourth side of the garden, on the south end, is the vineyard, which is surrounded by only a five-foot-tall wooden picket fence without barbed wire. Before Daniel goes to bed, he releases three bullmastiffs into the corridors between the black fence and the chain-link fence. Into the vineyard Daniel sends a fourth dog, some combination of pit bull, Rottweiler, German shepherd, and wolf, an animal as cruel and vicious as any animal on earth, or so Daniel told her. Daniel has given several names to this dog in his language, but in Spanish he calls him Black Heart. Black Heart was the topic of her mother's sternest lecture: *At night, don't ever open the door to the vineyard. Black Heart is on guard, and he's trained to kill whomever he finds.* "Even me?" *Anyone. Please, darling.* "Why would he kill me?" *Please. Never open the door.*

When they arrived in Argentina, Ed thought she should be curious about wine and empanadas and tango dancing. But Emily was curious about the guard dogs. How old were they? Were the three bullmastiffs brothers? Had the three bullmastiffs ever met Black Heart? Had Black Heart ever killed anyone?

Ed didn't know anything about them. "Ask Daniel," he said. So Emily did, in her bad Spanish. The next time they saw each other, Daniel pulled a tattered paperback Spanish-English dictionary from his back pocket. The print was so small even Emily had trouble reading it. The dictionary became a game between them, a game to see who could find the right word, who could speak it well enough so the other person understood. Daniel is only an inch or two taller than her five feet (she is the tallest girl in her class), and he has the blackest, straightest hair she's ever seen. His nose is large, and his nostrils seem, in proportion, even larger. Her mother and Ed call him Evo, because he supposedly looks like the president of Bolivia. Saturday is his night off. Sometimes on Saturday nights he stays home with Maria and sometimes he meets up with his Bolivian friends in Mendoza.

Often when Daniel returns late at night, she hears him singing, and this reminds her of her father, who loves to sing. Daniel's voice is light and sweet; her father's is low like a rumble or a growl. When her parents were married, the three of them would go camping every summer in southern

Ohio, and every night around the fire, her mother would play her guitar and her father would sing, his voice booming above the crackling flames. On the last couple of trips, Emily sang with him. Although her voice was as thin as air, it was beautiful, her father said, beautiful and enchanting. "You could sing a fish out of the water," he said. "You could sing a dog away from a bone."

In the week before she left for Argentina, Emily called her father every day, always when she thought his girlfriend wouldn't be with him. Even when she wasn't, their conversations were short. One time Emily called him and his girlfriend interrupted to ask him, "What do you think of this ring?" The last time she spoke to him, he was at a party and there was music in the background. "Remember this song?" he said, and she sang to show him she did. But she realized he had been speaking to someone else. Embarrassed, she hung up. The next day, she was on a plane to Argentina.

Emily hears a sound in the bougainvillea that covers the black iron fence on her left. Her heart springs into her throat. But it is only the stray tiger cat who visits some nights. Daniel calls him Romeo because he supposedly fathered all the recent litters in the neighborhood. He paws his way from the top of the fence, cascades down the purple flowers, and tumbles onto the grass. He is the thinnest cat she has ever seen, but her mother assured her he isn't starving. Emily didn't know what to call the two round pouches visible from behind when he lifted his tail. "Balls," Ed said, grinning. "Testicles," her mother said. "Please."

Romeo rubs himself against her leg, and she crouches down to pet him. His fur is like none she has touched before. It is thick and prickly like she imagines a groundhog's would be. "Do you know what I'm doing tonight?" she asks Romeo. "I'm going to visit Black Heart." He looks up at her, responding to her voice. "Don't worry. He's my friend. I've been visiting him in his cage. I sing to him." She pretends he says something. "He's not my boyfriend! He's a dog!" She laughs and shakes her head.

In her first week in Argentina, after they had become friends, Daniel brought her to see the dogs in their cages, located in the corridor between the two fences at the front of the property. They were like cages at the zoo, except they were no taller than her chest. The three bullmastiffs, who shared a cage, barked at her, but when Daniel scolded them, they whimpered like doves. When they reached Black Heart's cage, he attacked the bars, barking like no dog she'd ever known, like some hellbound creature from mythology. Surprised and frightened, she backpedaled and tripped. Daniel alternately spoke sympathetically to her and harshly to Black Heart. From where she'd fallen, she gazed, trembling, at Black Heart, who never ceased barking. She wondered how strong the bars of his cage were. She imagined them snapping and Black Heart pouncing on her and enclosing her neck in his mouth.

Black Heart looked less like a dog and more like a mammal from the period after the dinosaurs died. He was husky and broad-shouldered like a gorilla and his square face and dark, marble eyes seemed bison-like. He had scars everywhere—on his forehead, on his chest, in several places on his back—and she wondered what violent encounter each scar represented.

Thereafter whenever Daniel fed the dogs she accompanied him—except when her mother was around. Her mother didn't want her near the dogs. "They are not your friends," she said. "Okay, Emily? Okay?"

When she was with Daniel, she stood by his side, so close she could smell him. He wore cologne, but this didn't disguise his other smells, which she thought her mother would find repulsive but which she grew used to and found reassuring. As soon as Daniel fed the three bullmastiffs, which he did by sliding their bowls into a space on the bottom of their cage, they stopped being interested in anything but the food. But Black Heart wouldn't eat his food until Daniel and Emily retreated behind the garden wall. If they craned their heads around the wall to stare at Black Heart, he would bark like he smelled blood. To watch him eat, Daniel taped a hand-held mirror to a long stick and held it at such an angle that they could gaze into it and see him. He ate the brown nuggets with slow pleasure. She remembered the last time she ate dinner with her father, how he picked at the rotisserie chicken, finishing everything on the bones.

When Daniel lets Black Heart into the vineyard every night, he carries a bullwhip. The whip looks like a snake—*una culebra*—and Black Heart is scared of nothing in the world except the whip. Even so, he growls at it as if to say, Keep your distance or I will attack you. A week ago, as she leaned out of her open bedroom window, she saw Daniel leading Black Heart into the vineyard. Under his breath, he said, "One night he won't be afraid of the whip. And then what?" He looked up at her, surprised to see her. She smiled like she did when she didn't understand his Spanish.

"All right, Romeo," she says, "you be good. Be good to all your girlfriends." The cat darts off to the other side of the garden and disappears beneath the weeping willow tree, which in the night looks like a hunched giant with a thousand thin arms. She resumes her walk toward the door, but is stopped by a sound of "Who? Who? Who?" It is Boy, the white-faced owl, in his nook in the palm tree twenty feet above her. She always thought of owls as old, but this owl looks like a teenager—thus the name she gave him.

"It's only me, Boy," she says. If he could speak in a language she understood, she wonders if he would tease her like a brother would. Or would he say something like the man at the mall said to her cousin, who is fourteen but, with her breasts and European haircut, looks twenty?

"I'm going to visit Black Heart," she tells the owl. "It's all right. You'll see."

Some days when Daniel is out in the vineyard and Maria is at the market in Luján de Cuyo and her mother and Ed are napping under the thin-bladed ceiling fan in their bedroom or sampling wines in Chacras de Coria, she visits Black Heart in his cage. She used to bring him pieces of steak and chicken she slipped into her palm at dinner and saved in a paper bag beneath her bed. The first time, she tossed the pieces of meat between the bars of his cage and retreated behind the fence so he could eat them in private. When, on subsequent visits, she lingered, he snarled, growled, and barked at her but eventually, between his hostile sounds, devoured her offering.

One day, she sang to him after giving him his meat, and his vicious sounds ceased. Even with his gigantic, square head and his razor-blade teeth and his terrible scars, he looked familiar and approachable, like a misunderstood monster. The song she'd sung was one she'd heard often on Maria's radio. She didn't understand all of the Spanish words, but she could enunciate them clearly, and Black Heart cocked his head as if to hear better. As soon as she stopped, his face again became strange and hideous, and his barking shocked her ears until she fled, terrified.

The next day, she returned with only her voice. As long as she sang, he was silent, docile, calm. Content, even. Perhaps even happy.

Boy flutters his white and brown wings and swoops down toward her, his mouth open, his talons spread and pointed like daggers. As she ducks and covers her eyes, she feels the wind from his wings fill her hair. She shivers from fear and a strange pleasure before she hears a squeal, high-pitched and hopeless. She turns to see Boy pluck a mouse from the grass and retreat with his feast to the palm tree.

"You scared me, Boy. Maybe you wanted to? In fun, I mean. Like a brother would?"

The day she touched Black Heart, the air was a white mist. She couldn't see her feet. But she knew the path to his cage as if it were illuminated. When she stood before it, she couldn't see him; she could only hear his terrible bark. When she sang, his barking stopped instantly, as if she'd cast a spell. Piercing the bars of his cage, she held out her hand to him, palm open. She felt his mouth engulf it. She felt his teeth touch her skin. She thought he was going to bite down. But his mouth held steady. Carefully, she slipped her left hand into the cage so she could stroke his head and neck and back. His fur was like the leather of her father's jacket.

A moment later, she felt his tongue sweep the underside of her fingers and his teeth nibble, soft as a kiss, her fingertips. She felt her heart fly. She felt adored. For hours afterward, she didn't wash either hand.

During her last visit before tonight, as she sang a song she'd invented about a girl and a dog and the iron between them, he looked at her with what she swore was a plea. *I want to know you without bars between us.*

Ten feet from the door separating her and Black Heart, she stops. She can sense his presence. She hears a growl so soft it might be a purr. If she moves any closer, he will erupt and wake Maria, asleep in her tiny house. If this happens, her plan will come to nothing, and she will never again have the chance to visit him. Ed and her mother will keep her with them, even if they'd rather not. Besides, their time in Argentina is coming to an end. Another week, and they will be heading home.

She sings, softly at first, a sound like small waves hitting sand. He stops growling. She reaches the door. There are three deadbolt locks, the highest an inch beyond her reach. But she jumps and slaps it open. In jumping, her singing stops, and Black Heart growls. She slaps the second lock open, her singing coming jagged, and Black Heart continues to growl, his voice climbing in register the way it does before he attacks the bars of his cage. She tries to make her singing calm, but this is difficult because of her pounding heart.

She has one deadbolt left to open before she can turn the doorknob and release him into the garden. She gives herself a moment to doubt. The wisest part of her says she should go back to the house, go to bed. But her hand, which she can barely feel as her heart thunders, acts otherwise. It snaps the deadbolt to the side.

Stop, she tells herself. Think. If Black Heart were to attack her, Maria could do nothing. Daniel is in Mendoza with his friends. He might come home in five minutes. He might come home in three hours. And Ed and her mother? Even if they were to come, what could they do?

These reservations register the way the deepest fear does, like fingers squeezing her heart, but they cannot overcome her desire. She pulls open the door. Boy cries as if he's been wounded, leaps from his cave in the palm tree, and flies over her, his wings filling her hair with a warning wind.

Too late. Black Heart is at her side, so close she can feel heat coming from him. She thinks, I'm going to die. At the same time, exhilaration fills her. She feels like she owns the night. She turns, singing, and walks to the middle of the garden. Black Heart circles her, a slow loop on the grass, his eyes never leaving her. He might be dancing with her. Or he might be a lion circling its prey.

The moon blazes above her, and she feels powerful and magical and adored. Every so often, she touches Black Heart's back, at once smooth and rough. *I can sing all night.* But after a minute or five or ten—she has no watch, the night tells no time—her exhilaration fades into worry. She doesn't know how long she can stand here and sing. Perhaps she can make her way back to the house, open the door, slip in. It is only fifty feet from where she's standing. But when she steps toward it, Black Heart quickly moves in front of her and issues a clear, low sound, less a growl than a warning a human might give.

When Black Heart is at the farthest point in his circle away from the house, she again moves toward it. Again, he moves swiftly to block her. This time, his warning is louder and more insistent. She backs up to her original spot. She hears nothing but her voice against the inside of her ears and the swish of Black Heart moving in the grass. *My God*, she thinks, *I'll have to sing all night.*

She wonders if she should run toward the house. She wonders if she should shout Maria's name. But she fears—she knows—that if she broke off her song even for a second, Black Heart would attack her, devour her.

As she sings, she prays Daniel will come home. She prays Ed and her mother will become bored at the dinner and will drive the car into the middle of the garden to save her. She prays Maria will step outside and Black Heart will charge her, and this will give her the chance to flee. But the night radiates with brilliant indifference and fatigue weighs on her like something living, something growing. Her song has lost words.

When they find me, they won't know he loved me. They'll think I was a stupid girl who thought she could play with a mean dog.

She feels her eyes flutter from fatigue; she feels herself stagger. As in a dream, she feels Black Heart at her side, his head butting her thigh, insistent and strong. He prods her toward the vineyard's open door. A moment later, she is surrounded by grapes, silver-blue in the moonlight. Her arid mouth craves their delicious juice, but Black Heart jabs her and she keeps moving. She hears Maria calling her. She hears Ed's car limp up the gravel drive. She even hears, or thinks she hears, Daniel, or perhaps it's her father, singing in the distance.

The sounds fade. She wants to scream, but, so deep in the vineyard, she knows no one would hear her.

I'll find my way back, she vows, but stumbles, collapses. On her back on the grass altar, she sees, as if on a different planet, the snow-capped Andes. She discovers that, remarkably, she is still singing, in a voice charged with emotion. *I'm safe.* But—no—it is Black Heart, mouth at her ear, who is singing.

The Girl on the *Subte*

···

On the hot subway train, the girl stares at Karen as if studying her face, as if to discover whether she knows her. They are sitting across from each other, no one in the aisle between them. The girl's eyes are green, glimmering. A cat's eyes. Her cheeks are filled with freckles. The girl's family is sitting on her left. Her mother, with the same reddish-brown hair as her daughter, is talking about what they will eat tonight, what they will see tomorrow, what the weather must be like back home, in Vermont. "Snow, I am sure," she says brightly. "Snow everywhere." She spreads her arms and flips her palms up, as if to catch the falling snow. Between the girl and her mother sit her younger brother, pale and thin, and her father, who is wearing a black T-shirt with the word "Saints" written across it in gold.

The girl, who must be about twelve, continues to gaze at Karen, and if Karen's attention is sometimes drawn to the three high-school girls in blue and white uniforms standing to her left, the speed and register at which they speak Spanish making it seem like no language she has ever heard, or to the woman reading a Julio Cortázar novel in the seat to her right, or to the *Lonely Planet* guide to Argentina in her lap, it inevitably returns to the girl and her electric cat's eyes.

This morning at the Botanical Gardens, Karen saw dozens of feral cats lounging on benches and sleeping under laurel trees. They appeared well-groomed and well-fed, but whoever their keepers were hadn't spayed and neutered them. Karen saw two mother cats with their adorable, gamboling kittens. Karen has four cats at home in Sherman, Ohio, and if she happens to stop by the Cat's Meow on a day Animal Allies is showing off its latest refugees from kill pounds, she is always tempted to add one more to her menagerie.

The train stops at Agüero, and the high-school girls depart. The American family follows, the mother first. The father, bald and stocky like a circus strongman, wraps his arm around his son and steps off the car with him. The girl is looking at her palms, and Karen wants to warn her about her departing family. A moment later, the girl looks up, panicked, and moves toward the door. She makes a sound, something pleading but wordless. It's too late: the doors have closed. On the platform, the father looks back. The train slides off into darkness.

The girl presses her hands against the glass windows, murmuring, moaning. Karen jumps to her feet and moves next to her. "I saw what happened," she says.

The girl turns to Karen with watery eyes.

"I'll help you find them," Karen assures her.

The girl nods slowly, sadly, but says nothing.

"We'll get off at the next stop and wait for them. One of…I bet your father…I bet he'll come on the next train. I bet your mother will stay back with your brother in case they think you might catch the train going the other way."

The girl nods a couple of times. She rubs her eyes, and Karen sees they've become red.

"My name is Karen."

The girl smiles, a white flash, but again says nothing.

"Do you have trouble speaking? Are you—?" Karen looks in the girl's freckled face. The girl looks back, her expression half troubled, half curious. "I don't know sign language," Karen says. "I'm sorry. I barely speak Spanish, which I'm supposed to do fluently. At least according to my résumé." Karen laughs. "Do you read lips?" With her index fingers, Karen manipulates the sides of her mouth the way a clown might. The gesture, she realizes, is buffoonish, as futile as shouting would be.

Presently, they arrive at Pueyrredón. When the doors open, Karen gestures for the girl to walk in front of her, and Karen follows her onto the platform. "Let's wait here," Karen says, pointing to a wooden bench. Although hot and humid, the station doesn't smell of sweating bodies or decaying food. "I'm sure they'll be on the next car," Karen tells the girl, who nods, although Karen isn't certain she understood.

But when a subway car screeches into the station and releases its passengers, there is no sign of the girl's parents or brother. The girl glances at her; Karen can't tell what emotion is most prominent in the girl's face: confusion, fear, sadness, curiosity. "It's all right," Karen says, patting the girl on the knee. She doesn't know what to say next, so she repeats, "It's all right."

A few minutes later, another train pulls into the station, but although it, too, is packed, the girl's parents are not aboard. "Maybe they've gone straight to the police," Karen says. "I think we should go to the police."

At the last word, the girl's face turns pale. She clutches Karen's forearm, squeezing hard, and shakes her head, her hair flapping against her cheeks. "But your parents will probably have…" Karen begins, but the girl continues to shake her head and, at last, produces a sound, muffled but nevertheless distinct: "No. Please."

Karen can't tell whether the girl has a Vermont accent (if there is such an accent) or whether the tears she hasn't cried, but seems about to, have bled into her voice, distorting it. She imagines the girl's fear: strangers in uniforms, guns on their waists. "I know you're afraid."

"Hungry," the girl says, placing both her hands over her stomach.

Karen looks in her purse but finds no crackers, only her wallet, stuffed with credit cards and peso notes, her passport, *Lonely Planet*, and twenty-two pages of a manuscript she planned to work on over lunch. An associate professor of philosophy at Ohio Eastern University, she is writing a book about the uses of logic versus intuition in solving missing-persons cases. She hopes to include a chapter on political disappearances, with a focus on Argentina during its "Dirty War" in the late 1970s and early 1980s. But after three days in the country, she feels stymied by her Spanish, which she hasn't spoken regularly in a decade, and a familiar, persistent sense of dissatisfaction and unease about her work, her life, the world.

Another subway train rumbles into the station.

Karen was supposed to spend her first week in Buenos Aires with her sister, Beth, but Beth's oldest son, Ethan, fell ill with the swine flu a day before their departure, so Karen traveled alone. Beth is hoping to rearrange her schedule so she can come next week, but Karen doubts this will happen. Beth has three children, all of them under twelve, and Karen can't imagine her sister spending the days immediately preceding Christmas without them.

Another train empties without the girl's parents.

"Let's go back one stop, back to Agüero," Karen tells her, smiling with false cheer. "Maybe they're waiting." Karen doesn't believe this, but if the girl doesn't want her to go to the police, she doesn't know what else to do.

They ride back to Agüero, but there is no sign of the girl's parents, no sign of a single concerned person. A train empties and fills; another train arrives, expels strangers. The TV screen above the platform shows a serious woman in a brown suit speaking behind a newscaster's desk followed, incongruously, by a trio of babies batting at butterflies.

"What's your name?" Karen asks the girl.

The girl, unsmiling, answers, "Maria."

Karen says, "Let's find something to eat, Maria. Afterwards, we'll call the U.S. Embassy. All right?"

When Maria smiles, Karen glimpses crooked teeth. Her parents, she thinks, must be poor or opposed to braces. But if they don't have money, what are they doing in Argentina? Could they be missionaries? What religion objects to braces? Seventh Day Adventists? Christian Scientists?

But what kind of missionaries—what kind of parents—would abandon their daughter on the Buenos Aires subway?

Perhaps with her disability, whatever it is, she was too large a burden on her family. Karen tries to recall the father's expression as he looked back and saw his daughter on the train. Was he concerned or relieved? Sad because he had forgotten his daughter or sad because he was executing an unfortunate but necessary plan?

They leave the subway and climb into intense sunlight. Karen doesn't know where they are, but she doesn't want to pull out her *Lonely Planet* and thereby announce herself as a tourist here on the uncertain streets. They walk past a bookstore whose enormous front window reveals stacks of hardback novels about vampires. They walk past a pastelería, and Karen is tempted to buy a couple of medialunas or pengüinos. But feeding Maria sweets might spoil her lunch. Karen wants to do what is right with the girl. She imagines her parents' gratitude when they reunite with their daughter, imagines them praising Karen's considerate guardianship. At the same time, Karen wonders if they will be critical: "You could have gone to the police, but instead you went to lunch?" And Karen's response: "She was afraid of the police, and she was hungry. Besides, where the hell were you?"

Where the hell are they?

They continue to walk, and Karen apologizes to Maria: "I don't see a suitable restaurant, something casual and uncrowded." She wonders if Maria understands her. The sidewalks are filled with people. Some move quickly, purposefully. A couple of gray-haired men wearing glasses and leaning on canes talk outside a newspaper kiosk. Across the street is a theater, the life-sized poster under its marquee featuring a pair of middle-aged women, one with wild hair and extravagant make-up, the other in a neat blue business suit. The show, a comedy, is called *Mis Dos Madres*.

Karen knows where they are now, on Corrientes, in the theater district. The apartment she is renting is only two blocks west. Around the corner, on Montevideo, is a small, cozy restaurant Karen has been eyeing since coming to Buenos Aires. Karen smiles at Maria. "Another minute and we'll be sitting down, ordering sandwiches, and drinking lemonade."

The restaurant is called El Jardín, although nothing about it is particularly garden-like. They are seated toward the back of the restaurant, near an exit that leads into an alley or side street paved with cobblestones. The girl looks intently at the menu, which is in both Spanish and English, and when Karen asks her what she wants, she points to a chicken sandwich, French fries, a chocolate milkshake. "I hope it'll be okay with your parents," Karen says. "I'll call the U.S. Embassy as soon as we have a little bite to eat, all right?" There is a pause of a few seconds before the girl nods.

Their waiter is dressed in a white, button-down shirt and black slacks. His curly black hair and button nose, Karen thinks, would look attractive on a woman but makes him seem merely jolly. After Karen orders for both her and Maria, the waiter turns to Maria and says, in English, "Why so shy, young lady?" Maria looks at Karen before staring down at her lap.

He addresses his next question to Karen: "First time in Buenos Aires for the two of you?"

Karen thinks about explaining the situation. But it seems too complicated—she wonders how good the waiter's English is—and what if he immediately asked her why she hadn't called the Embassy or the police? What answer would she give?

"First time," she says.

He suggests an art museum they should visit, a tango show they should see. "And for your daughter, there is a children's museum up the street." He looks at Maria closely. "But perhaps she is too old. How old are you?"

Maria looks at Karen, and Karen detects anxiety or embarrassment in her expression. "She's twelve," Karen says.

The waiter nods. "Too old," he says. "With her eyes, it's difficult to tell her age. They make her look both young and immortal." He grins, as if expecting a compliment on his compliment. Karen obliges with a "thank you." She considers her own appearance. She was never beautiful, but save a gain in weight of fifteen pounds and the addition of an incalculable number of freckles on her face, arms, and back, she is the same un-beautiful she was in high school.

When the waiter is gone, Karen asks Maria, "Are you twelve years old?"

The girl doesn't answer immediately. "Eleven."

"You're tall for your age. Do you play basketball?"

"Football."

"Football? Wow. I don't know many girls who play football. On a team or just with friends?"

"Soccer," Maria says.

"You play soccer, too?"

Maria blushes and looks at her lap.

"I bet you're good at football and soccer."

There is something endearing about Maria's quick smiles and the way she looks down to hide whatever her face might reveal. If her parents have abandoned her...no, Karen can't imagine her parents wanting to abandon her. Even if she requires special education, surely the public schools in Vermont can accommodate her.

The waiter brings Maria her chocolate milkshake and French fries, which she pounces on. With a French fry at the edge of her mouth like a cigarette, Maria manages to articulate the softest "thank you" Karen has ever heard.

"You're welcome. You deserve it. You've had such a hard day. But we'll find your parents soon. This is only a little diversion so we can recoup our energy. Everything will be back to what it was."

Karen is about to ask Maria what grade she is in when the waiter arrives with two chicken and cheese sandwiches, toasted in what looks like pita bread or piecrust. The sandwiches are warm, the bread like an unsweet pastry, the meat inside soft and juicy and delicious. "What do you think?" Karen asks Maria, who has taken three swift bites of her sandwich. Maria reaches across the table to touch Karen's hand and says something Karen doesn't hear.

"I'm sorry," Karen says. "What did you say?"

A moment passes. The girl looks at her sandwich, then at her lap.

"I want to ask you something, Maria," Karen says. "It's about your parents."

Maria looks up. She looks sad. Or curious. Or indifferent. If Maria's face is a logic problem, Karen doesn't know its solution.

"Why did you and your family come here, to Argentina?"

Maria looks at her blankly.

"Are your parents religious people? Are they doing work here?"

Maria looks at her lap again. Karen tries again: "Or are you all here as tourists—you know, to see a different part of the world? When I overheard your mother talking on the subway...well...she seemed like an ordinary tourist, excited by a new country. And what would be the worst nightmare a family traveling in a foreign country could face—to lose a child in a big, anonymous city. So I was sure your mother or father would be coming on the next train, and I'm a little mystified they didn't."

Maria looks up, and it's as if she wants to tell Karen something but can't. "Go ahead," Karen urges her. "You can trust me."

Maria continues to gaze at Karen with pleading eyes. Or sad eyes. Or curious eyes. No, there is something urgent in them, something needy.

"Is something wrong with your parents? They didn't mean to leave you, did they? Or did they? You can tell me, Maria. I won't leave you, I promise. I'll stay right here." She taps the table, rattling the water glasses. "Whatever is happening to you, you can tell me."

Maria opens her mouth, hesitates, closes it.

"It's all right," Karen says. "I'll help you—whatever help you need. All right? Trust me."

Karen's cell phone rings, a purring sound from her purse. She places her purse beside her plate, reaches in, and pulls out her iPhone. Her sister is calling. But when Karen says, "Hello, Beth," she hears nothing. "We don't have a good connection," she says into the phone. "Let me move outside."

Karen places the phone against her chest. "This will be a quick call," she tells Maria. "I'll be right back. I'm not leaving you. Okay?"

Maria nods.

Karen steps outside onto the narrow cobblestone street, which despite being between tall buildings is filled with sunlight so bright Karen has to shield her eyes. "Hello?" Beth says. "Hello?"

"I hear you now," Karen says. She asks Beth about Ethan, and Beth says he is doing better, although she is worried about secondary infections.

"I'm sorry, Kare," Beth says. "I don't think I'll be able to come down."

"It's okay," Karen replies. "I found a traveling companion."

There is a brief pause, followed by Beth's hopeful, "A man?" Ever since Karen broke up with Matt four-and-a-half years ago, Beth has pushed her to find another lover. Two years ago, she tried to set up Karen with a man from Cleveland she'd met on a flight to Las Vegas. When the man called Karen to arrange a date, he admitted to being married, adding, "Not that it should matter."

"Not one little bit," Karen said, and hung up.

"No, not a man," Karen says, and she hears Beth sigh.

Karen and Matt, an art history professor at Ohio Eastern, dated for six years, and long after Karen understood Matt never intended to marry her, Beth joked with him, prodded him, even, behind Karen's back, pleaded with him to make an honest woman of her sister. In the last six months of their relationship, as she sensed its impending end, Karen stopped taking the pill without telling Matt. Every month, she waited, with increasing disappointment, to see if she was pregnant.

"Who is it, then?" Beth asks her. "Another middle-aged woman?" Whatever enthusiasm might have been in Beth's voice is gone.

"An eleven-year-old girl," Karen says. She explains the events of the morning. When she is finished, her sister hesitates before saying, "It's strange the parents wouldn't have come looking for her or contacted the police."

"I haven't gone to the police," Karen says.

"Why not?"

"Maria didn't want me to."

"Why not? What would she know about—. This is sounding a little strange, Kare."

"It isn't strange. It's sad. What if her parents wanted to abandon her? I told you she might have learning disabilities. Maybe they found them too much to bear."

"Maybe," Beth says doubtfully.

"What? What are you thinking?"

"Nothing," Beth says. "I'm going to go check on Ethan. Please call me after you resolve this situation, okay?"

"Yeah. Sure."

"And be careful."

"Careful of what?"

"I don't know. In general."

"All right," Karen says. "I will." They tell each other "I love you," and the conversation is over.

Karen turns around to face the restaurant, but all she can see in the window is her reflection, gold-tinted, grinning. Grinning? She strides toward the side door, pulls it open, and steps back into the restaurant.

Their table is empty. Their dishes remain in place, with Karen's half-eaten sandwich on one. Karen thinks Maria must be in the bathroom, and she is about to walk toward the back of the restaurant when she remembers her purse. She moves around the table to her chair, but her purse is gone. Her heart fires against her chest. Maria must have taken the purse with her to the bathroom, Karen decides. *Smart girl.*

The door to the women's bathroom is unlocked, the single room, no bigger than a shower stall, unoccupied. "Maria?" she asks, but it is only herself Karen sees in the square mirror, brown eyes wide, grin gone.

Karen leaves the bathroom. The waiter is at their table, and when he sees Karen he smiles with relief, "Oh, señora," he says. "I thought you had… run." He hands her the check, and she gazes at the numbers, which mean nothing to her.

"Have you seen the girl, the girl who was with me?"

"Your daughter?" he asks.

"The girl," she says. "Yes."

"I think perhaps she went into the street to look for you." He points to the front entrance, and she rushes toward it. Outside there is sunlight; there are strangers walking quickly and slowly. She walks up the block to her left; she returns and continues another block. No Maria. She looks in the cobblestone alley, shouting Maria's name.

When she returns to the restaurant, she looks for her purse under the table. She even falls to her knees, hoping to find it concealed somewhere. She rises and collapses into her seat. "What happened?" she asks aloud, although she thinks she knows. She cannot bring herself to declare so definitively, however. There is still a chance—isn't there?—that Maria will return, bearing her purse and a shy smile. "Come on, please," Karen says. "I'm not that big a fool, am I? I'm not…I'm not that fucking gullible."

Presently, the waiter returns. She catches him glancing at the check in her hand. "Would you like anything else?" he asks her. The cheeriness has left his voice. He is all business now.

She bows her head, shakes it, then looks up at him. His stone face reacquires a little of its openness. She explains what happened, and even before she is finished her story, he is nodding and saying, "I'm sorry. I'm very sorry. What a terrible trick."

The police station, two blocks from the restaurant, might have looked the same half a century earlier. Its concrete walls, painted baby blue up until about five feet, then giving way to gray, are pockmarked with holes. Karen sits in a narrow waiting room on a wooden bench, also painted light blue. She has her cell phone, and although she occasionally runs her fingers over Beth's number, she doesn't call her. She doesn't want Beth's sympathy or, worse, her implied I-told-you-so. She wants her purse, her wallet, her passport. She wants to confront Maria, or whatever the girl's real name is, yell at her, scream at her, punish her, something. She wonders if she might be able to find Maria, but Buenos Aires is a city of thirteen million people. She could spend a year—ten years—searching its streets, its parks, its subway cars, and never see her again.

After forty-five minutes, she is called into a cubicle in a gray room. A young man sits at a desk behind a computer so old it might as well be an Underwood typewriter. The man looks like he could be in one of her survey classes. Pale-skinned, he is wearing a red T-shirt advertising a rock band called Los Gatos de la Noche, and his long, black hair is either uncombed or is set in a style with which she is unfamiliar.

She is about to greet him when a police officer steps in. He is as short as she is, with tea-colored skin and pudgy cheeks that make him seem both child-like and menacing. His eyes are tiny and black. He cannot be thirty years old. The police officer introduces himself, in earnest English, as Juan Morales. He introduces the other man as Diego, without giving his last name. He points Karen to a seat in front of the desk as he stands beside Diego.

When he asks her what happened, she begins in Spanish, but after a couple of stumbling sentences, gives up. Morales translates perhaps a third of what she tells him to Diego, who punches at his ancient computer.

"Are you traveling with your family?" Morales asks her.

The answer, she would have thought, is obvious. "No."

"So alone?" he asks her.

The question annoys her, although she doubts there is anything hostile or judgmental in it. "So alone," she answers.

When she describes the scene on the subway—the parents and son leaving, the girl remaining—she detects a small smile on Morales' lips. "You think I'm a fool, don't you, Officer Morales?"

His smile vanishes. "For wanting to help a lost girl?" There is a pause, and she expects him to say more, something about the inadvisability of trusting a stranger, no matter how young, or how duplicity is everyone's game these days, even children's. But he only shakes his head. In the absence of his voice, it is her own she hears: *Sucker. Sucker. Sucker.*

After the interview concludes, Diego prints several copies of the report and Morales proceeds to sign and stamp them with the vigor of someone branding cattle. "What do you think the odds are of finding her?" Karen asks him.

Morales looks up from his stamping. He has a patch of dark blue ink on his palm. With an encouraging smile, he says, "We will do our best, and you are always welcome to come back and check with us."

"I'm leaving in ten days. Is there any chance, any chance at all, you might find her? Please tell me the truth."

He glances down at Diego, who continues to punch his computer keys. He looks back at her and sighs. "The truth is zero. Zero is the truth."

"Thank you," she says.

The woman behind the bullet-proof-glass at the U.S. Embassy, a cherubic Asian-American who looks twenty-two but is probably in her thirties, is sympathetic. She says tourist scams are as old as tourism, and because they evolve, it's difficult to prepare for them.

Karen isn't alone in being conned by a child, the Embassy woman says. A similar scam was pulled by a ten-year-old boy on a pair of tourists from California the previous week. "They brought him back to their hotel," she says. "He walked out with a suitcase stuffed with wallets, watches, laptop computers, iPhones, iPods. They were lucky to have clothes left."

The scam as practiced in Buenos Aires dates back to the early 1990s, the Embassy woman says, when a pair of unemployed actors trained street children to speak a little English and act disabled. Initially, all the children did was beg, but soon the actors were choreographing heartbreaking scenarios of accidental abandonment. "Our embassy eventually caught on and put up travel advisories," the woman says. "And the scam disappeared. But most scams have several lives. Like cats." The woman smiles faintly. "This scam is ingenious. It plays on the goodness in people, the instinct to help the most vulnerable. It's contrary to our nature to expect anything but innocence from children."

"So Maria is a street kid?" Karen asks.

"I wouldn't take it personally," the woman says. "It's a job for them, really. It's all about finding the moment when they can grab the purse or the wallet or the iPhone and scram."

Karen replays her time in El Jardín with Maria. For Maria, evidently, it was nothing more than a countdown to when she was left alone with the purse. *It couldn't have been only this*, Karen thinks, remembering the emotion in Maria's face, the desire she seemed to have to tell her something. *I made a connection with her. I wasn't simply a mark. Was I?*

"Anyone who's traveled much has a similar story," the woman says. "It'll be something to tell your friends and family back home."

When Karen calls Beth, it is out of obligation rather than urgency. She is back in her apartment on Corrientes, where she fortunately left a small stack of peso notes and her second Mastercard. Immediately upon returning to her apartment, she concealed her $105 emergency passport under a pot on a shelf in the kitchen. The Embassy woman told her she shouldn't carry it with her.

Karen sits on her bed, the mattress too thin and too soft.

"How did it all work out?" Beth asks.

Karen has been fighting an impulse to lie ever since she picked up her cell phone, and now it is too great a temptation. "She's back with her family."

"Really? Where the hell were they?"

"They went to the Embassy. They either panicked or didn't think she would be swift enough to get off at the next stop. She's eleven-years-old but functions like a five-year-old."

"Wow. Okay." Beth pauses. "They're lucky you were functioning like an adult. Nice work. Congratulations."

This, remarkably, or perhaps unremarkably, is all Beth asks about the matter. She talks about her sons. She talks about the eight-year-old girl with cerebral palsy who died of swine flu in the local hospital. She talks about what she's buying her boys for Christmas. Beth's voice is a soporific, and when Karen hangs up, she lies on her bed and puts the extra pillow over her head, blocking out the late afternoon light. But she cannot extinguish the noise—on the street six floors below, cars honk like they're in a parade—or her thoughts. She pictures Maria on the subway train, Maria in the Agüero station, Maria in El Jardín. Karen would like to blame the actor-couple who pretended to be Maria's parents. They were the ones who coerced her into doing what she did. But they were not the ones to whom Karen spoke. They were not the ones Karen fed. They were not the ones by whose side Karen would have stayed as long as she was needed.

I saw your face. You saw mine. We looked at each other. After this, how could you?

She throws the pillow off her face. *I'm going to find her. Goddamn it, if I have to spend the next ten days on a subway train, I'm going to find her.*

Finding a girl on a Buenos Aires subway train isn't like finding a needle in a haystack. It's like finding a specific needle in a sky-high and horizon-wide stack of needles. Even before she steps on the subway, Karen knows she is wasting her time. She knows she is forfeiting whatever research she hoped to do, whatever sights she intended to see.

On the first day of her Maria search, she skips lunch, and this will become her custom. It is no great sacrifice; the subway stations and trains are appetite-deadening. Línea A, Línea B, Línea C. Plaza Italia. Medrano. Plaza Misere. She studies the frescos on the walls at Carlos Gardel, Ríos, and Jujuy. From an old man who sits next to her one afternoon, his English as gnarled as the veins on his hands, she learns that only twelve cities in the world had subways before Buenos Aires: London, Athens, Istanbul, Vienna, Budapest, Glasgow, Paris, Boston, Berlin, New York, Philadelphia, and Hamburg. "I know all the dates they were opened," he says.

"What were they?" she asks because she has all the time in the world.

Smiling as if she might have doubted the depth of his knowledge, he tells her: 1863, 1869, 1875…"I will give you a tour of all of Buenos Aires," he says. "La Casa Rosada. La Boca. I will show you the cemetery where Eva Perón is buried. We can talk about a price for my services afterwards."

"I'm only interested in remaining here," she says. "Underground."

"The subway?" He looks puzzled.

"Yes."

He smiles faintly. "I am only a true expert on what is above." Two stops later, he is gone.

The people she sees on the trains and platforms remind her of people in her life or in her past. She sees her sister and her brother-in-law and an unfeverish Ethan. She sees three versions of her mother: young, middle-aged, and gray-haired, dour, and on the point of death. She hears her mother say to her, "Of course I wanted a career. I wanted ten careers. But you see how much energy you have left with two children and a husband who expects you by his side everywhere but in the john."

She sees no less than five versions of Matt, with his smile she once thought sweetly conspiratorial but now thinks was intended to suggest distance, irony, even disdain. She remembers how when he announced he was leaving—and it did feel like an announcement, as if he were addressing a class—she wished she could have told him she was pregnant, if only to surprise the horrible grin off his face.

Every morning, she eats the same breakfast in her apartment: Corn Flakes with Nido powdered milk. Her refrigerator broke the day before she met Maria, and although the apartment owner's phone number is pinned to a board on the inside of the front door, she doesn't call to complain. Her milk is lukewarm because the powder won't dissolve properly in cold water; it tastes faintly of the tin can it comes in.

For dinner, she always eats in El Jardín, perhaps as self-punishment for her naiveté and gullibility or perhaps in the perverse hope Maria will find her here, eating a chicken-and-cheese sandwich and drinking half a bottle of Doña Paula Malbec, fortification for her last several hours on the subway. Sometimes the waiter, whose name is Neruda, "like the great but, sadly, Chilean, poet," as he explained, stands for minutes next to her chair, talking to her, his English fluid and oddly elegant. In discussing Maria with her, he sometimes refers to her as "your daughter."

"I never knew my mother," Neruda says when she has a week left in the country. "She died two days after I was born. I had no grandmothers or aunts, only my father's...how do you say 'amante'?"

From *amar*, Karen thinks. *To love.* "Lover."

"Right," he says. "She was married but had no children. The only time she showed me affection was when she said hello or goodbye and gave me little kisses on my cheeks. But they were warm kisses, and she always smelled like spring."

Although less crowded at night, the subway is just as warm as during the day.

Olleros. José Hernández. Juramento.

Karen remembers Beth talking with her soon after her breakup with Matt about single women and sperm banks. Karen bristled at the implied suggestion, but she supposes fear more than pride had been her true obstacle. At thirty-eight, and without tenure, she found the idea of raising a child alone terrifying, and she hadn't given up hope of meeting someone who, within, say, two years, might become her husband and the father of her child. Now her old reasons seem cowardly and naive. She has new reasons: the comforts of inertia, the creeping exhaustion of old age, the freedom to travel anywhere she wants.

Malabia. Dorrego. Federico Lacroze.

Sitting on the A train to Carabobo, she remembers how, when Dan, her sister's husband, called to announce the birth of their second son, she didn't pick up the phone. She knew who was calling; the birth, a C-section, had been scheduled. Karen waited twenty-four hours to call back, and her sister never said anything about it.

I could be better to the people who care about me.

On the A train to the Plaza de Mayo, she sits across from an American family, a husband, a wife, a son, and a daughter. But the daughter isn't Maria. And when the train stops at Perú, they all leave together.

Plaza de Mayo. Back to Perú. Piedras.

The Argentine students in their white and pale blue uniforms fill the trains early in the morning, again at midday, again at dusk. They travel in groups of three, four, five, stand in the middle of the car, hold the handrails, talk swiftly and, to Karen, incomprehensibly. Karen always loved school uniforms, no doubt because she never had to wear one. Perhaps a similar formula applies to her feelings about children.

One day there are no students on the subway. Christmas vacation must have begun.

With three days left in the country, Karen listens again to Neruda speak about his father's lover. She would come sometimes to his soccer games, he says. She would never sit in the stands next to his father but would stand in a corner of the field, as if she was only passing by.

"Sometimes I would look up and she would be cheering me like I was magic," he says, picking up the bottle of Doña Paula Malbec and pouring her more wine. "And sometimes I did—I did feel like magic." He pauses to glance at the back of the wine bottle before returning it to the table.

"When I was fifteen, I had one last meeting with her, with my father, in La Boca. What a terrible neighborhood. Have you been? Tourists everywhere. This, of course, was why my father chose it as the place we would meet. Neither he nor his lover would be recognized because who in La Boca besides the waiters and tango dancers is Argentine?"

Karen offers him a seat, as she does every night, but, as always, he declines, saying, "I am working, thank you," although there is no one else to serve. "We had a meal, we watched tango dancing, and the time seemed to drag. I had the feeling my father's lover wanted to tell me something. But what?" He smiles, a little sadly. "Well, it was goodbye. She and her husband were moving to Bariloche. He had bought a hotel or a car-rental agency. Something. She looked at me and began to cry. And I began to cry, too. Why? I didn't know this woman well. Maybe I cried because I missed my mother. Or maybe I cried because this woman was the only mother I had ever known."

Neruda pours her more wine, although she hasn't had a sip since he last poured.

"I asked my father why she didn't divorce her husband, and he said the subject had never come up. What must they have talked about if not this?"

"You," Karen says.

Neruda smiles, nods. "Sure. Why not?"

Lavalle. General San Martín. Retiro.

Karen spends the morning of her second-to-last day in the country at the Retiro bus station. It is famous, Karen learned from Neruda, as a thieving ground. She wonders if Maria and her "family" might occasionally pull scams on tourists here. But as Karen moves from gate to gate, with announcements blaring and people in pin-striped suits and faded T-shirts rushing past her, she doesn't spot Maria.

Karen finds her attention drawn to the newspaper kiosks and their piles of magazines devoted to sex and soccer and to the CD stores, dark rooms filled with urgent rhythms and pleading love songs. At gate thirty-three, a tall man with blond, curly hair is looking around frantically, speaking what is probably Spanish but comes across as an unintelligible exclamation of surprise and disbelief. Karen is standing perhaps ten feet from him, and his eyes find hers. "My backpack!" he says in English. "It's gone! My passport was inside! My fucking journal!"

If sympathy is her first impulse, it is replaced quickly by mistrust. What scam might he be pulling? she wonders. Pretend your backpack is missing, win the tourist's trust. And then—what? "Borrow" money? She finds herself backpedaling, concealing herself within the crowd.

Retiro. San Juan. Constitución.

"You don't have to be a mother to be a mother," she told Beth once. Or did Beth tell her? Was it Beth comforting her or her justifying herself to Beth?

She thinks about how well the logic of this statement would hold up when applied to other endeavors:

You don't have to be a brain surgeon to be a brain surgeon.

You don't have to be an airplane pilot to be an airplane pilot.

You don't have to be a clown to be—

Well, this last one works. She imagines her hair dyed red, her face filled with white makeup. All she would need are the mournful eyes.

Or wouldn't this be a problem?

Plaza de los Virreyes. Varela. Medalla Milagrosa.

"This is my last full day in the country," she tells Neruda when he hands her the menu. "My flight leaves at 6:30 tomorrow evening."

"You will be going home alone?"

"Yes, alone."

He frowns. "I am sorry you are ending your vigil," he says and plucks her menu from her hands, although she hasn't ordered. It doesn't, of course, matter; he knows what she wants.

When he comes with her dinner and wine, she asks, "Did you ever hear from your father's girlfriend again?"

He uncorks her wine and pours a small amount in her glass. She follows the ritual and swirls it, sniffs it, looks for color. She tastes it and nods and he pours her more. "I hear from her every year, on my birthday," he says. "My father has been dead for eight years, and it doesn't matter. She still sends a card. She always signs it 'With love.' There is no return address, so I cannot write back." He shrugs. "There is comfort, I suppose, in knowing I am loved. Even by a ghost mother."

At night in the apartment, with the car horns making awful music on Corrientes, Karen tries to talk herself into ending her subway vigil now. She realizes she wouldn't know what to do if she spotted Maria anyway. Would she yell at her? Would she pull her off the train, sit her down on one of the benches on the platform, and chastise her in laughable Spanish?

Or would she say nothing and hope her face conveyed everything she wanted to convey?

Which is what?

When daylight breaks into her room, stealing whatever sleep she might have left, she rises and forsakes the ritual of a shower and breakfast. Likewise, she bypasses her usual starting station and walks over to Tribunales. The train arrives as soon as she steps onto the platform, an eight-dollar knapsack, her substitute purse, on her shoulder. The doors open, and Karen walks in. It is uncrowded, and she finds a seat across from a family. Two parents, a son, and a daughter. Maria. Her red-brown hair, her freckled cheeks. Her green cat's eyes catch Karen's eyes. If Maria draws back in surprise, her movement is so subtle as to be invisible. Then—and this amazes Karen—Maria smiles.

The emotions Karen imagined feeling have been overthrown by Maria's smile. Karen can do nothing but reciprocate. Her smile is cautious, tentative, but stupidly, strangely, grateful. Their smiles hold until the train stops at Callao.

Karen is sure that Maria and her "family," at risk of being identified as thieves and of having the police sicced on them, will rush toward the open doors. But although people exit, Maria and her family remain. The doors close. The ride resumes. With her eyes, Karen is asking, What are you doing? Maria nods at her before turning and whispering to the boy next to her, who whispers to the mother, who whispers to the father. This, Karen thinks, her smile fading, is the end. The signal has been given. At the next stop, they will flee.

And I won't have said a word to her.

She thinks she should pull her cell phone from her pocket and call Officer Morales. She should stand and point an accusing finger at the family. But if she ever had this impulse, she no longer does. Maria gives her another small smile.

She is seducing me, Karen thinks. *She is smiling at me so I don't follow them onto the next platform and shout for the police.*

Karen hears Maria's father mention the weather "back home" in Idaho. Her brother says, "Sledding." And Maria says, "Ice skating," as if she has a pond in her backyard.

"It's two days before Christmas," the mother says, and if Karen didn't know better, she would think her accent Idahoan.

Vermont. Idaho. What other obscure states are in their repertoire? Montana? West Virginia?

She has a new theory: They are rubbing it in, humiliating her with a near re-run of ten days before. Go, she wants to tell them. Go before I scream. The train reaches Facultad de Medicina. The man, the woman, and the boy stand and stride toward the open doors, exiting onto the platform. Karen waits for Maria to stand, and when she doesn't, her impulse is to tell her to hurry, she'll miss her family. Karen sees the man, the woman, and the boy in the window behind Maria, looking in. The man glances up at Karen and his face registers recognition followed by consternation, confusion. He moves quickly, as if panicked, toward the open doors.

What's happening? Karen wonders, her heart running like a train on the tracks. *Am I being played? Or am I part of the deception?*

The doors have shut. The father stands beyond them, tapping against the window, gesturing with a finger toward Karen, as if to warn Maria. But

Maria is gazing at her lap. The train leaves him and slips into darkness. Maria lifts her head to look at Karen, a smile, or a question in the form of a smile, on her face. Presently, Maria says something Karen can barely hear above the noise of the train. But Karen does hear it. It is her name.

She feels nothing she could have predicted. Although the Buenos Aires subway is as familiar to her now as the pounding of her heart, she doesn't know where she's going.

In the Village of Mourning

••

Outside the Purulhá market, where the bus had left her, Olivia stared at the mountains to the north of town. Pine trees adorned their peaks and sheer, scarf-like clouds curled down their sides. The vista appeared otherworldly in its serenity, and Olivia understood why Angela, her sister, said she could have lived here forever.

Turning from the mountains, Olivia walked south and stopped in front of Esmeralda's house, having remembered its dried-blood color from photographs. The house's front door was open, and Esmeralda was standing in the doorway, wearing a white cotton dress and no shoes. No photograph, Angela had often said, could do justice to Esmeralda's beauty. Her face was round and bright, a full moon, and her eyes were two brown, beaming stars.

Esmeralda strode down the dirt path lined on one side with blooming roses—reds, pinks, yellows, and whites—and on the other by wild tangles of bougainvillea and spread her arms and welcomed Olivia with an embrace. Esmeralda was warm, as if she'd been sitting in the sun or in front of a fire, and she smelled like coffee. "Angela," she said into Olivia's ear. "We were afraid. We thought…We were worried…But, *gracias a dios*, you are safe."

Olivia, separated in age from her sister by fourteen months and in experience by Angela's two years here, felt thrilled to hear Angela's name spoken, thrilled to have her sister alive again.

"When we heard what happened in New York and to the building where you worked…." Esmeralda didn't finish the sentence, but smiled in relief.

Olivia found herself being embraced again, and she looked down to discover two children, a boy and a girl half her height, holding her around the waist. They were Pablo and Milena, Esmeralda's five-year-old twins.

"They know you, even if they've never met you," Esmeralda explained. "I've told them all about you."

"And I think I know them," Olivia said, speaking the words her sister might have spoken.

A minute later, Olivia was seated on a wooden bench in the front room of the house, a mug of coffee in her hand. Esmeralda sat next to her on the bench; the two children sat cross-legged on the floor. Esmeralda smiled at her, a joyful smile of reunion. "Tell me what your life is like now," she said.

Olivia hesitated over whose life to speak of, her own or her sister's. Now, she thought, was the time to confess, to articulate the sad, prescribed words again the way she had to her sister's college friends and David, the married man with whom Angela had had a long, painful affair. But when she opened her mouth, she told Angela's story, speaking in the first-person of the hours she'd spent at her office in the tower, listening to presentations by start-up companies, their executives sometimes a decade younger than she was but seeming even younger, like boys in high school, some with acne, others puffing out their chests to be bigger than they were, the women in heavy make-up, hiding their baby fat behind blush.

She talked, too, about the apartment she and her sister shared on 116th and Broadway or SoHa, as they'd named it, South of Harlem. Angela earned enough to live in SoHo or any other area of the city, but she used a generous portion of her salary to fund women's development projects in Guatemala, Haiti, Fiji and, her latest effort, South Africa; besides, she liked the neighborhood. This year, when they both had found themselves without boyfriends or suitors of any kind, they started a Saturday night ritual of candlelight dinners in their narrow kitchen. They drank a bottle of wine, always a Merlot no matter the meal. If they hadn't collapsed with exhaustion, they ordered a movie, and the Jamaican boy on the red one-speed dropped it off and said, whatever the film, "Good choice." They watched it or they didn't, and whoever woke first the next morning made the coffee, and the smell, the warm, delicious smell, roused the sister who was asleep and they drank coffee and ate bagels and read the *Times* and the *Post* (because it had comics) until it was dark and they were hungry again and they had to think about the week ahead.

They weren't twins, although they'd been mistaken for them, especially as they'd gotten older; they had the same reddish-brown hair, the same oval eyes, the same wide hips their mother always praised as "child-bearing hips," although neither she nor Angela seemed destined to bear children. Angela was thirty-six, Olivia thirty-five, and with no man "in the picture," as their mother liked to phrase it (usually with a question mark), and no desire to have a child without a father, well, what good were such large hips? They would laugh sometimes about how they were going to be a couple of old maids living together into their dotage, eccentric sisters, the stuff of Southern fiction and bad sitcoms, and maybe they would have… Yes, they would have, certainly, they would have been happy together into their eighties if a plane hadn't come racing across the sky, piloted by men from halfway around the globe, and sliced the world in half.

In her senior year in college, Angela had applied to the Peace Corps.

The summer after her graduation, she was assigned here, under the cloud-crowded mountains. Olivia moved to New York to become an actress, and she'd had luck early—two TV commercials, an understudy's role in an off-Broadway play, a trio of cameos in a TV drama set in the Bronx—all of this tying her up so she couldn't visit Angela in Purulhá, as she'd promised. After Angela returned to the States, she earned an M.B.A. at Columbia, then started working on Wall Street. At age thirty, Olivia saw her acting stock fall. Her callbacks declined, then ceased. She turned a temp job in the public relations department at World Rock, an international development organization, into full-time employment. On the day Angela died, Olivia was driving alone to a recruiting event in upstate New York. She heard about what happened only at noon when, finished listening to an audio tape of the Royal Shakespeare Company's performance of *A Midsummer Night's Dream*, she turned on the radio.

"How did you escape?" Esmeralda asked. Olivia shook herself from her reverie, unsure when she'd stopped talking or what, exactly, she had told Esmeralda. "I flew," she thought to say, as Angela. She had wondered whether Angela was one of the people who jumped out of a window, hoping a wind might lift her to safety or a god or firefighter might catch her in impossibly strong, impossibly gentle arms or hoping only to make her death a choice, to jump and die rather than burn or wait to be crushed by concrete. Instead, she answered, "When I heard the plane hit, I ran down the stairs as fast as I could. Outside, I looked up. I saw fire, and I didn't look up again."

"Thank God," Esmeralda said, and Pablo and Milena repeated their mother's words.

Esmeralda brought her more coffee. When she was settled again in her seat, she asked Olivia how long ago she was here last. Olivia knew she couldn't retreat from being Angela now, and the thought brought her relief—more—a rush of happiness. "Five-and-a-half years ago," Olivia answered, "when I came to see how the cooperative was doing."

"Yes," said Esmeralda, who followed this with a knowing smile, "and to see Celestino."

"Who?" Olivia wanted to ask, but, remembering, she returned Esmeralda's smile. "Yes," she said, "and to see Celestino."

Angela had had a boyfriend in the Peace Corps, a fellow volunteer who lived on the other side of the country from her, but she was friends with Celestino, a medical student. Sometimes she accompanied Celestino to villages outside of Purulhá. He would treat patients and Angela would work with women's weaving groups, teaching them accounting skills and encouraging them to form a cooperative, and at dusk they'd walk back to

Purulhá together. At the end of one day, they were stopped by a handful of guerrillas, and the situation might have become perilous if Celestino hadn't volunteered to give checkups to the men. As, by flashlight, Celestino looked down their throats, Angela tried to entertain them by reciting the plotlines of Hollywood movies she'd seen, a superfluous task, as it turned out, because they'd seen all the movies she'd seen and could describe them in greater detail and with more animation.

But Olivia hadn't known that one of Angela's motives for returning to Purulhá half a decade ago was to see Celestino. This would have been during the time she, Olivia, was living with Paul, who'd had an enviable gig as Macavity in *Cats*. She and Paul were planning to marry in the spring, although what spring was never clear and became irrelevant when Paul left her for one of his feline co-stars.

"The week before you came, Geronimo was assigned to oversee a construction crew in the Petén, where he continues to work three weeks in every month," Esmeralda said of her husband. "You had broken off with the man in New York, and you thought...you thought Celestino might..." She smiled sadly. "But when you came, Celestino had just gotten married."

Olivia remembered Angela telling her about comforting Esmeralda over her husband's distant work assignment. She remembered, too, how for weeks after returning to New York, Angela seemed especially quiet, aloof, and wistful. Olivia had thought Angela was mourning David, but was she also ruing her missed chance with Celestino? It pained Olivia to think her sister had kept this from her.

"I had written to tell you about Celestino's marriage," Esmeralda said, "but you hadn't received my letter before you came."

The light outside the window behind her was suddenly cut off, as if curtains had been pulled, shades drawn, and Olivia heard the patter of rain on the tin roof. There was a single lamp in the far corner of the room; it cast a yellow glow on Esmeralda in her chair and the two children on the floor, sitting cross-legged and quiet, Buddha-like. "Celestino's wife died four months ago," Esmeralda said. "She was giving birth to their second child, but neither she nor her child lived."

"I'm sorry," Olivia said. She felt surrounded by grief, and she looked around, as if to find an exit, an escape. It was raining harder now, the patter a small torrent. She gazed down at the children, their eyes as bright and soothing as their mother's. She breathed deeply. There was a sedative scent in the air, the calming smell of coffee, roses, the very earth.

"Celestino isn't the way he was," Esmeralda said.

"No," Olivia said, shaking her head. "How could he be?"

Esmeralda asked her if she'd like to join her in the kitchen the way she used to, and Olivia followed her. The kitchen was as narrow as the kitchen she and Angela shared in New York. In the far corner, near a window the size of a small picture frame, was a two-burner gas stove. Esmeralda lighted one of the burners and put a flat pan on it. A moment later, Esmeralda handed her a ball of corn dough—masa, she called it—and said, "Do you remember how to make a tortilla?"

Olivia said, "I don't think so."

"It will come back to you," Esmeralda said. "It will be like—what did you always tell me?—like riding a bicycle." She laughed softly. "Of course, I never learned to ride a bicycle, despite your lessons, so I don't know if this is true."

Olivia watched how Esmeralda smacked the tortillas in her hands, quickly patting the dough into a thin roundness. She imitated her, and at first the dough felt heavy, sticky, and unmanageable. "Put a little water on your hands," Esmeralda suggested. After Olivia dampened her hand with water from Esmeralda's sink, she had an easier time shaping the dough into a tortilla. It was as if her hands remembered what she didn't know they'd learned.

Esmeralda put her tortilla onto the flat pan. "Go ahead," Esmeralda said, and Olivia placed her tortilla beside Esmeralda's.

When the pair of tortillas was ready, Esmeralda removed them from the pan without burning her long-fingered hands. "We'll make more," she said. "But the first two we must eat in celebration."

After they had eaten their tortillas, and beans and eggs and, as dessert, plantains in cream, they sat in the living room, listening to the cassette tapes Angela had left Esmeralda as a goodbye gift a decade ago. Olivia knew the songs well; she'd listened to them in high school, and the music conjured up parties ended abruptly at midnight by parents returning from the movies, old boyfriends, and one Christmas when she and Angela, bored with the festivities and the parade of relatives at their house, slipped outside to the tool shed with a boom box and a couple of joints, a present from Angela's college roommate.

Angela was a freshman, Olivia a senior in high school, and it was the first time Olivia had ever tried marijuana. But even after smoking the joint down to a stub, she felt no high, only vaguely ill, as if she'd stood too long around a pile of burning leaves. Angela, who had grown quiet after her first drag, turned down the music and spoke as if from a dream: "I miss you in the next room, you know? I didn't think I would. I thought I'd be distracted with new people and classes. But sometimes in bed at night I'll close my eyes and imagine I hear you rehearsing your lines from *Twelfth Night* and I'll want to shout, 'Shut up, will you?,' but only to annoy you because the truth is I always liked listening."

Although Angela never mentioned their conversation again—indeed, Olivia feared she'd forgotten it in her marijuana haze—Olivia decided to go to the same college Angela was attending, although she'd intended to go to a smaller school with a better drama program. They'd ended up rooming together during Angela's last two years and minoring in the same subject, Spanish, and spending a semester and a summer together in Spain. Then Angela was off to Guatemala and, a year later, Olivia graduated and moved to New York.

As the music played in Esmeralda's living room, Olivia felt grief seep into her like rainwater into a permeable roof. She felt she would need to run to the bathroom or out into the night, but Esmeralda spared her the scene by speaking again: "Last month, the women voted me president of the cooperative." She was, it seemed, trying to hide her smile and the pride it displayed; Olivia, distracted back to the present and her role, knew it was something to praise, and she knew that she, too, deserved praise because it was she, Angela, who had founded the weaving cooperative more than a decade before.

"That's wonderful," Olivia said, clapping her hands to emphasize the point. Pablo and Milena imitated her gesture and laughed. "How many women are part of the cooperative now?" Olivia asked.

"Fifty-two," Esmeralda answered. "We are weaving more than güipiles. The women are making tablecloths and baby clothes and shawls. We are selling in Cobán, of course, in the same market stall you helped us find. But we are also selling to merchants in the capital and Quetzaltenango. And a man from Mexico comes four times a year to buy our products, which he sells in the United States."

"Marvelous," Olivia said. And it was. But she found herself frowning.

"What's wrong?" Esmeralda asked.

Olivia called up a smile. "Sometimes so much can come of so little," she said. But she thought: *Sometimes so little can come of so much.*

So little? No, nothing. They hadn't recovered Angela's body or any part of it.

Esmeralda said, "It's late. You've had a long journey."

Ten minutes later, Olivia was lying in a bed in a small, square room. Moonlight pressed against the curtains in front of the lone window. In a pen outside, chickens rustled. Olivia closed her eyes, hoping to dream the dreams Angela would have. She dreamed of fiery buildings whose shattered pieces did not fall or rise, but hovered, suspended between the perilous ground and the wide blue sky.

Early the next morning, filled with Esmeralda's breakfast—eggs and tortillas and sweet bread and Corn Flakes in warm milk—Olivia walked with Esmeralda and her children to Celestino's house. Although Esmeralda spoke to her on the way, Olivia only half listened. She was thinking about how Celestino would recognize her or, rather, fail to recognize her. But when Celestino opened the door of his blue house, he said, with a hint of joy, "Angela?"

"It's me," she said, smiling. He invited them inside. Esmeralda excused herself, saying she needed to feed Pablo and Milena. She touched Olivia on the back, a warm, encouraging hand.

Celestino was taller than she, and his skin was a color like tea. His eyes were striking, a bright mix of gray and blue. "I am supposed to be in El Ángel at noon," he said. He gave her a shy, questioning smile, and she guessed it was supposed to convey some mutual history connected to the place. She wondered what Angela had done with him here. Or did his smile only acknowledge the similarity of the village's name to Angela's?

When he asked if she'd like to come with him, to help him, she nodded. "We'll have to leave now," he said, and she nodded again.

He looked at her with a gentle, appraising gaze. "Your hair is different," he told her.

"Shorter?"

"No, but with fewer curls."

"They'll come back in the humidity here."

"And your eyes..."

"Yes?"

He licked his lower lip. "Well, could they be green now instead of blue?"

"It's because of the landscape here. Everything's green." She smiled at him. "You look the same."

"Thank you. But in certain light, I see more gray hair than black."

They walked east out of town. When they reached the base of the mountain, they began a long, slow ascent. To his questions about her life, she told him what she had told Esmeralda, her conversation coming in fragments as she labored in the thinning air. He told her about his wife. His son was four years old, he said, and one morning he'd found him huddled in a corner, gazing at one of his old medical textbooks. Celestino hurried toward him, worried he might be staring at photographs of patients with malformed limbs or body-covering burns. Instead, he was tracing his finger across the large first letter in the word "médico" on the book's title page and saying "'M' como en María."

"María?" Olivia asked.

"His mother's name."

Olivia was about to speak words of sympathy, but she couldn't catch her breath. Celestino told her about the end of the country's civil war and the celebrations and the subsequent disappointment when, instead of soldiers and guerrillas, the people of Purulhá and everywhere now had to fear thieves and kidnappers, ex-soldiers and ex-guerrillas with no war to fight but still carrying guns.

They stopped in a grove of pine trees to drink water. In the mountains, the air was cool, and Olivia didn't feel at all thirsty. But when she lifted the bottle to her lips, she found she couldn't stop. If she didn't finish what was inside the bottle, it was only out of politeness. "It's all right," Celestino said to her. "I have more water in my bag." From his backpack, he pulled sandwiches and fruit, but half a cheese sandwich was all she could eat. "I'll save the apple for you," he said, returning it to his bag.

An hour later, they reached the mountain's peak, well-worn ground no larger than a sidewalk square; in its center was a small heap of smooth stones, a humble altar. Turning behind them, they could see Purulhá and several towns around it, even Cobán, forty-five kilometers distant. From this height, everything looked diminished, hemmed in by lush green mountains. In front of them was the village of El Ángel, a scattering of adobe houses and a soccer field with goals made of crooked tree branches.

Angela must have shown Olivia pictures of this village, because she recognized it—the short brick fence surrounding the white wooden church, the dirt trails running like veins between houses and past cornfields and down the other side of the mountain. "Here we are again in the Village of Mourning," Celestino said. "But I think it will be less sad than when you last saw it. In the past year, there have been three births, and some of the boys who escaped or were spared during the massacre are now grown men. So El Ángel is no longer entirely a village of widows and children."

They descended to the church, where a line had formed, mostly of old women but also a few children and one young man, perhaps twenty years old, with a straw hat and a cabbage-shaped nose. When the old women saw Olivia, they shouted Angela's name and raced up to her, holding her hands, embracing her. In quick words, they told her about the cooperative and the sales in Cobán, the capital, and the United States.

Celestino set up his examination room behind a screen in the church. A broad window allowed in light. There were three chairs and a long, thin table. Celestino handed her a three-ring binder, on each section divider the name of a patient. Before he examined a patient, he asked her to tell him what he'd written down previously about the patient and to write down what he said now. There was a rush of patients, and she barely had time to look up from the notebook, a relief because she was spared the sight of yellowed eyes and breasts burdened with lumps of cancer. Three hours passed, and she was putting down a final note when Celestino said, "There will be a few more patients when the men who are working in the fields return."

She stood up and looked behind the screen; the church was empty.

"I think I'll lie down for a few minutes here," Celestino said, indicating the table. "But if you would like to rest here, I will sleep in one of the pews."

"No, thank you," she said. "I'm not tired." This wasn't true; her limbs were heavy. But she didn't think she could sleep.

She handed him the binder. After gazing at a couple of the pages, he said, "I used to need a magnifying glass to read your writing, remember? Either my eyes have improved or you remembered my complaints and have humored me with larger letters." He smiled at her, although his eyes scanned her face, as if exploring it for something.

Quickly, she stepped outside. Clouds surrounded the village, but the soccer field, where a handful of boys and girls were playing, was sunlit. Olivia sat on a slope above the field, watching the game. When a boy scored a goal, he turned to her, and when she applauded, he smiled and waved.

She left the field and climbed to the mountain's peak. Too tired to stand, she sat down beside the stone altar. The clouds had converged over El Ángel, but behind her, the sun's light fell in a long blanket over Purulhá, giving even the dark green trees surrounding the town a golden cast. She wished the mountain had a steeper precipice or, better, a sheer cliff, so she might step to its edge and feel a little of what Angela felt so far above ground, so she might reach across the emptiness of air and catch her sister in the sky and hold her hands until, together, they either fell or flew. She had imagined Angela's death every day, but she couldn't imagine Angela dead. And now, in the Village of Mourning, she wouldn't have to. Angela wouldn't ever be dead here because she, Olivia, would be Angela. It would be her greatest role, and it would be effortless because it would be nearly true, as easy as pretending to be oneself.

More clouds encroached on the sky, rain seemed imminent, and a wind shivered across the soccer field and rose to touch her, but she wasn't cold. She was Angela.

Five days after the towers collapsed, when they were told there was little hope of finding Angela alive, her mother, distraught, exhausted, asked Olivia to call their relatives and Angela's friends, to confirm what they feared. She obeyed, even phoning David, the married man, at his office. Days later, she and her parents sat in a church six blocks from her parents' house, a Methodist church they had stepped into no more than twice before, and heard a minister they didn't know quote the Bible and speak Angela's name as if he'd seen her every day. When it was Olivia's turn to speak, she did, in brief, elegiac words she'd penned as if writing a scene. She didn't believe what she was saying. She couldn't. It wasn't right to give Angela up this quickly, this easily. At the funeral, Olivia was acting again, and badly.

It was after she'd found Angela's letter to Esmeralda in her desk—undated, with this line: "I hope to come see you, maybe before the new year," with a signature even—that she conceived her idea. She mailed Angela's letter instead of the letter she'd planned to write Esmeralda. She cut her hair to look like Angela's the last time Angela had visited Purulhá; she wore Angela's clothes; she adopted Angela's quiet laugh. In one place, at least, Angela would still be alive.

Olivia stood up, feeling grateful and excited. *You're here, Angela*, she said. *We never left each other.* She placed both her hands on her chest. *We're together.*

But even determined to see her performance last her lifetime, to preserve Angela in her living body, Olivia felt something fall on her, something heavier than the rain, which had begun tentatively, a few drops expelled from the sky. "Oh, God," she said, knowing this wasn't what she was supposed to say. "Oh, God."

She heard footsteps and turned to see Celestino climbing toward her with a happy quickness. Even in the opaque light, his eyes were bright. "Here you are, Angela," he said.

She knew what lines she should speak. Although they would be weighted by fatigue, as they should be after such a long day, they would show pleasure at his having found her here and at what their latest reunion promised. Nothing, it seemed, had been lost, not even the hope of Celestino's love. But when she opened her mouth, something other than what she intended left it, something halting and in a lower octave, choked and whispered. It was something like the first syllables of her name and Angela's run together.

"Here you are," Celestino said again, although this time without Angela's name and in a less jovial voice, a voice, perhaps, of accusation. Or was it of concern, of pity?

When she didn't reply, couldn't reply, he looked at her without suspicion, only a piercing tenderness. She wondered if he'd known her secret from the beginning, his grief unveiling hers.

"You must be hungry," he said, his words as soft as water. After reaching in his backpack, he pulled out an apple and placed it gently in her trembling hand.

part three

....

TRUTH

What to Expect When You Say You're Expecting

••

Between Monday and Friday of the second week of September, two of Sasha's friends told her they were pregnant. When on Wednesday of the following week, a third friend, in an explosion of enthusiasm, conveyed the same news, Sasha exclaimed, "So am I!"

She had intended to say what she had said to Becky and Emma upon hearing their happy news: "Wonderful! Terrific! Congratulations!" But somewhere between her brain, her voice box, and her tongue, her stock words of excitement and elation had changed costumes and had emerged into the air between her and Missy Witherspoon in the flowing white gowns of a lie.

A preposterous lie. A provocative lie. A lie she could only hope to sustain over time with a series of other lies. Her mouth would have to become a lie factory. She would have to become a student of her lies so as not to forget or contradict them. In order to sustain her lie, she might even have to lie to people she loved. She saw all of this instantly.

She knew that all she had to do to escape Lie-ville was to say, "I'm joking." But as she was about to take this corrective step, she comprehended the expression on Missy's face. The I'm-a-woman-whose-belly-is-blooming-with-child glow had faded, replaced by a mixture of perplexity, disappointment, you-stole-my-spotlight pique, and a doubtless unrelated urge to pass gas.

Seconds ticked by. Even so, there was still time for Sasha to step back from the edge, to shake her head in her I'm-your-oddball-friend kind of way, and return the spotlight to Missy, whose petite, narrow face and thin, nearly translucent hair evoked at its best a preadolescent princess and at its worst a constipated mouse. But Missy's expression was so baffled and therefore so satisfying Sasha couldn't bear to see it restored to prideful glee. "Isn't it wild?!" Sasha exulted. "And I don't even know which one of my one-night stands to thank!"

For the record, Sasha, who was thirty-four years old, had slept with four men in her life, the most recent of whom, Greg, over an eight-year period during which they a) never married; b) never conceived; and c) never traveled out of North America. Toronto was their farthest, and most romantic, destination, although Sasha toured the city alone because Greg was attending a conference on the future of solar power in military weapons design. He was an odd, but apparently not unprecedented, combination of tree-hugger and hawk. He had promised her marriage and children at least fourteen times. He broke up with her to marry a Russian émigré named Svetlana who was doing groundbreaking research on wind-powered aircraft carriers.

In the wake of her breakup, and after having made a valiant go—or perhaps a haphazard and sputtering go—of earning a living as a folk musician in San Francisco, where she and Greg had shared a two-bedroom apartment with a bathroom-window view of the Golden Gate Bridge, Sasha returned to her hometown of Sherman, Ohio, to become the music teacher at East Elementary School. Her father played golf with the county's school superintendent.

The beautiful thing about returning home was the chance to reunite with people she liked in high school. Or it would have been a beautiful thing if all the people she liked in high school hadn't moved to places like New York and Los Angeles and Buenos Aires and left her stranded as if on a deserted island (which Sherman, population: 42,189, sometimes resembled) with everyone she hated in high school. Sasha didn't hate them anymore. She loathed them. But she loathed lonely nights in her one-bedroom apartment, located smack in the middle of the college-student-dominated section of Sherman called Partytown, even more, and so she joined her new—and newly pregnant—friends at their weekly girls' night dinner at the Waterfront Grill and sympathized with them over their morning sickness and their husbands' over-the-top servility in the presence of their soon-to-be-bulging bellies.

By the next girls' dinner, Becky and Emma knew Sasha's news. After Becky gushed, "Do you know what this means? Between us, we'll be having quadruplets!", they settled down to interrogate Sasha about the identity of the baby's father.

"Well, he's likely a man," Sasha said, gazing around the table at six wide eyes and three pairs of lips already poised to transmit whatever was worth repeating all over town.

"Well, of course he's a man," said Emma, a redhead who taught biology and coached field hockey at the Sherman Learning Academy.

"I wouldn't say, 'Of course,'" Sasha said.

"How could it be a woman?" asked Becky, whose face was as round and jovial as a cartoon moon. "That's—"

"There was this one night," Sasha interrupted. "It was dark from start to finish. Dark at the club. Dark at his—or her—or its—place. And on the bed-side table, I noticed what looked like a large syringe, which, as I think about it, seemed to be filled with a murky white substance."

"Maybe it was a glue gun," said Missy, whose husband was a carpenter.

"I don't know," Sasha said. She turned to Becky. "When you had your turkey basting, what did the...uh...instrument look like?"

Becky and her husband, Art, had been trying to conceive for several years before they abandoned conventional measures. The turkey-basting gave Art's lethargic sperm a crucial head start, and Becky was pregnant the same month. Becky disliked discussing the way she had become pregnant as much as she liked discussing her pregnancy. "It looks like what the name implies," she answered, frowning.

"That's what I was afraid of," Sasha said, blinking as if staring into the bright light of revelation.

"Do I understand this right?" asked Emma. "You slept with someone whose gender you're uncertain of? Someone who may have impregnated you with a kitchen utensil?"

Sasha lowered her gaze to her bowl of half-eaten chef's salad.

"Where did this person pick you up, the Inside Out?"

The Inside Out was Sherman's only gay club. But because it played the best music of any dance club in town, it was popular with heterosexuals as well. Sasha looked up from her plate and nodded.

"In that place, you could get pregnant by sitting on a toilet seat," said Missy, her voice rising to the octave of outrage.

"There are other candidates, right?" Emma asked. "Didn't you say you weren't sure which one of your anonymous liaisons to blame—I mean, to credit—for your pregnancy?"

Emma, Missy, and Becky leaned over their meals in order to better hear Sasha. But what fertile stranger could Sasha invent who would top the mystery and outrageousness of her turkey-basting beau?

On the television above the bar at the other end of the restaurant, three men sprinted toward a gold finish-line tape. "There were three men," Sasha said.

"All right," Emma said. "Take them one at a time."

The racers broke the tape simultaneously.

"But I didn't take them one at a time."

All three of the men raised their arms in triumph.

"Get out!" Becky said.

"They were triplets," Sasha said. "Identical triplets."

"Get out!" Becky said again.

"Wait a minute," Emma said. "Triplets? You're putting us on, Sasha. I'm willing to buy the weird pickup artist at Inside Out. But triplets?"

Sasha sighed heavily. She bowed her head. She pretended to wipe tears of shame from her eyes. She thought about how her life had come to this—to lying to people she never would have been friends with if she hadn't been so lonely. She felt real tears crowd her eyes.

"It's all right," Emma said.

"No, it's not all right," Missy said. "It's kind of sick and immoral, but we're your friends and we're here to listen."

Sasha looked up. "I was jogging down by the river, and these young men came jogging up to me. I thought they would pass me, but they slowed down to talk." Sasha sighed again, this time wistfully. "They were all handsome—square jaws, thick, shimmering hair, bodies as sleek as sports cars."

"They aren't from here," Emma said. "No man in Sherman qualifies in even two of those categories."

"They were from Minneapolis or St. Paul," Sasha said. "They were here to attend some kind of conference and were staying in the Hotel Sherman." She paused. "Which is where this might have happened." With a smile containing both bemusement and pride—or their imitation—she patted her belly, filled modestly with lettuce, ham, and cherry tomatoes.

"You had unprotected sex with triplets?" Missy asked. "Odds are at least one of them had a venereal disease."

"And you'll never know which one impregnated you," Becky said.

Over the remaining hour and fourteen minutes of their dinner, Sasha tried to turn the conversation toward her friends' pregnancies, but they summed up their conditions in a few words: "Chocolate cravings." "Already my jeans don't fit." "I throw up twice in the morning, once before breakfast, once after. Then I'm good."

After Missy and Becky excused themselves to use the bathroom, Emma leaned over the table, her red hair inches from the yellow flame of the centerpiece's lone candle. "What was it like?" she whispered.

"What was what like?" Sasha said.

Emma looked behind her, down the trail Missy and Becky had blazed past a bald man dining alone. There was no sign of their return. "Having three men at once."

Sasha nearly said, How would I know? But her lie returned to her before she could speak. She paused to consider what sex with three men at once might be like. "Crowded," she answered.

"Isn't it?" Emma said with a laugh.

"You...?" Sasha began.

"In college. But only with two. Cousins." She leaned back in her chair. "The whole experience wasn't very elegant. I have a theory about where the phrase 'Three's a crowd' comes from."

Emma leaned over the table again and whispered, "And if three's a crowd, what does that make four?"

"A mob?" Sasha ventured. Or, she might have added as Missy and Becky returned to complete their quartet, *only dinner with friends at the Waterfront Grill.*

Her father had heard she was pregnant. "You didn't want to tell your old man?" he said as they ate lunch at the Sky Lake Country Club. Her father played golf here three times a week. Sometimes he would finish eighteen holes before ten o'clock, then sit on the restaurant's patio overlooking the 18th green and shout advice to the golfers below.

Sasha looked like her father: the same long, narrow face; the same almond-shaped eyes; the same widow's peaks, which in his graying hair looked distinguished and in hers looked like female pattern baldness, even if her hair had been this way since she was three. Because daughter and father looked alike, friends, acquaintances—even strangers coming in from the golf course—assumed they must have a close relationship. The truth was Sasha didn't like her father. He had divorced her mother when Sasha was a junior in high school, and two years later her mother was dead of lung cancer. Her mother never smoked; her father did—profusely and in every room in the house.

As an executive with Ohio Life, Health, and Auto, her father was charged with finding reasons to reject medical claims. The fine print in his company's contracts gave him the right to turn down claims for any one of 1,248 pre-existing conditions, and he did so with an Evangelical devotion. While Sasha had long suspected her father's malevolence, he displayed his true wickedness when Ohio Life, Health, and Auto refused to pay for her mother's cancer treatments. The company said she had lived within eighty feet of a gas station for two of the previous ten years, disqualifier number 439. Her father wouldn't so much as write a letter of protest.

The only reason Sasha continued to speak to her father, much less eat with him at his country club, was money. Her rectitude became amazingly limber in front of cash. Gazing across the wooden table from her as a golfer cursed his missed putt below, her father shook his head in disapproving sweeps. "I understand the father is black," he said. "Is that true, Sasha?"

Her jaw fell.

"Don't tell me," he said, holding up his left hand, which, three-and-a-half hours after his round, was still enclosed in a golf glove. "Let me just write you a check."

"For what?" she asked.

"The abortion."

"Why would I want— "

"Or for a year's supply of diapers. But God help me, if the kid is browner than that sand trap"—he pointed to the golden half circle behind the 18th green—"don't bother asking for my blessing."

Sasha felt a surge of righteous outrage. She stood up and pointed her long index finger at him. "How dare you threaten to shun my baby!" she said. "You will be there for him, and I don't care whether he comes out looking as black as your heart!"

She expected her father to deflect her anger with a smooth disclaimer or a vague promise. But he seemed to be cowering in his seat. She had never spoken to him like this before. It was satisfying, liberating. "And until you start to embrace your inner grandfather and ditch your outer racist," she said, "I refuse to accept another penny from you."

"But...but—"

"Baby's on board," she said, patting her stomach. "Are you?"

At times over the next few weeks, Sasha thought to end her phantom pregnancy with a phantom miscarriage. But the truth was she wanted this baby, phantom or real. A miscarriage would have devastated her.

She bought several books on pregnancy. *What to Expect When You're Expecting* became less a manual of deception and more a day-by-day catalogue of wishes. From time to time, she even wondered if she was, in fact, pregnant—immaculately, like Mary. Because how else to explain her occasional early-morning queasiness, her at-least-twice-as-much-as-usual flatulence, her strange desire to watch Baby Bach videos and knit blankets?

For every subject taught at East Elementary School, there was a voluminous curriculum the teacher was supposed to follow. But a week after declaring herself pregnant, Sasha misplaced the enormous blue binder containing this information. She could have blamed her absentmindedness on her pregnancy, but at school she hadn't shared her happy news.

In the absence of a curriculum, Sasha improvised. For a performance of the opening of Beethoven's Fifth Symphony, she had her sixth graders pretend to be an orchestra and use their mouths to imitate violins, violas, cellos, double basses, flutes, oboes, clarinets, contrabassoons, trumpets, and trombones. She had her fourth graders act out the liberation of Moscow from Napoleon's army to the music of Tchaikovsky's 1812 Overture. Her first graders wrote their own rap songs and used their desks as percussion instruments. Only two students had to be sent to the nurse because of bruised palms.

East Elementary School's student population was an eclectic mix. The children of doctors at Ohio Eastern University Hospital studied with the children of immigrants from Sherman's Spanishville, an area of town settled by people from El Salvador, Guatemala, Honduras, Mexico, and Nicaragua. English wasn't the first language for most of the latter children, but in Sasha's music classes, it didn't matter. Sounds trumped words.

In her kindergarten class, she handed the children recorders, kazoos, bongo drums, and the rest of the school's limited instrument collection and asked them to express their feelings—sad, happy, angry, shy, indifferent—with sounds. When they were done, María, whose birthmark around her left eye made her seem like a six-year-old boxer, said, "Now your turn, Señorita Sasha. Make the sound of what you feel."

Sasha considered the happiness she might have felt if she were pregnant, a happiness tempered with concern about the future. In such a circumstance, she would play "Ode to Joy," although with a tremolo in every fifth note.

The classroom had gone quiet. Twenty-one faces, beaming with curiosity, gazed up at her. It was one thing to lie to her friends who weren't her friends. It was one thing to lie to her father who wasn't much of a father. But her students deserved the truth. "May I?" she asked María, pointing to the recorder on María's desk. María nodded, and Sasha brought the instrument to her lips. Presently, her fingers and breath found in sound what she never could have expressed in words, her music like a lullaby mixed with the blues mixed with something experimental and unfinished.

On a Friday a week later, she decided on the Better Late than Never plan. She would seduce a tourist in the bar at the Sky Lake Resort, go with him to his room, and engage him in wild, spectacular baby-making sex. Or tame, boring baby-making sex. The next night, she would repeat the process with the same man, if he was around, or with a new partner. The following night, she would do the same. Friday, Saturday, Sunday. Three nights, three chances to become pregnant. She was in mid-cycle. It was the perfect time.

Sky Lake used to be the summer refuge of Ohio's political and business elite. Ulysses Grant was said to have written the opening to his memoirs in a cabin on the lake. Warren Harding was rumored to have had at least two affairs during his sojourns here. Nowadays, the Resort hosted annual meetings of the state's body shop and plumbers' associations. Sasha had no illusions of procreating with a British royal or a Saudi oil baron.

The bar was built to look like the interior of an old ship, with wooden floors and porthole windows offering vistas of the lake. The bartender dressed in a captain's outfit, complete with cap. Sasha sat at the end of the bar in a yellow dress, staring into her glass of pinot grigio. The one sip she'd had was unpleasant enough to relegate it to a prop for the rest of the night.

An hour passed before a suitable candidate showed up. He was on the short side—if he stood on his tiptoes, he might be able to kiss her—but he was impeccably dressed in a linen suit. He must have showered within the last half hour: his blond hair was damp and combed. Even from three seats down, Sasha could smell him, like a battlefield of clashing colognes.

The stranger spent a long time staring at himself in the mirror behind the bar. When his gaze turned to Sasha, she wondered if he was looking at himself in her eyes. Apparently so: he tapped down an uncooperative strand of eyebrow hair. In response to her question, he told her he was here on business—he sold equipment to gyms and health spas.

"Are you as fit as you look?" she asked him, her voice the purr of a cat as channeled by a woman who grew up with two hound dogs and a goldfish.

"I'll show you," he said.

Three minutes later, they were in his room. And three seconds after this, he was in the bathroom, promising a swift return.

There were two double beds in the room, and over the next twenty minutes Sasha alternated sitting on each. Several times, her future baby's father, whose name, she had learned on the elevator ride up to his room, was Owen, shouted from the bathroom, "I'll be out in a minute."

She looked at her watch. She looked at the carpet. She looked at the television on top of the dresser. The screen reflected, in brownish-green, her desperate face. She wanted to go home and pick up her guitar and write a rock opera about mothers who had never had children.

The door of the bathroom flew open. Owen was wearing a white muscle-man T-shirt and red shorts so tight they might as well have been painted on. It appeared he had applied baby oil to every inch of his exposed skin. Even his nose glistened.

"This could be you," he said.

"Okay," Sasha said. "But could I have the baby without the oil?"

Owen didn't acknowledge her joke. "This could be every one of your students. With Owen's Master Muscle Machine, their bodies will be as beautiful as their brains."

"I teach music," Sasha said. "I teach music to kindergarteners."

"I thought I heard you say 'college.'" Owen shifted poses, so he now looked like Atlas with the world on his shoulders. "It doesn't matter. There's no reason six-year-olds can't use my machine in pursuit of physical perfection. And when their parents see the results—bingo—you'll sell double the number of models."

"The last time I sold anything was in high school, and I almost got arrested. Of course, I was selling pot, but—"

"Wait here."

He slipped back into the bathroom and emerged with what looked like a flattened black bowling ball. "Ta da!" he said. "This is it. Owen's Master Muscle Machine." He explained: The outside of the Machine, which, she observed, wasn't a machine at all, was made of silicon; the inside, said Owen, was composed of a substance "indistinguishable from Play-Doh."

"So if it rips open, I can make a gingerbread man or build a castle?"

Owen smiled and patted down another loose eyebrow hair. "Because my Machine can be manipulated into hundreds of shapes, you can use it as a free weight, a medicine ball, even a theater prop, such as a hump."

"Have you cleared this with Quasimodo?"

"He wrote one of the testimonials." He grinned and struck another pose. "The Machine's Velcro straps enable it to be tied around any part of the body, allowing the user a muscle-targeted workout. It's simple, elegant, and expensive enough to make you rich on the ten percent you receive on every model you sell."

"Wait a minute," Sasha said. "I just came here to have sex."

But he was thrusting a four-color brochure into her hands. It featured Owen in several semi-strenuous poses with his shape-shifting product. "As you see, they come in pink, black, blue, and rainbow, and in ten- and twenty-five-pound models. I could send you off with two dozen tonight. I bet you have more than twenty-four students. What do you think?"

He smiled at her, and his smile wasn't as oily as his body. There was even something vulnerable in it, something hopeful and sweet. She realized it was going to be hard to disappoint him. "Could I buy one model, you know, to try out?" she asked.

Five minutes later, she walked out of his room with a ten-pound, sky blue Owen's Master Muscle Machine. She wasn't even on the elevator when she realized that, affixed around her waist with its Velcro straps, it was exactly what she needed to imitate a swelling womb.

When she met Becky, Emma, and Missy at the Waterfront Grill in the following weeks and months, she matched their swollen bellies with her swollen belly. She matched their delight—"Oh, I feel him kicking!"—with her delight ("I swear I have a marching band in here!"). She overthrew their disgruntlement—"Peter is as horny as a bunny rabbit, but there's no way he'll be burrowing before the baby's born"—with her stupendous satisfaction: "You would be shocked to know how many men want to please a pregnant woman in bed. And half of them don't expect reciprocity!"

She suited up in Owen's Master Muscle Machine whenever she visited her father. One day, he asked to feel her belly. "All right," she said. "But only from outside my shirt. My skin is extraordinarily sensitive."

With his hand over Little Owen, as she had secretly named her protean womb, he exclaimed, "I feel movement! Active tiger, isn't he?" He grinned. The bottoms of his teeth were brownish-yellow. His years of smoking hadn't left him unmarked. "When you were a baby, I used to bathe you every night," he said.

"No, you didn't," she said.

There was a pause. They were standing next to their table in the Sky Lake Country Club restaurant. He looked older than she remembered either of her grandfathers ever looking. Could he be older than they were when they'd died?

Her father nodded. "You're right," he said. "Maybe I just wish I had."

Sasha had told her friends and her father that she was due in April—April 1st, to be precise. She laughed every time she thought of her due date. Eventually, however, she knew it would be she who would look like the fool.

When Sasha pictured her friends and her father discovering her deception, she imagined telling them, "It was a metaphor." But if asked what the metaphor was, she wouldn't have an answer.

Becky, Emma, and Missy were all due in March. At the end of February, they agreed to suspend their weekly dinners at the Waterfront Grill. At their last meal, they filled the air with rapid-fire reports on the status of their health, their marriages, their maternity leaves. Becky said she would be using her grandfather's stopwatch to time contractions; Missy said she had test-driven six different routes to the hospital; and Emma mentioned the music she planned to listen to in the delivery room ("Dolly Parton, because it was the music my mom used to sing to me when I was a baby"). After a while, they fell silent, and Sasha supposed they were contemplating how, in a few weeks, their lives would be utterly, perhaps magically, perhaps miserably, changed. It was an awesome notion to consider: One body becomes two bodies. A couple becomes a trinity.

Sasha put a hand against her counterfeit belly. "Sometimes," she said, "I wish it was all over."

The music teacher at East Elementary was required to produce the Spring Extravaganza, an hour-long program to be performed for students' families on an evening in the second week of April. Sasha learned this on the first day of March. She foresaw disaster.

By the third day of March, however, she had a plan—a grand vision of an elementary-school opera. It would be called *Winter to Spring*, and depending on what season they represented, her students would dress up as icicles and snowmen or bumble bees and crocuses. She would have them write little musical numbers based on the seasons, from chilly recorder sounds to thunder-crashing symbol smashes to bird-like whistles from the school's new pair of piccolos.

She rehearsed with her students during every music class. But this, she decided, wasn't sufficient to avoid catastrophe. She considered holding rehearsals after school, but she didn't want to exclude students who rode busses, most of whom lived in Spanishville. So she received permission to hold rehearsals during lunch period. This way, all students could participate, even if they blew macaroni and cheese into their woodwinds.

On the Friday of the first week of March, Sasha returned home to a phone call from Emma: Missy had given birth to a boy, eight-pound, six-ounce Peter Jr.

On a Tuesday afternoon in the second week of March, Sasha's father collapsed over a plate of Cajun-fried shrimp at the Sky Lake Country Club. He was dead by the time the ambulance brought him to the Ohio Eastern University Hospital, where Sasha met his cold, ashen, but reassuringly peaceful corpse. On her way back to the hospital parking lot, Sasha ran into Becky, who flashed her a smile and said, "Contractions. One minute, fifty seconds apart." As another contraction radiated from her womb, she doubled over, and a sound like a triumphant horn issued from her. "Excuse us," said her husband, who was wheeling a pink suitcase the size of a coffin, "baby makes us gassy."

Sasha wasn't wearing her imitation womb. But her billowy brown dress no doubt hid her flat stomach—if Becky and her husband had even been looking.

In her car, an ancient Honda more faithful than any man she'd been involved with, she thought about her father. If he had died any time before this year, she wouldn't have cried.

Later the same day, when she stepped into his house in the mountains above Sky Lake, she found in his living room a small, flat box. It was propped against one of the walls. When she opened it she saw it was a crib, made of honey-colored oak. She gripped one of the rails like a baby might, with both hands.

Three minutes after Sasha returned home, Emma called to say Becky had given birth to a boy, nine-pound, six-ounce Art Jr.

"On the literal level, it's about the death of winter and the birth of spring," Sasha explained to Max, a divorced father, during the dress rehearsal in the school's cafeteria. The dress rehearsal was being held after school; several busses were on standby to ferry the bus-riding students home. "But it's also metaphorical," Sasha continued. "It's about all kinds of renewal. Spiritual. Psychological. Political. Philosophical." If hyperbole were a crime, she thought, the cuffs would be slapped on her now.

Max, whose daughter played a snowball, nodded like he was hearing her explication of Mahler's Resurrection Symphony. His black hair was cut in a Prince Valiant haircut, although if he was younger than forty, it was by months, not years. As Max continued to nod, there came a shout from the stage: "My mommy had her baby last night!"

Sasha looked up to see María, who appeared in *Winter to Spring*'s final scene as a butterfly, standing at the front edge of the stage like a diver at the end of a diving board. "When I told my mom I wanted a baby girl, she said it wasn't my decision. But I wanted to be a girl, and look—I'm a girl! And so is my new sister!"

Max glanced at Sasha, his smile wide and warm. "Wonderful dialogue," he said.

"I wish I'd written it," she said.

A moment later, Max said, "You've put in a ton of work on this. Someone ought to buy you dinner."

An hour after Sasha returned home, Emma called from the hospital. "I've named her Emma Jr.," she said of her eight-pound, four-ounce baby girl. "I'm joking! Her name's Sophie! But she does look like me—except she's 114 pounds lighter. You'll love her!"

So it was over, she thought, plopping down in her living-room chair, which offered a view out the window of a tire swing in her neighbors' yard. All three of her friends had completed the nine-month obstacle course and had reached the finish line. They had won their delicious, warm, sobbing, stinking prizes. All Sasha had to show for her nine-month gestation was a chaotic elementary-school opera. "It's a metaphor," she said to the unoccupied tire swing. "I gave birth to amateur art."

"This is fantastic," Max whispered to Sasha as they stood at the back of the auditorium during the last scene of the one and only performance of *Winter to Spring*.

"I'm glad you think so," Sasha said, although all she could see were the mistakes. The butterflies were supposed to dance around the flowers, who were supposed to play the same three-note melody while a quartet of bumblebees sang, "Spring is here! Spring is here! Spring...is...here!" But the flowers had also begun to dance, leaving their instruments behind, and occasionally flower, butterfly, and bee collided. If Sasha had been a movie director, she would have yelled, "Cut!"

"Fantastic," Max repeated as the curtain fell with a thud and a profound puff of dust. She glanced at him and saw he was being neither flattering nor sarcastic. This is what happens, she thought, when parents have a living stake in an event. The mundane becomes the marvelous. When she spoke to Emma the previous night, her friend spent at least three-and-a-half minutes waxing wonderful about Sophie's first bowel movement.

"Would next Friday be all right?" Max asked.

"Friday?"

"For your celebratory dinner. Your dinner of thanks."

"Thanksgiving?"

"A thanksgiving for all you've given our children."

"Great," she said as applause filled the cafeteria. All of the students were now crowded on the tiny stage, bowing and bumping into each other. A snowflake toppled off the front edge, where, fortunately, she was caught by one of the parents. Called to the stage, Sasha was handed six pink roses, their thorns exposed. Her post-performance speech consisted of a single word: "Ouch!"

There were refreshments, including sugar cookies in which the "cookies" part seemed at best wishful thinking, and in a corner of the auditorium, near the custodian's closet, Sasha thought she saw a couple of parents sharing a flask. Eventually, the party moved outside. It was only eight-thirty—*Winter to Spring*, for all its operatic grandeur, had lasted a mere forty-three minutes—and people seemed in no hurry to go home. On the basketball court, a huddle of parents puffed on cigarettes.

Outside the side gate, on the sidewalk beside the street where the car line to drop off and pick up students formed before and after school each day, Sasha spotted María and her mother, who was carrying her newborn daughter in her arms. María waved and said, "Come meet my new little sister!" In the illumination from a streetlight, the baby looked more precious than even a baby should, with her rosebud lips and stunningly enormous mop of black hair. "This is Angelina," María said. "I call her Poopy Diaper."

"It was a beautiful show," said María's mother, whose name, Sasha remembered, was Blanca.

"Thank you," Sasha said.

Blanca stuck a hand in her pocket. "I think I left my program inside. I want to give it to María's grandmother." She gazed at Sasha. "Would you mind holding her?" Even before Sasha could answer, Blanca put Angelina in her arms. "She's no trouble when she's sleeping. I'll be back in a minute."

Blanca strolled across the basketball court and back into the school building. María dashed after her.

I have my baby, Sasha thought, gazing down at the cuteness in her arms. *I could run.*

A handful of cars passed in front of her, parents and their children at last making their way home. When a familiar gold SUV slowed as it neared her, she thought the occupants were parents intending to thank her again. But when the driver-side window came down, she saw Becky behind the wheel. From the passenger seat, Missy leaned over.

"We thought we recognized you," Becky said. "We were over at…" Becky's eyes had moved from Sasha's face to what was in Sasha's arms. "Did you have your…"

"Is that your baby?!" Missy exclaimed.

Sasha stole a swift glance behind her, but neither María nor her mother was coming.

"Oh my God!" Becky said.

"Shows what we know," Missy said. "We thought you were faking it. You know, crazy Sasha, up to her old tricks!"

Do I have this reputation? Sasha thought to ask. Instead, she held up the sleeping baby, swaddled in a pink blanket.

"How cute!" Becky said. "Which one of the men, do you suppose—"

There was a light tap on the horn from the car behind them. A line of traffic had formed.

"We'll talk!" Missy said.

"Sure," Sasha said.

"Wow," Becky said. "She's beautiful!"

"They all are," Sasha said, gesturing to the school behind her. Her eyes fixed on a snowflake and a crocus dancing next to the jungle gym, their performance continuing after the curtain. They were moving as she had taught them, but with a grace and enthusiasm all their own. She gazed at the dancers for so long, and with such absorption, that she missed her friends' goodbye.

Authorship

....

"I need to be first author," Bill said.

Catherine wondered if he would say please. His mouth opened again, his expression turned pleading, and his eyebrows arched in a near rainbow, but in the space in which he might have spoken the word, he only sighed.

"Bill, it was my idea, my research, my work," she replied, stating the obvious. "Of course I appreciate your suggestions and additions on the first couple of drafts. But this was my baby from the beginning."

Bill and Catherine, married seven years, were sitting in their living room, on the couch Bill had owned since his undergraduate days at Boston College. It was, as Bill liked to boast, durable, having survived five moves, and because it was black, its stains were disguised. Every so often, however, she caught from it a whiff of his bachelor life.

Several times she had lobbied to replace the couch. He always said, "When I have tenure."

Tenure was the true subject of their conversation now. Bill was in his critical year at Ohio Eastern University. In four months, he would need to turn in his tenure file to his department chair. In nine months, at the end of the school year, he would know whether he had been granted tenure or a one-year, terminal contract.

Last spring, the university's president had replaced the dean of the college of arts and sciences with a woman from Cornell who, adhering to the letter of the college's guidelines, had immediately rejected two tenure candidates. But Catherine hadn't been concerned. She wouldn't have thought Bill, even as casual as he could seem toward his research, capable of falling short of the minimum publication requirements. On their short walk to this afternoon's beginning-of-the-school-year departmental picnic, however, Bill had reminded her of the new dean's by-the-book strictness. Under his breath, he added, "I could be her third victim."

"What do you mean?"

"I'm one good publication short. My chair said if I've buried a brilliant analysis or a groundbreaking study under my bed or on my hard drive or—hell—up my ass, it's time to excavate."

"What are you talking about?"

But they had arrived at the picnic, during which Bill became so drunk he told three of his colleagues how Catherine, on their wedding night—at the pinnacle of their lovemaking, no less—had shouted the name of her dissertation adviser. "I guess she always wanted a professor in her bed," Bill remarked, laughing, as his colleagues threw quick, uncomfortable glances at Catherine. "The question is whether I was the one — "

"Enough, Bill," she said, and his colleagues scattered toward the swing set and softball field.

Soon afterwards, they were walking home, under a gray evening sky. She upbraided him for his behavior at the picnic, but she saved most of her ire for how he had mishandled his research and scholarship, how he had jeopardized his job, how he had made their future in Sherman, their future in any academic community, tenuous. "I had no idea, Bill," she said. "You lied to me. By keeping me in the dark about your research—or lack of it—you lied."

Inside their house, on the couch, Bill, sobered by coffee and her anger, delivered his plea.

It was August, and the days were humid and hot. Nights offered little relief. Above them, the ceiling fan, black like the couch, spun lazily. Its faster speeds were broken. Bill had turned off all but the light beside the piano, on the other side of the room. He always said playing the piano helped him clear his mind so he could think about his research. Now she recalled long afternoons when he never left the piano bench, his fingers thumping across the dozen songs he knew by heart.

Bill's face was dark red, as if he were having trouble breathing. "I know it's asking a favor," he said. "A big favor."

"A favor?" Catherine said. "I'd say it's more than a favor."

Putting Bill as first author on the article, which had been accepted for publication the week before, would be academic fraud, she knew, although of a peculiar and difficult-to-prove kind. But even more unsettling, his request was an acknowledgement of his proximity to failure, which was a failure in its own right.

"You're right, you're absolutely right—it's more than a favor." Bill spoke quickly, his gaze on the piano. "I'll return the favor—the super favor, whatever we're going to call it—with my next article." He amended: "Or the next article I have accepted by a top journal." He bowed his head, as if realizing the inadequacy of his proposal. Bill hadn't published in a major journal since graduate school, and then only as the second author to his adviser. Catherine had researched and written her article not because she needed the publishing credit (she worked part-time for a local NGO) but because the subject compelled and inspired her—and because it revived, often joyfully, the scholar in her.

"If you and I were colleagues instead of a married couple, this wouldn't be an issue." Catherine spoke in an even-tempered voice, disguising the tone she was inclined to use. "This is my article, and by granting you second authorship, I've acknowledged the contributions you've made. But, Bill, your contributions don't come close to equaling what I did."

"We aren't colleagues," Bill said. "We're a husband and wife who happen to have degrees in the same field. And isn't marriage about lifting up the other person when he's down?" He glanced at her. "If I'm first author on this article, I'm all but guaranteed tenure and we can start doing what we talked about—buying a house, taking an overseas vacation, having...having a..." For a moment, it seemed he'd forgotten the word. "Baby." He took a breath before continuing: "This isn't only about me and tenure. This is about us and our future."

He shifted his body. Outside, a fire truck raced past, its alarm screaming. The house they rented was on one of Sherman's main streets in a student-dominated area called Partytown. "We have to think about what's best for both of us, for the couple," he said. "Of course I don't like the idea of claiming the majority of credit for the article when you did the hard work, but this is a unique situation. Does it seem like I'm asking for the world by asking to be first author?"

For her article, Catherine had enlisted former classmates who were working in hospitals, health clinics, and youth centers across the country to collect data. If she were to grant Bill first authorship, some of these friends, most of whom were Bill's friends, might want to know why. None would require the long explanation she would be obliged to give the journal's editor. "After considering the contributions each of us made...." Or: "While I generated ideas for the article, it was Bill who..." She resented the tone she would have to take, the lies she would tell. Researching and writing the article had taken her three-and-a-half years; Bill had spent at most five nights on it.

Bill turned toward her. "Consider the conditions you enjoyed so you could do your research," he said. "I was the one working full-time, bringing in the bulk of our income. I was your infrastructure." His eyes held hers for a moment before his gaze returned to the piano.

"We planned how we would divide up the work of the household before we moved here," she said. "Our plan, as you must remember, included having a baby."

"If we'd gone ahead and had a baby," he said, "we—you—we wouldn't have written the article, and we'd be looking at an even more precarious tenure situation."

She bristled at his ultimate choice of pronoun but aimed her ire at another part of his argument: "If we'd had a baby, the stakes would have been higher. Maybe you would have worked harder."

She registered the surprise and hurt on his face. "I *have* worked hard—you know I have." He glared at her, but the intensity in his eyes faded quickly. "I've been stuck with inconclusive data. Your data didn't suffer from the same shortcomings." He caught his breath, released it. "We're fortunate it didn't."

He touched her thigh, thought better of it, withdrew his hand. Never thin, she'd gained twenty pounds since they'd moved to Sherman. It was as if her body hadn't heard about their change of plan, but, having presumed childbirth, had grown matronly in the phantom aftermath. Meanwhile, the alarm on her biological clock had been ringing for months.

Catherine was thirty-eight-years old. In the last year, she'd taken to dyeing her hair to avoid looking like her mother.

With his robust shoulders, orange-brown hair, and cherubic face, Bill, two years her junior, was the best-looking man she'd ever dated. She'd met him in graduate school, and they'd married the summer after they defended their dissertations. Although she was the only student in her class to graduate with high honors, she agreed that Bill should be the one to pursue an academic career. Now her old reasons for deferring to his ambition—the pressure to publish, the insularity of academia, her desire to be a consistent presence in her yet unconceived children's lives—didn't seem sufficient.

Bill leaned back, leaned forward, sat upright, but said nothing.

Catherine thought of Silvia, a friend from high school who'd given her husband one of her kidneys. But Silvia's situation was different, she thought. For Silvia's husband, it was a question of life or death.

Yet to be denied tenure at Ohio Eastern University, which wasn't exactly Harvard or even the Harvard of the Midwest, could mean the end of Bill's academic career. Catherine also understood how humiliating it must be for Bill to ask her for first authorship, and perhaps there was, because of this, a degree of courage in his plea.

"What do you think, Cath? I mean…" Bill stopped, his gaze moving from her face to the floor.

She remembered their wedding-night lovemaking and her (admittedly, embarrassing) invocation of Saul Mathews, her dissertation adviser. In his early forties, with distinguished speckles of silver in his hair, Saul had been named an endowed professor the year before she graduated, although no one could have guessed his talent and ambition from his office, which was decorated with drawings by his twin sons and, after hours, resonated with earnest sounds from his steel-stringed guitar. Had she married Bill hoping he would be like Saul, someone who could succeed spectacularly while seeming to be casually wrapped up in everyday pleasures? Had she shouted Saul's name like a wish she'd been holding secret?

A motorcycle on the street outside sounded like a chainsaw. Even minutes later, she thought she heard it, splitting the night.

Half of my life is over.

Catherine turned to Bill. His mouth was open, like a baby's awaiting a food-filled spoon. Yet there were lines at the corners of his eyes, spreading like skeletal wings. The years they'd promised to each other had once seemed abundant.

Moments passed, and beneath her anger, Catherine felt sadness. She pretended to brush something from Bill's shoulder. He looked at her hopefully, and she wondered what might be salvaged from her old dreams.

"Are you sure that by being first author you'll be guaranteed tenure?"

Bill released a breath he might have been holding all evening. "There are no guarantees. But first authorship on a provocative article in one of the field's top journals? The dean wouldn't only have to be hard-assed but idiotic to say no."

"So if it's all but a sure thing, we can start looking to buy a house soon?"

"Tomorrow, if you want," Bill said brightly.

"And our vacation?"

"This summer. France. Italy. Rwanda." He shot her a smile. "And don't forget I'll be due a sabbatical."

"And," she said, "we can go ahead and get pregnant."

His response wasn't as quick: "Sure."

She said, "We can start tonight."

His eyes fell and struggled to reclaim her face.

"I'm in mid-cycle," she said. This wasn't, strictly speaking, true. But she wanted to leave no haven for his ambivalence. "It's the perfect time."

"So no diaphragm?" he asked.

"You make it sound like we'd be leaving behind a friend." She paused and noted the doubt on his face. "All right," she said, "forget it."

"No," he said, and he pressed his hand onto her thigh, as if holding her to her concession. "Let's go upstairs." He tugged her off the couch and pulled her toward the staircase. Now haste seemed his goal, as if he wanted to outrun any second thoughts either of them might have.

"We can enjoy this, you know," she said, struggling to keep up with him. "This shouldn't be a chore."

"I know," he said. In an easier voice, he repeated, "I know." They were in the bedroom now.

"I'll call my editor tomorrow," she said. She met his eyes. "And we'll keep having sex until I'm pregnant. Agreed?"

He nodded and unbuckled his belt. Already, she felt dirty and desperate. Even if only she and Bill would ever know about their bargain, this felt like too large an audience, too many witnesses to their humiliation.

"Listen, Bill," she said, her voice raspy. "If one day you have doubts, or feel guilty, about what we agreed on tonight, I don't want to hear a word, all right?"

Bill slid a finger across his lips, then, with the same finger, crossed his heart. Catherine tried to smile.

Moments later, they were in bed, undressed.

And moments after this—too soon, Catherine thought, and not for reasons of her pleasure but for the significance of what they had both surrendered—the deal was sealed.

The Meet

∙∙∙

The father saw the first runner crest the hill. The runner wore red, like blood, like the blood of every runner he'd defeated, including the father's son, twice this year, four times last year. The father's son was two lengths behind the lead runner, and the father said, perhaps to himself, perhaps to the fathers around him, perhaps to God, "This time—no. This time, I win. I mean, my son—my son wins." So the father, in his jacket and tie—he'd come to the middle-school cross-country meet from a sales meeting—jumped onto the course as his son neared and, racing beside him, screamed, "Catch him! Faster! Go, go, go!"

The father of the lead runner observed this unorthodox cheerleading, and he worried it might motivate the second-place runner to pass his son. Seeing no choice, and also relishing an excuse to do what he'd wanted to do at last year's county championships, where his son had come in a humiliating sixth place, he sprinted beside his boy, yelling, "Don't you dare let him catch you! Run, damn it! Run!" He had taken off his shoes in the cool fall grass; they'd been itching from a persistent case of athlete's foot, although his only athletic feat in the past few months was walking up three flights of stairs one Wednesday morning when the elevator at his law office was out of order.

The father of the third-place runner saw what the two other fathers had done, and he didn't want his son to be at a disadvantage. His son was disadvantaged enough, he believed, having inherited the opposite of a killer instinct from his mother, who regularly allowed cars into traffic ahead of her and offered generous tips to mediocre waiters. "Faster!" he shouted, matching his son's strides. "Third place is for losers! This race is ours!"

We, the other fathers on the sidelines, refused to be outdone or out-maneuvered or out-bullied. We, too, joined the race, striding alongside our sons, urging them on in a language we hadn't spoken in years. Yes, even the father who had declared from the start—of the race, of the season, of his life—that he didn't care about winning, that what was most important was trying one's best and savoring the journey and making sure the means were celebrated as joyfully as the ends—even he un-pretzeled himself from his yoga pose, tossed aside his peace pipe, and thundered into the torrent.

Several mothers joined the race, some confused into thinking it was an opportunity to spend quality time with their sons. One mother, however, discovered she could help her son's cause by tripping his opponents' fathers. Another—she had large breasts and her T-shirt did nothing to disguise the fact—seduced several of us into believing the race continued across a creek, through a cornfield, and over the edge of a fifteen-foot retaining wall. A third simply wanted to show she was a better runner than anyone on the course, and she would have shot into first place if one of the fathers hadn't tackled her.

The father of the boy who had been bringing up the rear (and perhaps even, sad to say, walking) was now driving him to the front of the pack on an all-terrain vehicle, its tires spinning grass and dirt onto the competition. Before the ATV driver and his son came within honking distance of the leaders, however, a father stuck out his arm and clothes-lined both riders, sending them flying backwards into twenty-sixth place.

Another father—a pharmacist or a doctor or a dealer—injected something into his son's left buttock, and the boy ran faster than he had ever run, but whether because of the injection or because he wanted to avoid his father's next syringe no one could say.

One boy didn't have a father. Some of the mothers wondered if this was an advantage.

We ran hard and fast beside our sons. If they had been horses, we wouldn't have spared the whip. They needed to learn toughness, and we would teach them. This was a crucial race, a decisive race. This was the third race of the season! Bad things come in threes, and we didn't want to be three-time losers. We'd lost enough. We'd lost poker games. We'd lost bets on the Super Bowl and World Series. We'd lost out on promotions and prizes to younger men and dumber men and men who were in all ways superior to us (which made us feel no better about losing to them). One of us had lost his taste for life and was thinking of checking into a psychiatric ward. Another, who was spending money like he had it—which, to our distaste, he did, thanks to savvy investments—had lost all modesty and moderation. Yes, we'd even lost abstractions: fearlessness, fidelity, faith. A few of us, the most unlucky, had lost children, to illness or accidents or, in the case of the retired major, married to his second wife, twenty years his junior, to war. It was all the more important, therefore, that the children we did have keep pace with our wildest dreams and defeat our most haunting nightmares.

"Go! Don't slow down! Faster, faster, faster!"

When we realized there wasn't much distance left in the race, we had mixed feelings. On one hand, we were tired and looked forward to a rest. On the other, we had so much for which to make up, so much to correct and avenge, and so little space, and therefore so little time, in which to do so. For one father, there was the humiliation of being the only boy cut from his junior high basketball team. For another, it was the shame of being fired from his job last week. For a third, it was the embarrassment of his recent failures in bed with his wife, whom he was sure was having an affair. We had suffered failures of omission and commission and diminution. We had failed spectacularly and quietly, publicly and privately. After our failures, some of us had cried. Some of us had pretended we hadn't tried. The grimmest of us, the fathers with the deepest wounds, wished—with a terrible ache—that we had died.

But it wasn't only failure that motivated us. There was jealousy, spite, hatred. A father of a runner in blue was the next-door neighbor of a father of a runner in yellow, and he was tired, goddamn sick and tired, of watching from his kitchen window every Sunday morning as the yellow-shirted runner's father washed his late-model Mercedes in his driveway, lathering it like he was putting whipped cream on a naked woman. Yes, much of what motivated us was sex. We wanted our sons to win so the mothers who were watching (and, in some cases, running) the race no longer looked at us as the bearers of pot bellies and thinning and receding and graying hair but as the still-youthful progenitors of the victorious who could, with an invitation no more indelicate than a kiss, revive their lives with ecstasies unimagined. We weren't over-the-hill. We were about to catch a second wind!

The course was now crowded and chaotic, and there was nothing the officials or the coaches could do to restore order. Besides, half of them had joined the field, desperate to do what they'd long wanted to: Show these boys what it was to be a real runner, a real man. When you're this close to the end of the race, son, you don't hold back, you kick like a racehorse, you sprint like you're heading home to a naked woman in your bed or, in the case of East Middle's coach, a naked woman *and* a naked man, you…

But where is the finish line? Wasn't it supposed to be around this corner? Or was it the next corner? Or the next? We're breathing like we're in a steam room on top of a 20,000-foot mountain. We are losing our wind and our will. Is one of us walking? Has one of us fallen on the grass? Is one of us slipping off into the forest over to the right, hoping no one will notice?

And where have our sons gone? Have they outrun us? But they were here only moments ago, by our sides, breathing the same air we breathed, their hearts beating to the same rhythm. Are you happy, son, wherever you are? Is this the race you wanted to run?

Perhaps we have outdistanced them. Yes, that must be it. This shouldn't be a surprise. From the start—in our hearts, in our groins—we recognized our superiority. We are the alpha males to our sons' breathless, boneless betas. We hoped to make them kings, but they're still only princes, fumbling around our thrones.

Who's going to win the race? What does it mean to win? Will winning do everything we want it to? Or will winning be only another disappointment, something we'll need to run another race to transcend or forget?

Why these doubts? Haven't we outraced doubts? We are the captains of our fates, the masters of our souls, the champions of—

Now here's the finish line. At last. But whose idea—whose joke—was it to make the banner black?

Pistachio

••

August 1, 2008

Dr. Edward Morton Ladybing III
Director
Harvard University Press
Cambridge, Massachusetts

Dear Dr. Ladybing,

Let me begin by reiterating how grateful I am to be included in the circle of screeners for your "American Thespians of the 20th Century" series. I have read all ten volumes you've published thus far, including your latest, Marlon Brando's revelatory diary of his thirteenth year. If old wives' warnings about masturbation were true, Brando would have had to play Stanley Kowalski with dark glasses and a walking stick!

About your invitation to review a memoir by the stage actor Felix Kapoodle, I must admit to having misled you when, in our telephone conversation, I said, "Of course I've heard of Kapoodle! Hasn't everyone?" As someone who has devoted his professional life to the study of 20th century and contemporary American theater, and as someone who teaches in a university located in Mr. Kapoodle's hometown, I was appalled to think I might not be familiar with this actor of even minor importance.

Now, however, I can answer truthfully that I do know Mr. Kapoodle—perhaps better than anyone in the world, for in the interest of writing a thorough review of Mr. Kapoodle's memoir, I engaged in a fact-checking mission so far-reaching it must be unprecedented. It is my great pleasure to enclose my review.

Sincerely,
Dr. Gerald T. Small Jr.
Assistant Professor
Department of Drama
Ohio Eastern University
Sherman, Ohio

Felix Kapoodle's *My Dream Career on Stage: A Memoir*
Reviewed by Dr. Gerald T. Small Jr.

Felix James Kapoodle was born on Halloween of 1943 in Sherman, Ohio. In the early summer of 1961, he moved to New York City, where he lived until he returned to Sherman in the fall of 2003. He died last year on J.M. Barrie's birthday (May 9). Little else about his life as he depicts it in his 724-page memoir can be called the undisputed truth. In fact, the research I did contradicts parts or all of his memoir's most salient recollections. Furthermore, if one agrees with Mr. Kapoodle's detractors, the accomplishments his memoir goes to great lengths to celebrate should be viewed as abominations against the theatrical arts, if not as outright crimes.

I, however, do not share this opinion. Having spent the better part of eight months working to separate what is fact and what is fiction in Mr. Kapoodle's memoir, and having undertaken the less laborious but even more difficult job of arriving at a judgment of his place in 20th and 21st century American theater, I have come to have a profound respect for both Mr. Kapoodle and his unflinching vision of what theater could and should be. In this scholar's opinion, Mr. Kapoodle deserves to emerge from the dark wings of theater history and assume his rightful place on stage.

The Circus

Mr. Kapoodle declares he fell in love with theater at age five after seeing clowns from the Ringling Brothers Circus perform a skit based on Anton Chekhov's *The Three Sisters*. The skit was intended as mere incidental entertainment between the elephant and human cannonball acts during a show at the Sherman Fairgrounds in July of 1949, but, Mr. Kapoodle writes, "the performance struck me like a knife-thrower's errant blade to the heart." Instead of longing to go to Moscow, the three clowns long to join the circus. In the end, the clowns make the happy realization that they are already in the circus. "The three sisters in Chekhov's drama could have made a similar realization—Moscow, after all, is a state of mind as much as a place," Mr. Kapoodle writes. "Too bad Chekhov was such a sourpuss."

Sherman's daily newspaper, *The Advocate and Post*, makes no mention of Ringling Brothers appearing in town in July of 1949. However, a regional circus, the Dingling Cousins, did occupy the Sherman Fairgrounds for three consecutive summers beginning in 1948. (The Dingling Cousins attempted to return a fourth time, but as their train was approaching the town line, it derailed, and most of the wild animals aboard, including a troop of spider monkeys, escaped—to take positions, as the joke became, in local government and law enforcement agencies.) Whoever their employer, the three clowns made an enduring impression on the young Kapoodle. Revising masterpieces would come to be his claim to fame—or infamy.

Mr. Kapoodle acquired his "stentorian, reach-the-rafters voice," he writes, thanks to his parents, who, by his reckoning, made him spend three out of every five weekday afternoons of his childhood at the top of Sherman's Main Street reciting Bible verses and anti-Communist speeches. On occasion, Mr. Kapoodle writes, he "slipped into a Shakespeare medley, quoting in swift succession from *Antony and Cleopatra*, *The Tempest*, *Romeo and Juliet*, and a dozen other plays." About his parents, he writes, "In a backwards way, I owe all my success in theater to them."

Maybelle Jones, Mr. Kapoodle's only living sibling—he was the youngest of six—disputes Mr. Kapoodle's portrait of his childhood. "Felix's problem was the opposite of what he claims," Mrs. Jones told me outside a methadone clinic in Cleveland. "He was ignored his entire life. On the day he was born, our mother was taking a bath and didn't realize she'd given birth. I don't think she even knew she was pregnant. Three of us took showers before Sandra—she's the oldest—noticed him at the end of the tub, all red and helpless and hungry. For a week, maybe longer, my mother was sure he was something the cat had dragged in."

Attention Must Be Paid

Mr. Kapoodle claims to have "invented the very notion of live theater" at the Sherman Alternative High School in his role as president of the Alternative-to-Mediocrity Players. Yearbooks published during Mr. Kapoodle's time at the high school, however, make mention of only three extracurricular groups besides the two-person yearbook staff: the Pigeon Predators, a bow-hunting club specializing in inner-city prey; the Neo-Prussians, a group whose members greeted each other with the cry, "Heil Bismarck!"; and the school's football team, seven of whose members were arrested in Mr. Kapoodle's senior year after failing to understand that their coach's injunction that "football is war" wasn't to be taken literally.

In his junior year, Mr. Kapoodle, who was of average height and remained on the gangly side for all but the final decade of his life, claims to have achieved the unprecedented feat of performing all twelve roles in *Death of a Salesman* during a single, sold-out performance at his high school's 500-seat auditorium, which also functioned as the school's cafeteria and boys' locker room. A small notice in *The Advocate and Post,* however, reveals that the performance actually occurred on the tulip-lined walkway to the school's front door. Moreover, the article said, Mr. Kapoodle spoke only a single line from the play—a line he repeated "at least 4,000 times," according to the newspaper—"Attention, attention must finally be paid to such a person." (*The Advocate and Post* speculated about whether Mr. Kapoodle's singular performance might qualify him for notation in *The Guinness Book of Records.* It did not.)

Over two weeks in April of his senior year, his memoir claims, Mr. Kapoodle performed the entire Eugene O'Neill canon, culminating in a performance of *Long Day's Journey Into Night* in Sherman's Metropolitan Theater. He was assisted in his endeavor by two of the football players who'd been involved in the "Friday Night Massacre." The football players, Mr. Kapoodle writes, had "discovered redemption and reward" in acting out the bit parts O'Neill had created as "warm-up acts to the haunting monologues of his immortal protagonists, whom I, of course, portrayed with heretofore unheard of energy and conviction."

My interviews with the two ex-football players, conducted face-to-face but through glass and via telephone at the Northeast Ohio Maximum Security Prison, revealed that participation in the O'Neill marathon was a mandatory part of their plea bargain agreement with the local prosecutor. Everyone in the production read their parts off scripts weekdays from three to five in the deserted basement of the Sherman Public Library.

Denied

Mr. Kapoodle devotes an entire chapter of his memoir to his acceptance by the Yale School of Drama and his subsequent decision to turn the school down. In fact, Mr. Kapoodle was never accepted into the venerable institution; he applied for and was denied admission nineteen times in twenty-three years. After Mr. Kapoodle was rejected for fifteen straight years, the school's long-time director, Dr. Peter Yardley, who this past fall celebrated his 70th year at the university, notified Mr. Kapoodle that his application would be considered only every two years. In all of his rejection letters, Dr. Yardley emphasized two reasons for denying Mr. Kapoodle admittance: 1) Mr. Kapoodle's undergraduate degree, granted by the Luxembourg Correspondence School of Ballet and Theater, gave him "suspect preparation for serious dramatic study"; and 2) Mr. Kapoodle's audition tapes showed he was "at best, a pathetically bad actor."

Deception and Recognition

Although Mr. Kapoodle doesn't admit as much in his memoir, he forged a letter from Dr. Yardley in which he had the esteemed director, theater scholar, and professor call him "a daring actor, a charismatic actor, an actor who, frankly, was too great for even our great school."

In addition, Mr. Kapoodle fails to acknowledge that he used this forged letter to secure his first professional acting job, the understudy to the grave-digger in a Martin Middleton production of *Hamlet*. Mr. Middleton, whose production was scheduled to do a four-city tour (San Francisco, Chicago, Washington, D.C., and Boston) before reaching Broadway, said he hired Mr. Kapoodle on the basis of the letter alone. "I didn't have time to audition him," Mr. Middleton told me when we spoke in his room at a retirement home in Connecticut. "My gravedigger understudy quit to join his family's funeral home business—true story—and Kapoodle's résumé and letter were on top of my desk. After what Kapoodle did, I held on to the letter—in case I wanted to file a lawsuit."

In his memoir, Mr. Kapoodle describes the episode thusly: "At last, someone had recognized my genius. Martin Middleton and I may have had our artistic differences, but I'll always give him credit for his keen eye for talent."

Peanut, Pickle, Pretzel…Pistachio!

Mr. Middleton said all would have gone smoothly for Mr. Kapoodle had he been content to do what he was hired to do: "The young man who played the gravedigger [Anatole Paul, who would later return to France to star in pornographic films] was in good health and probably wouldn't have missed a performance. Kapoodle would have had 'Broadway actor' on his c.v." But during what Mr. Middleton described as a better-than-average performance on the company's opening night in Boston, Mr. Kapoodle burst into the final scene, before the duel between Hamlet and Laertes inaugurates a bloodbath, and declared, "I am Pistachio, Hamlet's long-lost brother, and you will now have to fight the two of us. Look out, freaks!"

Members of the company weren't sure whether Mr. Kapoodle intended actual harm with the fencing foil he was holding. Not taking any chances, they fled the stage, leaving only Hamlet, Horatio, and "Pistachio." "What a surprise to see justice so quickly done!" Mr. Kapoodle proclaimed in his invented version of the traditional play-ending couplet. "And who knew it could be so much fun!" The three men on stage bowed, and the audience exploded in a deafening mixture of boos and cheers. Back stage, there was debate about whether to do a curtain call, but because Mildred Piles, the actress who played Ophelia, had phoned the police and they had since arrived to confront Mr. Kapoodle, the curtain call was abandoned.

In his memoir, Mr. Kapoodle defends his improvisation: "The theater aristocracy, which includes most directors and even the most talentless of prima donnas, is far too wedded to archaic traditions such as following the script. True advancement in the theatrical arts comes about by exploding the mold and leaping outside of the box. Sophocles did a radical thing in his day—he put an extra actor on stage. I am not claiming to be the innovator Sophocles was, but I have created and defined for all time the part of Pistachio. No blackballing by any director or theater company can take that away from me. As far as sullying the work of theater's greatest genius—I'm speaking about William Shakespeare, although God knows Martin Middleton had a stratospherically high opinion of himself—well, the Bible tells us 'Ye shall have no other gods before me.' For the theater aristocracy, Shakespeare is the golden calf.

"Personally, I don't think there's anything wrong with giving old Billy's tragedies a jolt of the new, not to mention the happy. *Hamlet* was only part one of my master plan. In *Julius Caesar,* I was going to play a sophisticated plebeian who undermines Marc Antony's funeral oration by pointing out all of his sneaky rhetorical tricks. In *Othello*, I planned to play the part of Ricky Rodriguez, a Latino musician who holds thrice-weekly classes in racial sensitivity and thereby prevents a whole fifth act of gratuitous carnage. That theater goers never saw these versions of Shakespeare's tragedies is the real tragedy."

Mr. Middleton, on the other hand, described Mr. Kapoodle's improvisation as "the epitome of unprofessional. If the theater world were the criminal justice system, Kapoodle would have received the death penalty."

Although Mr. Middleton was worried that Mr. Kapoodle had killed his version of *Hamlet*'s chances on Broadway, this didn't prove true, at least not initially. The play opened to sellout crowds, and many of the theater-goers quoted in a story in *The Village Voice* admitted to being in attendance only to see the character they referred to as "Peanut," "Pickle," and "Pretzel," as well as by his correct name, "Pistachio." Mr. Kapoodle had been dismissed from the production, however, and the audience saw only what one of its numbers told *The Voice* was a "workaday performance with a too predictable ending."

If there is a case to be made for Mr. Kapoodle's memoir's inclusion in the "American Thespians of the 20th Century" series, it rests largely on his invention of Pistachio. Commentary on the role is limited, however. The four contemporary theater critics who wrote about Mr. Kapoodle's performance described it as a fiasco; in the words of *The Boston Globe*'s E. Major Martin, what Mr. Kapoodle did was "an amateurish prank, stupid to the core, and not even sophisticated enough for high school."

As for current scholarship on Mr. Kapoodle and his career-defining role, while I stumbled upon a pair of references to the actor on anonymous Marxist literary blogs—one celebrates his "overthrow of literary royalty and bourgeoisie," the other touts his "revolutionary theatrical vision"—I had the peculiar sensation I was reading Mr. Kapoodle's own words. When I discovered a reference to "Kapoodle" on a Belgian web site, I was, of course, excited. But this "Kapoodle" proved to be the brand name of a remote-control stuffed dog, which in my enthusiasm for this project I ordered, to the tune of $99.49.

Actor and Audience

Aside from Mr. Kapoodle's brief turn in *Hamlet*, he earned no money from acting. Subsequently, his only theatrical "performances" in a New York theater were his carefully scripted outbursts as a member of the audience, usually from the back-row balcony. During a performance of *Oedipus Rex* at the Juan Lopez Theater in Brooklyn by the Canadian troupe Maple Leaf, Mr. Kapoodle shouted, "She's your mother! You killed your dad! I know a good therapist!" In his memoir, Mr. Kapoodle gives himself credit for inaugurating the role of "The Voice of Truth and Compassion" in *Oedipus Rex*. The police report makes it clear that his "voice" was unwelcome.

Although theaters in all five boroughs soon had post-office-style warnings featuring Mr. Kapoodle's face plastered all over their facilities, he occasionally sneaked past unsuspecting ticket takers. He interrupted a performance of *A Streetcar Named Desire* at the AMA Theater in Manhattan by announcing that he was Chet Huntley, Blanche DuBois' mythical Texas oilman millionaire, and he was going to "sic some lean, mean cowboys" on Stanley Kowalski. "How painfully often had *A Streetcar Named Desire* been performed before my bold and necessary revision of it?" Mr. Kapoodle asks readers of his memoir. "Frankly, to see Blanche raped yet again by that thug was going to make me puke up Polish sausage. It was time to turn this tragedy into a miracle play." Although Mr. Kapoodle again claims he was part of the acting company that put on the performance, it is clear from the police report that all his lines were shouted from row ZZ, seat Y.

While it would seem logical that scholars of audience-inclusive theater would examine every outburst of Mr. Kapoodle's career, neither Viola Winegarden at UCLA nor Richard Pope at NYU—nor any of their dozens of disciples—so much as mentions Mr. Kapoodle in their volumes of scholarly work. (Ms. Winegarden's romance novel, *Drama Queen*, written under the nom de plume Violet Wine, does include a character named Felix K., whose life-long ambition to re-write *The Crucible* as a Halloween farce can only be a bizarre coincidence.) Of course, Mr. Kapoodle never acknowledged that he was a part of any audience, which might have forced these scholars to examine with even greater care the question of where the line between actors and audience should be drawn.

The Art of Everyday Life

Poignantly, Mr. Kapoodle lists his "longest and least acclaimed" role as the protagonist of *The Peter Pan Deli*. This was, Mr. Kapoodle declares in his memoir, "extemporaneous theater at its most subtle and subversive. The cast and I pretended to be the employees of an Upper West Side deli. In our interactions with our 'customers,' we brought to life the gritty, soul-trying, heartbreaking, and occasionally—very occasionally—joy-filled drama of life in the most vibrant and most tragic city in the world."

As my interviews with the owner and several former employees of the Peter Pan Deli confirm, however, Mr. Kapoodle wasn't playing a role at all. He was, in fact, the deli's chief sandwich maker and bagel slicer and had been ever since his move to the city following his graduation from high school. He usually worked the 6 a.m. to 2 p.m. shift, which left him time to catch a 2:30 matinee on Broadway, if he was so inclined.

"I was paying him to make egg salad and bologna sandwiches—or whatever the hell the customer ordered," the deli's owner, Frank McGuire, told me from behind his cash register. "If he was spending his time acting on the job, then he owes me money. I may be ninety-three-years-old, but I still know how to dial up a lawyer."

"If it was all a big drama, I didn't know nothing about it," said Lenny "Quick Hands" Smith, who backed up Mr. Kapoodle on sandwiches and was also the deli's main lottery ticker seller.

Another employee, Bruce "Too Much Mayo" McMahon, said that while he didn't recognize at the time that Mr. Kapoodle was acting, it made sense to him in retrospect. "Sometimes he would stand on the counter next to the condiments and pound his chest and ramble on about how someone named Willy Loman should have been let in on the ground floor at Nike and somebody named Nora only needed a job suited to her intelligence to feel good and why hadn't anyone worth a doll's house offered her one? We thought he was touched. It's funny to think he was only acting."

Homecoming

A month before his sixtieth birthday, Mr. Kapoodle moved back to Sherman, seeking, as his memoir puts it, "to bring to the town of my birth a little of the magic, not to mention the expertise, I'd acquired in my glorious days on the boards in New York." Three weeks after his return, he auditioned for the role of King Lear in the Sherman Players' staging of the Shakespeare play. "There was no question I would get the lead," Mr. Kapoodle reports in his memoir. "I was born to play Lear." While Mr. Kapoodle, who by now had rounded into a mini-Orson Welles, complete with gray hair and beard, did secure the lead role, it was due entirely to his résumé, comprised of "five pages of lies and fantasies," according to Margaret Wilson, the play's director and the vice president of the Sherman Community Arts Center.

"I was overwhelmed by his so-called accomplishments, and if his audition was less than stellar, I thought I had excessively high expectations," Ms. Wilson recalled. "But as we were nearing intermission of our first performance, Kapoodle, as Lear, gathered his three daughters to him and said, 'We're not leaving this stage until we succeed in being a happy family again.' What followed was forty-five minutes of the most bizarre improvisation I've ever seen. He had the three sisters say what they liked best about each other, what their first happy memory of each other was, what their fondest wish for each other was. He even had them take turns falling backwards into each other's arms. At the end of this, he said, 'Now I am satisfied, and I shall lie down and die!' And he did!"

Wilson said students in Ohio Eastern University English classes whose professors had assigned them to see the play handed in papers calling Shakespeare "touchy-feely," "New Age," and "the inventor of the group hug."

"The professors assumed their students had skipped the play and had indulged in hallucinogens instead, and so they handed out Fs like candy on Halloween," Ms. Wilson said. "I had to call the English Department to explain the situation."

Ms. Wilson thought that after the first performance she had Mr. Kapoodle's promise to "play the role the way Shakespeare wrote it," but the second performance proceeded exactly like the first with the exception that at the end, Mr. Kapoodle's Lear declared he was giving up his kingdom to join the Peace Corps. "It's true that Shakespeare was guilty of a few anachronisms," Ms. Wilson said. "He put bells in Rome, for example. But the Peace Corps? 'Ask not what your kingdom can do for you, but what you can do for your kingdom'? It was ludicrous."

Ms. Wilson had fantasies of killing Mr. Kapoodle. "But then I thought he might have liked it," she said, "especially if I pulled the trigger during the play. He would turn both Lear and himself into martyrs, and I wasn't going to give either of them the satisfaction." So Ms. Wilson let Mr. Kapoodle finish the last four shows, although she stayed clear of the theater during the performances. "The only way I would have shown up," said Ms. Wilson, "was if the second coming of Lawrence Olivier had arrived to rescue my hijacked play."

In his memoir, Mr Kapoodle says *Lear* proved a "luminous exhibition of my dramatic range and improvisational genius." He was stunned, therefore, when no other roles were forthcoming, despite his numerous attempts to secure parts at community theaters all over Ohio. "Directors are notoriously jealous of superior actors because superior actors make directors superfluous," he writes. "I was punished for being too damn good."

Love and Longing

Mr. Kapoodle claims to have made "long, sensuous love" (he uses this phrase thirty-three times in his memoir) to thirty-three women, most of whom were (and some still are) big names in the New York theater community as actresses, directors, producers, and well-heeled theater aficionados. None of the six women who answered my requests for interviews claimed to have heard of Mr. Kapoodle, and five threatened lawsuits on the spot. (The sixth was glad someone was still thinking of her in "that way" and invited me to dinner.)

There is a distinct note of pathos in Mr. Kapoodle's declaration that, given his "intense and demanding career, I never had time for a wife, much less children. It is too late now—I am exiled from the theater and am in the twilight of my life. This is no time to make up for lost time by marrying one of the nubile college women who eye me with undisguised desire whenever I walk in front of their sorority houses on Park Street. But how I long sometimes for a son or daughter with whom I could share, for example, my addition to *The Glass Menagerie* of a second gentleman caller who sweeps into the Wingfields' St. Louis apartment, marries Laura on the fire escape, and moves the whole family to a house on a golf course outside of Atlanta. Alas, fatherhood will forever remain a dream."

The End

In his return to his hometown, Mr. Kapoodle secured work as a custodian at Sherman High School, where, while mopping the girls' third-floor bathroom, he suffered a fatal heart attack. Missy Whippleworth, who'd been hiding out in one of the bathroom stalls for the previous six hours, overheard his final word: "Curtains." He had sent his memoir to the Harvard University Press three days earlier.

Conclusions and Reflections

While it is impossible to evaluate Mr. Kapoodle's claim that he is "the most gifted actor who ever lived in obscurity"—could it not be said that most stage actors today, performing in the obliterating shadows cast by film, television, and the Internet, live in obscurity?—it is possible to provide a tentative evaluation of his impact on the theatrical arts. He is the only 20th-century and contemporary American theater actor who, with premeditation and no word of warning to the play's director, dared change a classic text in order, as he described it, to make the experience of watching a tragedy "less tragic." While he has had few, if any, imitators in the theater world, screenwriters have long felt at liberty to alter classic works to provide a so-called Hollywood ending. Several sources told me that Mel Gibson was considering concluding his film version of *Hamlet* with Pistachio saving the day. Apparently, Mr. Gibson opted against this finale out of concern that, as Hamlet, he would be outshone by "a nut." (The logical response to Mr. Gibson is, "It takes one to know one.")

On a socio-political note, Mr. Kapoodle's instinct to re-conceive tragedies as dramas with happy endings taps into what might be seen as an ascendant American phenomenon, which became prevalent at the end of the 20th century and the beginning of the 21st. One need only look at the United States' recent military ventures, its treatment of prisoners in the war on terror, or its see-no-problems approach to environmental degradation and climate change to understand how tragedy is re-packaged as something benign. But unlike a government that refuses to admit to the tragic consequences of its decisions in the name of anaesthetizing voters and remaining in power, Mr. Kapoodle, I believe, intended in his revisions of the masterworks of ancient and modern theater to have a deeply cathartic impact on theatergoers—a different, but no less authentic, catharsis as the kind Aristotle defined in his *Poetics*. Expecting to witness profound tragedy, theatergoers would find themselves jolted by Mr. Kapoodle's alterations into accepting the idea of an uplifting, even miraculous, ending, not just for Shakespeare's or Ibsen's or Tenneessee Williams' characters but for themselves.

If Mr. Kapoodle's memoir were to be published by the Harvard University Press, a step I enthusiastically endorse, it would inevitably need to be positioned as a disenfranchised artist's look at the world of American theater. (In addition, it would need numerous annotations, which I would be happy to provide.) Mr. Kapoodle is the antithesis of every successful actor, director, and playwright America has ever produced. In a comparison he might appreciate, he is the Willy Loman of the American stage, a forgotten man striving to make a name for himself—indeed, to triumph—while "riding on a smile and a shoeshine." That he failed, and failed miserably, was almost inevitable. It can be safely said that he had no talent. But did he own a rare, perhaps even unique, vision of a canonical repertoire cleansed of tragedy and replaced with large, generous outcomes? Certainly. And did he possess a dream? As big as the country he lived in.

Truth Poker

....

Congressman Stevens greeted my father and me at the door of his house in northwest Washington, D.C., in a dark suit with a red handkerchief—the kind magicians use—in its breast pocket. He was tall and I was short, even for a ten-year-old, and he crouched to look at me. As his radiant blue eyes held mine, I felt I was the only person who mattered to him. I would never like him, but from the beginning I saw how my father could.

Congressman Stevens stood and introduced me to his nephew, Ralph, who was two years older than I. Ralph was as lean as a scarecrow, and with his gray eyes and mouse brown hair, he was as plain as Congressman Stevens was handsome. My father put a hand on my head and ruffled my curly hair. "Have fun," he said before he and Congressman Stevens strolled off toward the wood-paneled dining room.

Ralph gave me a smile. "You like baseball, right?"

I nodded, and he motioned me toward the back of the house. We passed a piano with photographs above the keyboard of the congressman, a blonde-haired woman, and twin teenage girls.

Ralph noticed me staring. "My aunt and cousins," he explained. "They're in England or France this summer. My aunt doesn't like my mom." Ralph cupped his hand to my ear and whispered, "It's because she's so pretty. Look." From the brown leather wallet in his pocket, Ralph pulled a black-and-white photograph. His mother was standing on a shore, the ocean crashing behind her, wind in her light hair. Her legs were crossed and her hands were on her hips. Ralph, I saw, had inherited her teardrop eyes.

The photograph, Ralph explained, was taken on Redondo Beach, near where they lived. Ralph said his mother moved to Los Angeles when she was eighteen to become an actress. "And I'm sure she would have been if I hadn't come along to steal the show." He smiled. "Fortunately, she says it's a very, very good show."

We walked out the back door and onto a long, wide lawn with three red maples at the end. A handful of tennis balls and a pair of baseball bats were scattered on the grass. Ralph explained the rules: Whoever hit the most balls to the red maples on the fly won. "What team do you want to be?" he asked me. Of course I wanted to be the Indians. Before my father and I moved from Cleveland to Washington in May, we had been regulars at Municipal Stadium. Three years before, we had cheered on the Indians to the 1948 World Series championship. "I'm the home team," Ralph said, and we began our game.

I was beating him by six runs when my father and Congressman Stevens appeared at the back door. The congressman had changed out of his suit into shorts and a T-shirt. "Adults against the young men?" he proposed, striding out onto the lawn and picking up a bat. My father, who was dressed in jeans, removed his short-sleeve, button-down shirt and followed the congressman into the yard. In his T-shirt, he looked as fit as a lifeguard. His hair was black and curly like mine.

Congressman Stevens hacked at the baseball with the abruptness and impatience of someone swatting at a fly. In contrast, my father blasted every pitch into the red maples. Because of him, they beat us easily.

My father and I stayed for dinner. Congressman Stevens employed a cook, and at the four-seat kitchen table, we ate roast beef and corn bread and what struck me at the time as an exotic vegetable: asparagus. My father wasn't a big talker, so the three of us listened as Congressman Stevens told stories about big-league players he knew.

After Ralph and I finished our meals, Congressman Stevens suggested we play a board game, a half dozen of which were stacked on a bookshelf in the living room. Sitting cross-legged on the carpeted floor, Ralph and I played a few games of checkers and a game of chess. After putting the games back on the shelf, Ralph discovered a deck of cards. "Let's play poker," he said. "We'll place bets."

"I don't have any money," I said.

"We won't bet with money."

"What will we bet with?"

"The truth." He explained: The person who won the hand could ask the person who lost the hand anything. "And no lying," Ralph said.

I was familiar with basic poker, but Ralph had special rules, and I didn't understand them all. One-eyed Jacks were important, but I didn't know how. I lost the first three hands, and Ralph asked me what I missed most about Cleveland (Indians' baseball games, I said, although I missed my grandmother more), what I liked least about Washington (our apartment, which was small and was located below neighbors who fought all the time), and whether I had ever seen the Pacific Ocean (no).

In our next hands, we both had a pair of threes, but Ralph had an ace to my king. "It's my question," he said. A silence followed, although I had a feeling he knew what he wanted to ask. "What were you doing when you learned your mother was dead?"

So he knows, I thought. And although it was obvious how he knew—his uncle had told him—I was stunned into muteness. I still hadn't spoken by the time my father and Congressman Stevens walked into the room. "Sorry to break up the poker party," the congressman said.

Before my father and I stepped into the humid night and the waiting cab, Ralph whispered into my ear, "You'll tell me next time, right?" When I turned to him, I expected to see a cruel grin. But his lopsided smile suggested only curiosity. So I nodded.

My mother came from one of Cleveland's oldest and wealthiest families. Her grandfather had been the city's mayor at the turn of the century. My father grew up in a working class, Catholic neighborhood of East Cleveland, where people spoke more Lithuanian than English.

My parents met at the Westwood Country Club in Cleveland the summer my mother graduated from high school. My father was working as a caddie, and one day he spotted my mother sunbathing on an inner tube in the pool. He borrowed a swimming suit, sneaked past whoever was guarding the entrance against outsiders, and dove in.

When my mother and father married in the winter of the same year, my mother's parents disowned her. I was born four-and-a-half months after their wedding. I never met my maternal grandparents.

One summer morning, when I was seven, my father and I were tossing a baseball in my grandmother's backyard, the silence broken by the smack of the ball in our mitts. Suddenly, as if he had been waiting until we had thrown the ball exactly twenty times or thirty times, my father dropped his mitt and strode toward me, his eyes looking everywhere but my face. He stretched out an awkward arm and placed his hand on top of my Indians cap.

I knew he was about to tell me something about my mother. For the last few weeks, I had heard her shouting and crying at night in my parents' downstairs bedroom, and the two times I tried to investigate, I encountered my father at the dining room table, staring blankly at himself in the mirror above the buffet. Both times, without a word, I turned back to my second-floor bedroom.

"Your mother died today," he told me. I didn't cry—my father hated my tears—but I felt my heart contract as if it had been scalded or stung. He said she had fallen off the balcony of a hotel downtown—an accident. But I discovered the truth when I overheard my father speaking with my uncle later the same day: My mother had jumped out of a window in her father's office on the thirty-third floor of the Terminal Tower.

After my mother's death, my father and I moved out of our small house on Euclid Avenue and into my grandmother's house off 185th Street. My grandmother's English was little better than my Lithuanian, but we communicated in other ways—through food, for instance, which she bestowed on my plate in generous mountains and which I devoured with loving thoroughness.

I never knew my grandfather, who died when my father was a child. Of his three siblings, my father liked only his younger brother, Peter. Joseph, my father's older brother, had children, but I rarely saw them.

When, on New Year's Day of 1951, my father told his mother he was moving to Washington, she protested loudly. Because the conversation was in Lithuanian, and because I was on the basement stairs behind a closed door, I had a difficult time understanding it. I thought I heard my grandmother say, "Leave him here with me."

I loved my father, and if I needed proof that he loved me, it was that he'd brought me with him to Washington. At the same time, he resisted my becoming too close to him, as if someday he might, in fact, have to leave me behind.

The next time my father and I visited Congressman Stevens' house, Ralph led me into the living room, where the deck of cards was waiting. Before we played, he repeated the question he had asked at the end of my last visit. As before, I didn't perceive anything cruel in his inquiry. Rather, I sensed a tender interest, the interest of someone examining a friend's scraped knee or bloody nose and asking, "How bad does it hurt?"

I hadn't spoken about my mother in a long time. My father never mentioned her, and I never felt the license to do so. If it was painful to talk about her now, it was also exhilarating, as if in speaking about her, even about her death, I was with her again. I withheld from Ralph only the truth of how she had died.

Ralph won six straight hands, and each of his questions was about my mother. When, at last, I won a hand, I didn't know what to ask him. I was used to keeping my questions to myself. "What do you want to be when you grow up?" I managed.

Ralph sighed. "You can ask anything," he said. "*Anything*. And because it's the rule of the game, I have to answer with the truth."

There was no one to stop us from talking about whatever we wanted when we weren't playing Truth Poker, but I wondered if Ralph had been prohibited from asking about certain subjects and was using the game to circumvent the restriction. "Well?" he said.

But I couldn't think of another question.

He sighed. "I won't be a politician," he said at last. "And I won't be a star baseball player. But I'll come to your games." He smiled. "My mom said I should be a head-shrinker because I listen to all of her problems."

"What's a head-shrinker?"

"It's a Hollywood word. It means...I don't know...a doctor who makes your head feel better, I guess."

"By shrinking it?"

He shrugged.

A few minutes later, we walked outside. It was dusk, hot and humid, and even little exertions—swinging a bat, trotting after a ball—caused us to sweat. As the sky turned from blue-gray to black, my father and Congressman Stevens stepped onto the back lawn. "It's late," my father said. "Too late to go home. We've been invited to stay the night."

The room where Ralph slept was decorated with black-and-white, framed photographs of Cleveland Indians and Cleveland Browns players. I knew every one of the baseball players, and I told Ralph what each of them had batted, and how many games the pitchers had won and lost, the previous season. Congressman Stevens had set up a cot next to Ralph's single bed, and as I climbed in, I caught Ralph tucking the photograph of his mother under his pillow. When he caught my gaze, he merely smiled.

A few minutes later, Congressman Stevens and my father stepped into the room. I was reminded of the difference in age between the two men. Even as a ten-year-old, I thought my father looked young, his hair thick and ink black, his face unlined. Usually, my father tucked me into bed, told me a story or a joke, and kissed me goodnight. Sometimes he stayed longer, often in silence, until I fell asleep. Now he only waved and shut the door.

In the dark room, Ralph said, "Let's pretend we're playing Truth Poker. What's in your hand?"

"I don't know," I said.

"Imagine you're holding cards. What do you have?"

"Three kings?"

"I have four aces," he declared. I pictured him smiling. "What was the best day you ever spent in your whole life?"

I could have told him about sitting with my father in the bleachers at Municipal Stadium during the fifth game of the 1948 World Series. But instead I spoke about how on my sixth birthday, my mother allowed me to skip school and the two of us went to the zoo. We ate ice cream and cotton candy, and as we walked past cage after cage, my mother's hand in mine, she told me a story about the magic day each of the animals would break free.

When my father and I lived in Cleveland, he would ride off in the morning with his brother Peter, a tool belt strapped around his waist, and return in the evening, smelling sometimes of sawdust and sweat. If it was summer, I would spend the entire day with my grandmother, throwing balls off the roof of her garage. On Sundays, she held my hand all the way to church, as if I might try to escape. (Perhaps she had reason to fear: My father had stopped attending.)

In Washington, I don't remember a single time my father went to work, although there were a few occasions when he would leave me alone in the apartment for an hour or two. Once he was gone from lunch until nightfall and came home to find me, exhausted with worry, sleeping on the kitchen floor.

When we were in the apartment together, he spent most of his time playing his phonograph—usually jazz and swing, but sometimes opera. The women's haunted voices reminded me of the nights my mother cried. I read comics or sports books or played with my collection of baseball cards, doing quiet broadcasts of the games I imagined.

The next time my father and I were guests at Congressman Stevens' house, Ralph and I ignored the new board games his uncle had bought us in favor of Truth Poker. In answer to another of my inconsequential questions—about becoming a soldier one day—Ralph told me his father had been killed in France during the war. "But I never knew him and he wasn't married to my mother," he said. "She has boyfriends. They give her earrings and stuff, and sometimes they even give her money. One is really old, maybe a hundred. Another wears an eye patch. My mom and I call him Pirate."

We were stretched out on our stomachs on the living-room floor and I waited for Ralph to deal the cards. But he held the deck in his left fist, his fingers secure around it. "My mother says I shouldn't ask about my father," Ralph said. "There's nothing to know, she says." With his thumb, he rubbed the top card of the deck. "But I sometimes wonder. I can't help it." He flicked a card in front of my waiting hands. "Mom's with one of her boyfriends now."

"Where?"

"Mexico." He looked off. "She goes away sometimes. Sometimes to work, sometimes to be with her boyfriends."

He flicked another card at me. "It's nice your dad takes you with him to his meetings."

"His meetings?" I asked.

"With my uncle. He's a manager or vice president of my uncle's shipping business, right?"

"Right," I said, as if I had merely forgotten.

Ralph won the next several hands. Even when his questions weren't about my mother, I often invoked her, as if to make up for the years I hadn't been permitted to speak her name. I felt an unfamiliar pleasure, and I couldn't have said what was more responsible for it, my memories or Ralph's friendship.

My father and I became regular visitors at the congressman's house, where we usually spent the night. If it wasn't raining, Ralph and I would play baseball before retiring to the living room. We talked about piloting airplanes and joining the circus—Ralph said he wanted to be shot out of a cannon at least once in his life—and my dream to play shortstop for the Indians. We talked about teachers we liked and teachers we hated. Ralph mentioned a couple of his classmates with whom he'd gone to movies. He mentioned a neighbor girl with whom he'd built a fort in the woods behind the girl's house. My only friends were the boys I had played baseball with after school on the asphalt parking lot at the end of my grandmother's block. I knew little more about them than how far they could hit a ball.

One night Ralph told me he had learned from his mother how to do a dance called the Dead Drop. He sprung from the living-room floor and motioned for me to do the same. His gray eyes were laughing as he said, "Pretend I'm a gangster and you're my girl and we're dancing in a dark, smoky nightclub." A second later, Ralph placed his left hand in my right and wrapped his right arm around my back. He leaned into my chest. "Put your free hand on my shoulder," he said. "Okay, good. Now imagine slow, slow music."

He moved me in circles around the living room, and I felt competing feelings of embarrassment and happiness. "Now," Ralph said, "imagine a shot. Bam!" Groaning, he fell into my arms, entrusting me with his weight, which I supported as best I could. Our faces were level, and it occurred to me he might kiss me. In anticipation, I blushed. But he said, "Now you realize your dress is covered with blood and you drop me like a sack of potatoes." So I did, and he groaned as he fell to the floor, and we both laughed.

I looked up to see whether my father or Congressman Stevens might have been watching from a doorway, but we were alone. "Now I'm the girl," Ralph said, and we resumed our game.

Later, long after we were supposed to have fallen asleep, Ralph and I talked about when we could see each other again after he left Washington the following week. Perhaps I could come alone or with my father to California, he said. Perhaps he and his mother could make a trip east over Thanksgiving or Christmas. Under the worst scenario, we would have to wait until the following summer.

It was the beginning of July, and my father arranged to have me spend a last night at Ralph's house before Ralph returned to California. This time, I would be staying over by myself. On the afternoon of the sleepover, as my father stood in front of the bathroom mirror, brushing his hair (combs always stuck in his curls), I again asked him why he wasn't coming.

"I have a date," he said.

The idea of someone replacing my mother seemed both terrible and desirable. I didn't want to betray my mother; at the same time, if I could have found someone like her, with her soft hands and comforting voice, I thought I might be happy. But even as I contemplated the benefits of having a stepmother, I wondered about the likelihood of acquiring one. "Do you like her?" I asked.

"Of course I like her," my father said. "I wouldn't be going to dinner with her if I didn't." From his look, I could tell he expected me to ask no more questions.

It was a little after one when we arrived at Congressman Stevens' house. The congressman and Ralph were finishing lunch, and they invited us to eat dessert. "It's angel food cake from one of my constituents," Congressman Stevens said. "Perks of the office." It tasted insubstantial but sweet, like a cloud of sugar.

After we finished, Ralph led me outside so we could play baseball. The day was overcast and humid, and we didn't play with enthusiasm. An hour later, my father stepped outside to say goodbye.

When we returned inside, Congressman Stevens was on the phone in the kitchen, and I could hear him from the living room, where Ralph and I sat on the carpet to play Truth Poker.

"So you liked Paris? Tell me."

Ralph shuffled the cards.

"And London?" The congressman laughed. "I never found London appealing either."

"Your play," Ralph said. I threw down two cards and Ralph dealt me two back.

"I knew Italy wouldn't disappoint you."

Ralph threw down a single card, picked up one.

"Next time, we'll all go—you, me, the girls, your mother. Or maybe we'll leave your mother at home." He chuckled. "I'll make it a fact-finding mission—to discover the secrets of Italian cuisine."

It was his wife to whom he was speaking, I guessed. There was a false cheerfulness to his tone, what he said seeming like lines he knew he should speak but didn't feel. It was, I realized, the way my father had sometimes spoken to my mother.

"Certainly, darling. Certainly. Wait. Could you hold a minute?" There was a pause, and I heard a door close.

I wanted to ask Ralph whether his aunt ever cried during the middle of the night. But I doubted Ralph would know. Besides, my pair of Jacks lost to his two queens. It was his question: "What would be the first thing you would say to your mother if she came back to life?"

My talks with Ralph had revived my mother in my mind, so it wasn't hard to imagine her resurrected in body. With animation, I described the car ride she and I would set off on, our journey taking us past cities, over mountains, and across deserts, all the way to California. "We could go swimming on Re-Doughnut Beach," I said.

Ralph laughed. "It's Redondo Beach, But I like Re-Doughnut better."

Later, in my cot, still excited by my imagined journey, I couldn't sleep. I could hear Ralph's soft but distinct breathing, more like moans than snores. I wanted a drink of milk, something my father often gave me when I was restless or woke up from bad dreams. As I stood up in the darkness, I heard a car door slam. Was the congressman going somewhere?

After I left Ralph's room, I walked downstairs. I didn't go to the kitchen but slipped into the living room and stood in front of the far window, which overlooked the front walk. As if I'd conjured him, there was my father, striding toward the house. I expected him to knock. I was prepared to throw open the door with a smile.

Instead, my father opened the door, stepped inside, and turned toward the dining room. I began to follow him but stopped when the dining-room lights came on. I concealed myself behind an umbrella stand. I couldn't see into the dining room, but I heard the congressman say, "Good evening, Dan. Beer?"

"You read my mind."

I heard the pop of a bottle cap.

"Did my boy go to bed all right?" my father asked.

"Without a peep." There was a pause. "Is all your sleight of hand necessary, Dan? He's only ten."

My father's reply was a whisper: "I told you I think he's beginning to understand what's happening here. Ralph, too, I'm sure."

"Fine, fine," Congressman Stevens said. "One illusionist shouldn't question another's tricks."

There was a long pause before the congressman said, "Celia called to-night. She's back in the country—in our house in Shaker Heights, as a matter of fact. I told her I would join her in a few days, after Ralph leaves."

"You told me she wouldn't be home until Labor Day."

"She said her mother was tired of traveling; so were the girls. They skipped Spain and Portugal." After a moment, the congressman said, "I should spend a little time in my district anyway. In the summer, a first-term congressman can't afford to cavort with anyone but his constituents. I was foolish to think we could have the summer all to ourselves."

"You told me you would be divorced by now," my father said.

"I told you I would be separated by now. And if Celia had stayed in Europe, we would be separated—by the Atlantic Ocean." The congressman sighed. "We've had a nice time here, haven't we, Dan? Like a little family? Like you wanted? Now reality intrudes." He paused. "Celia and the girls will be living in Cleveland and I'll be living here. I'll go back to Cleveland on most weekends, of course, and I'm sure they'll visit me here a few times. But compared to what you and I have had to work around in the past, this is easy street."

A silence followed. "I'll need some money before you go," my father said.

"Of course," the congressman said softly. "We'll take care of it soon. In the meantime, here's a start." I heard him digging in his pocket. I heard his fingers caress clean bills. "You might think about finding a part-time job, something to keep you out of trouble."

"You and I had an arrangement when Michael and I moved here," my father said.

"I haven't forgotten."

There was an extended silence, and I realized they had left the dining room. When I returned to Ralph's bedroom, he was where I'd left him, but his eyes were open. "Bad dream?" he asked.

I considered telling him what I'd overheard downstairs. But when I opened my mouth, I found myself saying, "My mother didn't fall by accident. She jumped." I began to cry. Worried what he might think of me, I tried to stop.

Ralph left his bed and kneeled beside my cot, his face inches from mine. "I know it hurts," he said. "I know it hurts because I used to think that whenever my mom left, she was never coming back. Sometimes I would sit on our doorstep and wait for a man dressed in black to show up with the bad news. Sometimes when she goes away now, I'm still afraid it'll be the last time I'll ever see her."

I was lying on my stomach, and my left hand was hanging off the cot. He put both his hands around it. "Maybe that's why I asked you all those questions about your mom," he said.

"Why?"

There was a silence. "Because I wanted to know what it would be like."

"Why did she do it?" I asked him. "Why did she...?" I couldn't bring myself to say "kill herself." The phrase seemed brutal, so unlike the mother I knew.

"My mom had this friend, an actress," Ralph said. "She wasn't given a part in a movie she wanted and a few days later her boyfriend ran off with another girl. She was sad. So she drove off the side of a cliff. All the way into the ocean."

I absorbed this story in silence. "But my mother had me," I said. "If she had me, and she was still sad..."

"My mom said it's like a darkness. It fills your head so you can think only dark thoughts. It covers your eyes so you can see only the dark. You can't think about anything good. You can't see anything good. Your mom couldn't see you. She couldn't see your dad."

"But my dad," I said. "He..." I didn't know what to say about him.

"Your dad will look after you until you're a man. And then..." Ralph squeezed my hand before releasing it. "And then you're going to be a famous baseball player."

This was what I needed to cheer me up. My tears stopped, and believing what he had told me, and imagining the homeruns I would hit, I fell asleep.

When I woke up the next morning, Ralph was back in his bed, his mouth open, faint sounds coming from it. I walked downstairs to find my father at the kitchen table, drinking coffee. He wasn't wearing shoes. "I came early," he said, looking out the window at the red maples in the backyard. He turned to me. "Did you have a good night?"

Half an hour later, as my father and I stood in the doorway to leave, Ralph and I shook hands like adults and said goodbye with the coolness of strangers. But before my father and I walked toward the idling cab, Ralph said, "Wait a minute." He dashed off and returned with the pack of cards we had used to play Truth Poker. As he pressed it into my palms, he dipped his lips to my ear. "I cheated sometimes to win," he whispered. "I'm sorry."

"Thanks," I said, as much for the confession as for the cards.

Without Ralph, the summer dragged. During the day, my father and I would sometimes walk to the National Mall. In the Museum of Natural History, I stared at dinosaur bones. My father recited off plaques how long ago the dinosaurs lived, but I couldn't fathom such large numbers. I was ten years old. I would be eleven in October. Ralph was twelve and would be thirteen in May. My mother died when I was seven. These numbers were tangible.

Twice late at night, as I was in bed, I heard visitors come to our apartment door. Both visitors were men, both with voices deeper than my father's. When the second man shouted something, my father tried to shush him. The man said, "I didn't pay to be quiet."

One Sunday, my father took me to a Senators' game. We had seats in the bleachers, but having any seat in the ballpark would have thrilled me. We shared a box of Cracker Jacks, and in the bottom of the seventh inning, Eddie Yost, the third baseman, hit a long drive our way. My father came within inches of catching the ball, but another curly-haired man, his neck and face roasted from the sun, had a glove and snagged it. I found myself crying inconsolable tears, as if we had been denied something precious. My father, embarrassed, escorted me out of the stadium.

I calmed down, and on our walk home, my father told me he would be going away for a few days and I would be staying with Bertilda and her family. Bertilda, a short, stocky woman with shining dark skin and a birthmark like a heart under her left eye, lived with her husband and four young children in the apartment below ours.

"Where are you going?" I asked him, but I knew the answer. I'd seen his bus ticket.

"Cleveland."

"To see Congressman Stevens?"

He didn't answer for a moment. "Congressman Stevens lives here now," he said. "Uncle Peter is working on a project and needs my help."

I knew he was lying, and I was sure, or almost sure, he knew I knew. But he and I said nothing more.

At Bertilda's, I slept on the couch in the living room. Even at night, the house was noisy. Bertilda had a three-month-old baby, and her husband, who called me "Fastball," must have worked late shifts because he would come home at dawn, fumbling at the lock and singing.

Upon his return from Cleveland, I noted my father's pleasure, his uncharacteristic ebullience. "How was your work with Uncle Peter?" I asked him.

He looked puzzled before smiling again. "Successful," he said. And without pausing, he added, "When are the Senators playing at home again? I'll buy us box seats this time."

We next visited Congressman Stevens' house on a hot, humid evening in the last week of August. I was supposed to have stayed with Bertilda, but her baby was sick. Congressman Stevens answered the door in a red silk bathrobe. When he crouched to greet me, I could smell his breath, and the smell—at once fiery and fruity—made me recoil. When I looked past Congressman Stevens to peer into the dark living room, he reminded me that Ralph was back home with his mother. "Oh," I said, surprised to find my hopefulness so transparent.

Without Ralph, I soon became bored. All the games in Congressman Stevens' living room required two players, and I couldn't play Truth Poker against myself, although, hoping for Ralph's return, I had brought the cards. My father and the congressman were in the kitchen, and I tiptoed out of the living room and into the sunroom. I was so close to the men I could hear the tinkle of ice in Congressman Stevens' drink. I heard my father say, "You told me she would be staying in Cleveland."

"She changed her mind." Ice crashed against the side of the congressman's glass. "We'll make do. We have before. It'll be fine—you'll see."

"What's your plan—to meet up with me in hotel rooms between votes? I thought we had an understanding."

Ashamed of my father's emotion—he sounded like I did when I was about to cry—I retreated to the living room, where I set up the chess set and engaged the knights in jousting matches, angrily crashing them into each other. I hoped my father would come to tell me we were going home. But evening became night, and my father told me we would be staying.

As I lay in Ralph's bed, I remembered him tucking the photograph of his mother under his pillow. He carried her picture like an icon, something to cherish and guard. I fell asleep wondering what I could have done to save my mother. In my dream, I was at the zoo, and at the end of a long path, I spotted a tall, thin cage. Inside was my mother. She was wearing a white dress and her eyes were wet with tears. As I stepped up to the bars, she opened her mouth to tell me something, but I already knew what it was.

I sprung from Ralph's bed and ran down the hall past five or six doors to the room where I knew I would find my father. There was a chain guard, which I didn't notice until I'd broken it by hurling my body against the door. Congressman Stevens' bedroom was as large as our apartment, and against the back wall was a king-sized bed. My father awoke immediately, disentangling himself from the congressman's pale body. "What is it?" my father asked. "What's wrong?"

"You killed her!" I shouted. "She thought you loved her but you never did! You wanted her money!" I followed this with other declarations, the strongest of which was: "I hate you and I hope you die!"

My father scrambled to put on his clothes, and soon we were riding home in a cab at a time of night or morning I wasn't to see again for a decade or more. Neither of us said a word.

In the first week of September, we moved back to Cleveland. My grand-mother was living with her oldest son, so we stayed with my father's sister and her husband. My uncle had emigrated from Lithuania before the war and spoke in an accent so thick I frequently had difficulty understanding him. In Lithuania, he had been a professional cellist. In Cleveland, he drove a bus. He and my aunt had no children.

Every evening, my father made a show of spreading the Help Wanted section of both the *Press* and the *Plain Dealer* in front of him and circling promising listings in red pen. Work was available—I twice heard my uncle offer to take him down to the Cleveland Transit System's office—but my father said he had a particular job in mind.

I was sure my father never planned to find a job in Cleveland, sure he could no longer live with me because of what I had discovered and what I had said in the discovery's aftermath. No one he knew in town—Father Urbanitis, his mother, even his brother Peter—would have offered him any-thing gentler than my condemnation.

When he told me he was leaving, I couldn't find my voice to tell him it wasn't what I wanted or needed. I was as tight-lipped and stoic as he had always expected me to be. We were standing in my aunt's kitchen, adorned with sunflower wallpaper and overlooking the backyard, which my uncle had turned into a vegetable garden. "Your aunt and uncle will be good par-ents," he said, his gaze leaving my face and settling somewhere out the window.

If I begged him to stay, I spoke my pleas not to him but (that night, at the foot of my bed) to God.

My father intended to go to California. "Hollywood," my uncle said as we sat around the dinner table the evening after my father's departure, eating ham. "Maybe he will find work in movies." When my uncle chewed, his entire face moved in contortions of pleasure. We would eat ham—my uncle's favorite meal—twice a week until I was seventeen and started my freshman year at Ohio State, courtesy of a baseball scholarship.

My father wrote me several times, although he was as taciturn on paper as he was in person. My letters to him were diary-like notations of what I had done the previous week. Whatever feelings I had about his absence I left off the page.

My father never reached California. Twenty-one months after leaving Cleveland, he was working on an oil rig off the coast of Louisiana, one of the first of its kind, when ninety-five-mile-per-hour winds blew him and two co-workers into the Gulf of Mexico. Their bodies were never found.

Over the years, I often thought about Ralph. Once, in high school, I even sat down to write him a letter, intending to send it to him care of Congressman Stevens. But I suspected the congressman wouldn't be inclined to forward it. Later, I sometimes imagined Ralph surprising me by coming down from the stands after a game in one of the minor league baseball parks I visited as a player and, beginning in my mid-thirties, as a radio announcer, and the two of us talking near the third base coach's box as the grounds crew worked around us, smoothing the roughed up infield. Even as my life moved on—to major league announcing and other distractions—I continued to imagine a reunion with Ralph, although at this point in my life he had become an abstraction. Or several abstractions: Friendship. Childhood. Honesty.

My friends were baseball people, players, managers, and announcers who lived the game outside the ballpark as much as they did inside it. If our conversations didn't revolve around baseball, they usually didn't last long. Even the women I dated and the two I married I met because of baseball. They worked in teams' PR departments or were sisters or cousins of players or waited tables in restaurants frequented by baseball personnel. But if baseball afforded me the predictable variations of what happened on its diamonds, and if the friendships I made as a result of my involvement in the game had a comforting consistency, I sometimes felt unsettled, unsatisfied, unfulfilled. To this list, I might have added unknown. As far as my friends and lovers knew, my aunt and uncle were my parents and always had been. After my father's death, they had adopted me, and their last name had become mine. I had buried the boy I'd been.

Congressman Stevens' obituary appeared in the newspapers the week after my second divorce was made final, when I was fifty-eight years old. He had served ten terms in the House of Representatives before losing a close race for the U.S. Senate. In his last public years, he had served as the U.S. ambassador to Australia. He was survived by his wife, his twin daughters, and his four grandchildren. The obituary made no mention of his sister or nephew, but I didn't need prompting to remember Ralph. And two weeks after his uncle's death, I saw him.

I was in LaGuardia Airport, on my way back to Cleveland after broadcasting an Indians-Yankees game, and when I stopped at a newsstand, he was standing beside me, flipping through *GQ* or *Esquire*. He'd lost most of his hair, and the rest of it had turned silver, but his face was the same, unlined, boyish. He had the same bright gray eyes.

I had fifty-five minutes before my flight. I could have bought him a drink. We could have talked. But even as I felt an old, sweet anticipation, as if at receiving an invitation to share my heart, I failed to say so much as his name. Perhaps I was scared he wouldn't remember me. Perhaps I was scared of all I might have said to him and all I might have felt. Perhaps I was scared that Ralph would call the boy I'd been to testify for or against the man I'd become. Without a glance at me, he was gone, merging with the human traffic rushing down a wide concourse.

In the anonymity of the airport, I could have had what my mother, when I came to her with a scraped knee or a bleeding nose, used to call, with a silliness intended to lighten my mood, a deep weep. I'd remembered this phrase of my mother's only now, and perhaps its recovery—something gained when I'd lost so much—turned back my tears. Or perhaps I remained dry-eyed out of habit, my father's expectation of stoicism, as usual, fulfilled. There were, anyway, no arms to hold me, no smiles to cheer me up. I bought a couple of newspapers, found a seat at my gate, and waited to hear my row called.

But I wasn't sitting more than a minute when I felt a hand on my shoulder and turned toward a familiar voice, deepened by the years but no less enthusiastic: "I was walking down to the water fountain when I could have sworn I was staring at a good friend from a lifetime ago. But I said to myself, 'There's no way he could be…Surely he can't be…'" Ralph grinned at me like he'd just won another hand of Truth Poker. "Hell, but it is—it's you!"

The Autumn House Fiction Series

....

New World Order • Derek Green

■ *Drift and Swerve* • Samuel Ligon

Monongahela Dusk • John Hoerr

■ *Attention Please Now* • Matthew Pitt

■ *Peter Never Came* • Ashley Cowger

Keeping the Wolves at Bay: Stories by Emerging American Writers • Sharon Dilworth, ed.

Party Girls • Diane Goodman

■ *Favorite Monster* • Sharma Shields

New America: Contemporary Literature for a Changing Society • Holly Messitt and James Tolan, eds.

Little Raw Souls • Steven Schwartz

■ *What You Are Now Enjoying* • Sarah Gerkensmeyer

■ *Come by Here* • Tom Noyes

■ *Truth Poker* • Mark Brazaitis

■ Winner of the Autumn House Fiction Prize

Design and Production

••

Cover and text design by Kathy Boykowycz.

Text set in Stone Serif, designed in 1987 by Sumner Stone. Heads set in Frutiger Bold, designed in 1975 by Adrian Frutiger.

Printed by McNaughton & Gunn, Saline, Michigan.